"Wonderfully written . . . I highly recommend this tale."
—*Romance Reviews Today*

"An amazing, intoxicating love story . . . Definitely an author to keep your eye on." —*Romance Junkies*

"An outstanding novel . . . twists and turns that will keep you on your toes and a brilliant ending that will warm your heart. I encourage you to read this exceptional book."
—*The Road to Romance*

"This book is extremely HOT! Ms. Carew had me squirming in my seat while reading this story. This book was so great I want to read more stories by this author." —*Coffee Time Romance*

"Fast paced, erotic, and romantic . . . a definite keeper!"
—*Just Erotic Romance Reviews*

"An enchanting and entrancing story of love and forgiveness . . . a definite recommended read." —*Love Romances*

"A story of impossible love and unexpected scorching sex . . . The ending will have the reader gasping for breath. . . . I look forward to following this new series with great interest."
—*eCataromance*

"Carew really knows how to bring the reader into the lives of her characters. This story is one any reader will want to pick up time and time again." —*Fallen Angel Reviews*

"A wonderful book from the very first page. I could not put it down. . . . A great read!" —*Enchanted in Romance*

TWIN FANTASIES

Opal Carew

St. Martin's Griffin
New York

TWIN FANTASIES. Copyright © 2007 by Elizabeth Batten-Carew.
All rights reserved. Printed in the United States of America.
For information, address St. Martin'sPress, 175 Fifth Avenue,
New York, N.Y. 10010.

www.stmartins.com

Library of Congress Cataloging-in-Publication Data

Carew, Opal.
    Twin fantasies / Opal Carew.—1st ed.
    p. cm.
    ISBN-13: 978-0-312-36778-7
    ISBN-10: 0-312-36778-3
    1. Twins—Fiction.

PR9199.4.C367 T86 2007
813'.6—dc22   2007013050

10 9 8

To my husband, Mark,
who fills my life with love and happiness

To my two sons,
because I love them so much!

ACKNOWLEDGMENTS

A very special thank-you goes to Colette, who critiqued, complimented, and encouraged me throughout the writing of this and many other books. She was the resounding voice who assured me I would make it where I needed to go. She prodded when I needed it and got me back on track when I got lost. Colette, we may not be born of the same parents, but I consider you my sister.

Thank you to my sons, Matt and Jason, for understanding, even when you were toddlers, that Mommy needs time to write, and now that you're teenagers, that my writing time is important.

Emily Sylvan Kim, you are the best agent ever and I thank you for taking a chance on me, then giving me the best opportunity of my life.

Rose Hilliard, you are a wonderful editor, and I thank you for your patience, encouragement, and generosity. It's clear you believe in me and together I believe we're an indomitable team.

Thank you to two friends who have helped me learn and grow as a writer, who critiqued my work and made it shine, and whom I miss having in my life. Trish and Vicki, I appreciate all the help you've given me over the years.

TWIN FANTASIES

CHAPTER 1

JENNA WATCHED AS the tuxedo-clad groom handed a tall stemmed glass to Suzie, his bride, then leaned in and kissed her on the curve of her neck, below the ear. His hand stroked along her shoulder, left bare by the exquisite beaded ivory-lace bridal gown she wore. Her eyes glowed as she smiled at him.

Clearly, Suzie and Glen were deeply in love. Jenna felt her stomach clench, missing her own man terribly.

The band started playing one of her favorite songs, triggering an intense craving to swirl across the dance floor with Ryan, the man she loved. Unfortunately, *he* had chosen not to be here.

She was still angry that he'd backed out at the last minute. A trip to Toronto to fix some problems his clients, Bryer Associates, were having installing the new software his company had developed for them. It's not that she didn't understand the demands of running a business, it's just that this was the latest in a string of broken plans.

She had been looking forward to this wedding and the chance to indulge in an entire evening in Ryan's arms as they danced the night away. Preferably followed by hours of hot sex. She'd barely seen him over the past two months, and they hadn't made love in more than three months. She *desperately* wanted a night of hot sex!

Cindy, Jenna's best friend, nudged her elbow.

"Look, here comes that hunky attorney, Kurt."

Jenna glanced around to see the blond, blue-eyed attorney who'd sat beside her at dinner approaching them, carrying a highball glass and two stemmed wineglasses clasped between his fingers.

"Hello, ladies." He deposited the glasses on the table, then picked up the two white wines, handing one to Jenna and one to Cindy. "I thought you might like something to drink."

"Thank you." Jenna appreciated his attentiveness, but wished it was coming from Ryan. She sipped nervously, afraid he'd ask her to—

"Jenna, would you like to dance?" he asked.

Cindy, who'd been trying to cheer her up all evening, nudged Jenna's elbow, the insistent look in her emerald eyes encouraging Jenna to go.

She ignored Cindy and shook her head.

"Thanks, Kurt, but I don't think so."

He took her hand and drew it upward, leading her into a slow twirl.

"Come on, Jenna. I'm a great dancer," he coaxed.

"I'm sorry, but I'm involved with someone. I wouldn't feel right."

"Just one dance couldn't hurt," Cindy interjected.

Jenna wasn't so sure. She longed to be held in Ryan's arms, to be cherished and loved, but she was angry at him, too, and befuddled by a myriad of mixed thoughts and feelings. In fact, she'd been entertaining very serious doubts about their relationship.

Kurt drew her hand to his mouth and his lips brushed her knuckles as he placed a lingering kiss on her fingers, sending her blood into a slow simmer. Kurt was an extremely attractive man. He was also intelligent, witty, and attentive. A killer combination. If she allowed herself to be swept into his arms, she might be tempted to forget she was in love with Ryan. With several glasses of wine already dimming the memory, and the heat of this attractive man surrounding her as he led her around the dance floor, she might decide that *being* loved was more important than *who* was doing the loving.

Not that she'd ever sleep with a man she'd just met.

"Are you sure?" Kurt asked.

Before she had a chance to answer, Mona, the bride's mother, approached and linked arms with him.

"Kurt, you promised me a dance." She smiled at Jenna and Cindy. "Girls, you wouldn't mind if I stole him away for a moment, would you?"

Cindy and Jenna had known Suzie and her mom since high school and Jenna had always liked the exuberant, lively woman.

"Of course not," Cindy answered.

"I'll be back," Kurt promised as Mona led him away.

"When he comes back, you should dance with him," Cindy said, waving at them.

"No, I shouldn't. In fact, I shouldn't have come without Ryan."

Not that he'd given her much choice.

"Of course you should have." Cindy patted her arm. "Just because Mr. Boring doesn't want to have any fun doesn't mean you shouldn't. That gorgeous new dress should not go to waste."

Cindy smiled in the direction of the three groomsmen standing by the bar watching them.

"If you don't want to dance with Kurt, pick someone else. All the guys are eyeing you."

Jenna shrugged. She had noticed the men glancing at her, but their appreciative stares only made her uncomfortable. She had bought this dress to entice Ryan's gaze and keep him focused on her and what they would do after the reception.

"It would serve him right if you found a new guy to replace him right here, tonight."

"Cindy, I'm not going to—"

Cindy squeezed Jenna's arm. "I know, but it's too bad. You deserve to be treated better."

"He's just been busy, that's all."

"On a Saturday night?"

"I told you, he's working under a deadline. The new software has to go live first thing Monday morning. He's been fixing the bugs for the last couple of days and he's testing everything tonight. He flies to Toronto tomorrow—"

"Sunday!"

"Yes, Sunday, so he can install the software and make sure it works on-site."

He would then stay for another week or so to train the users of the system and to be on hand if any further problems occurred. Jenna had no idea when she'd see him again.

"And what about last month. And the month before."

Jenna sighed.

"He has a business to run."

"Yes, and you have a life to live. Hopefully, not all alone. If he doesn't make time to be with you, what's the point in staying together?"

Cindy's words echoed Jenna's thoughts over the past few weeks. What *was* the point? Maybe Jenna was just holding Ryan back? If he was free of feeling he had to spend time with her, he could throw himself into his work all he wanted.

Jenna noticed Kurt approaching.

"Here he comes," Cindy said. "Are you sure you don't want to—?"

"I'm sure."

"Do you mind if I do?"

Jenna smiled. "Not at all." She opened her purse and rifled around inside it, looking busy to avoid Kurt's gaze. His smile waned a little, but Cindy beamed at him invitingly.

"Cindy, would you like to dance?"

"I'd love to."

Jenna watched as the two crossed the room to the glossy wooden dance floor. As Kurt took Cindy in his arms, Jenna longed to feel Ryan's arms around her, to feel his lips on hers, to feel his body sliding on top of her. She longed to feel his hard maleness sliding into her.

But more, she longed to feel wanted by him again.

The heat of the room suddenly became unbearable. She tilted her glass, downing the wine, then plunked it on the table and strode toward the door.

RYAN TYPED THE compile command. As the result flashed across the build window on his computer screen, his mind wandered to Jenna. He'd actually managed to go several hours without thinking of her. A new record.

What was Jenna doing right now? Probably swirling across the dance floor at the reception in the arms of some hot, hungry stud hoping for a night of passion in her bed. Jealousy flared through him, but he knew, deep in his heart, he could trust his Jenna.

Damn, but he wanted to be with her right now. He wanted to hold her in his arms. He could imagine her in the gorgeous red dress she'd purchased for the wedding, the slinky fabric caressing her curves, accentuating her generous breasts. As she twirled around the dance floor, the skirt would swirl up, revealing exciting glimpses of her long, shapely legs. His groin tightened at the thought of her body swaying against his, her breasts crushed against his chest, her hands stroking over his shoulders.

After a few dances he would suggest they go back to his place, where he'd strip off the lovely garment to reveal her delectable naked body. Adrenaline rushed through him as he imagined her naked breasts under his hands, her nipples rising into his palms, pushing at them as though seeking escape. He would draw them into his mouth and she would moan softly. His cock pushed against his jeans, demanding release.

He stroked his hand over the bulge in his pants. Damn, every time he thought about Jenna his body reacted like a horny teenage boy's. He wanted her all the time. She was an obsession.

Love. It could be damn inconvenient.

As he remembered her hands stroking over his stomach, her fingers encircling his erection, then her delicate lips sliding over the head of his cock, he groaned. He wouldn't give Jenna up for anything, but he simply had to find a balance in his life. He couldn't spend every moment with her, no matter how much he wanted to. He needed to make his business work. He needed to be a success. Like his brother, Jake.

Ryan adjusted himself in his jeans, attempting to relieve the pressure. His erection waned a little as he thought about how embarrassing it would have been if his brother had still been here and noticed his raging hard-on. Thank God he'd sent Jake on his way half an hour ago, since there were only a few final details to handle. Certainly not enough to keep them both busy.

Jake and Ryan were both software architects, but they'd each started their own company. Ryan had called Jake in on this because Jake had more expertise with the particular operating system the client used and there had been some strange interface errors occurring.

Ryan glanced at his watch. Ten thirty. If he could finish up here in another half an hour or so, maybe he could head straight to the Westerly Inn and meet Jenna at the wedding reception.

JENNA STEPPED OUT of the ballroom, leaving the glitz and glamour behind. In the brighter lights of the atrium, she drew in a deep breath and sighed. She glanced around hesitantly.

Ryan never seemed to have time for her anymore. She couldn't understand why he had backed off so completely, but he had and Jenna had to face facts. The hot passion they'd shared a year ago had slowly dwindled over the past few months.

Her heart compressed as she realized she was close to making a decision she had been struggling with for weeks. She didn't want to be alone, and she'd felt more alone while dating Ryan these past few months than she'd ever felt while single.

She loved him, she had no doubt about that, but it was becoming increasingly clear that he didn't love her back. Not enough, anyway. Her heart ached as she finally started to face the truth.

They both seemed to be hanging on, but what was the point? The relationship was over. Ryan seemed to be waiting for her to end it, so it was up to her.

Cindy stepped out of the ballroom, followed by Kurt.

"Jenna, are you okay?"

A tear welled in Jenna's eye and she dashed it away. She opened her mouth to say something, but her throat choked up and she couldn't utter a word.

Cindy whispered something to Kurt and he disappeared into the throng of the wedding reception.

"Oh, honey." Cindy curled her arm around Jenna's and led her to a quiet corner near some tall plants. "What's wrong?"

JAKE STROLLED ALONG the atrium, attracted to the lively dance music drifting from the ballroom. He'd finished dinner at the hotel and didn't feel like sitting in the lounge alone listening to the piano. His gaze settled on the profile of a gorgeous young woman in a red satin gown sprinkled with glitter, who was chatting to a friend. She looked unhappy and he would have loved to sweep her into his arms and lead her around the dance floor in an attempt to bring a smile to her lovely features. He wasn't the type to crash parties, though, so he decided to just stand and watch her a little longer.

The following morning, he would be accompanying his

twin brother to Toronto to help him install his new software at Bryer Associates. Jake would ensure Ryan got the patches installed and would help with any last-minute problems that might occur during the on-site installation.

Jake had flown to Ottawa from his home in Montreal in his little Cessna aircraft. He and Ryan had met for lunch and they'd spent the afternoon debugging the code. Everything was fixed and tested now, but Ryan, obsessive as always, was spending the rest of the evening testing and retesting every aspect of the system.

Tomorrow, Jake would fly them both to Toronto for the meeting. Jake would return after the installation was completed on Sunday, but Ryan would stay a while longer to ensure everything went smoothly.

Right now, Jake intended to relax and enjoy himself.

"I . . ." JENNA GULPED, then tried again. "It's not going to work out with Ryan, is it?" She glanced at Cindy's face and the tight line of her friend's lips told Jenna all she needed to know. Tears pushed at her eyes. "I'm going to have to . . ." Her throat clamped tight, muffling a sob. She sucked in some air, then continued. ". . . to break up with him."

She hated the finality of hearing the words out loud.

Cindy slid her arms around Jenna and gave her a hug.

"Sweetie, I'm sorry."

Cindy drew away and opened her small satin bag, then fished out a clean tissue. She handed it to Jenna, who dabbed at her eyes.

"He just seems to have lost interest in me."

"You did tell him about your sexual fantasies, right?"

"Yes. Last weekend."

"You included the virgin captured by the pirate?"

Jenna nodded.

"And the sex with a stranger?"

"Uh-huh."

Cindy shook her head.

"I can't believe he didn't jump your bones on the spot."

Jenna remembered how Ryan had closed up when she'd told him, putting an even greater distance between them. Rather than being aroused into a spontaneous sexual romp, he'd called the night short and left in a hurry.

"So when are you going to do it?" Cindy asked.

"As soon as he gets back, I'm going to—"

"Omigod, Jenna, I don't believe it." Cindy's gaze angled over Jenna's left shoulder and locked on something.

A sudden prickle scurried up her spine.

"What is it?" Jenna turned around to see a pair of deep blue eyes staring at her.

Her heart did a backflip and a smile turned up her lips.

Ryan!

THE WOMAN IN red flicked her head around, the wisps of dark hair around her face fluttering lightly. Her gaze locked with Jake's. His breath halted for an instant as her eyes widened, then her lips curled up in a smile, transforming her lovely face to one of pure, ethereal beauty. For several seconds, they simply stared at each other. Finally, he drew himself from the sensual daze and strolled toward her. Her smile grew.

"Hi. My name is Jake."

She stared at him, her brow furrowing. Her friend giggled,

then nudged her with her elbow and whispered something in her ear. He thought he heard something about a stranger and a fantasy. The smile on the woman in red's lips broadened and he hoped whatever fantasy this woman had, he would be the stranger to satisfy it.

"My name is . . . Aurora."

"Pleased to meet you." He offered his hand and she wrapped her fingers around it in a firm handshake. He drew her hand to his lips and kissed her knuckles, the feel of her soft skin against his mouth causing a stir in his loins.

The friend giggled again. "And I'm Cindy." She gave Aurora another nudge. "I'm going to go now. You two have fun." She turned and headed toward the ballroom door. "Nice to meet you . . . Jake."

He nodded politely to the young woman as she left, then turned back to Aurora.

"Are you here with anyone?"

She smiled seductively. "I had a date, but he canceled at the last minute."

He raised an eyebrow. "I can't believe any sane man would stand up such a beautiful woman."

She laughed and he loved the sound of pure joy trimmed with bells of delight in her voice. He made a mental note to make her laugh often.

He heard the strains of a slow, sultry number begin.

"Would you care to dance?"

"I'd love to."

He curled his hand around hers, loving the feel of her long, slender fingers twined around his, and led her into the dimly lit ballroom, then onto the dance floor. He turned to face her. Her sinfully sexy red dress clung to every curve of her incredible figure. The strapless top conformed to her full, round breasts, then skimmed in around her trim waist. The skirt flared softly over her hips and swirled to the floor. She stepped forward and he took her in his arms, his heartbeat accelerating. Her hands slid over his shoulders and she smiled up at him, her blue eyes soft and dewy. As her fingers curled through his hair, a tingle danced along his spine. She rested her head against his shoulder and her sweet, delicate herbal smell filled his nostrils. Her lips brushed his neck, sending his senses into a spin.

As they moved to the music, she snuggled closer still—far closer than he could have hoped. His groin tightened as her breasts pressed against him, her nipples hard pebbles against his chest. His hands skimmed down her bare shoulders.

Good Lord, this woman had a powerful effect on him. He prayed the music wouldn't end soon, because it would be embarrassing to step off the dance floor just now.

CHAPTER 2

JENNA COULDN'T BELIEVE Ryan had come to the party after all. And pretending to be a stranger to play out her sexual fantasy was a delightful, romantic, and extremely sexy surprise. Her whole body fluttered inside at the thought that he would be making love to her tonight.

Surely, that was his intent. Unless he decided he had to rush off.

She pressed herself closer to him, stroking his back. She could feel a ridge growing against her belly. The song ended and another slow song began. He propelled her around the dance floor with confidence and grace. She'd had no idea what an exceptional dancer Ryan was. The song ended, replaced by one with a faster beat. He loosened his hold on her, but she didn't want to lose the closeness. She pushed herself onto her tiptoes, pressing her mouth near his ear.

"What I'd really like," she murmured, "is to be alone together."

Jake's pulse skyrocketed at the suggestion. He'd never met such a bold woman. She pressed her body closer, applying friction to his rapidly expanding erection, sending hormones exploding through his body.

"I have a room." The words came out before his brain had time to intervene.

She stared at him intently and he feared he'd misunderstood. Maybe she had only meant to suggest going out for a drink together.

He held his breath, afraid he'd blown it. Her eyes glittered and her smile blossomed once again and he breathed a sigh of relief.

"What are we waiting for?" she purred.

He spun her around and planted her in front of him to hide the huge bulge in his pants, and pointed her in the direction of the door. They hurried to the corridor off the atrium, then toward the elevator.

He pushed the Up arrow, then slid his arm around her waist and drew her close. Luckily, no one else waited with them. As the display above the elevator counted off the floors, he nuzzled her neck. He couldn't believe this beautiful young woman was going up to his room with him. They had barely met. Still, there was no denying the wild attraction between them. Had she had too much to drink? He didn't want to take advantage of her, but he didn't want to let her go. Although he could smell the subtle aroma of wine on her breath, she didn't seem at all inebriated.

One of her hands rested on his outer thigh and she stroked him with delicate fingers. His cock throbbed. His gaze rested on the swell of her breasts and he imagined peeling away the red silky fabric to reveal them in their naked glory. Her nipples peaked beneath the fabric. He tightened his free hand into a fist, keeping it occupied against the need to reach out and touch her.

Lord, but she was a sexy woman. He'd never wanted a woman as much as he wanted her right now.

A ding indicated the arrival of the elevator. When the door slid open, he hustled her inside. The doors whooshed closed behind them and finally they stood alone in the small space. He wanted to drag her into his arms, to devour her lips, to slide his hands all over her body, but he held back. He didn't want to spook her.

His arm slid around her waist and she pressed against his side. She nuzzled his ear, then wrapped her arms around his waist and snuggled close, her body pressed against the length of his as the floor numbers slowly—painfully slowly—counted up.

To his surprise and delight, Aurora couldn't seem to stop touching him. She stroked her hands up the button placket of his shirt, then toyed with the knot of his tie, neatening it. One of her hands slid down and around his waist while the other lightly slid around his forearm, stroked over his upper arm, then toyed with the hair curling over his collar. She nuzzled under his chin, then kissed the pulse point at the base of his neck.

Breathing became difficult and blood rushed to his already engorged cock. He wanted to sweep her into his arms and kiss her senseless. No, what he really wanted to do was slide his fingers under that sexy strapless top and tug it down, revealing her rigid nipples. Then he'd lean her back over his arm and draw one hard nub into his mouth, toying with it under his tongue until she moaned in ecstasy.

Another ding and the slowing of the elevator alerted him to the fact that the doors were about to open. He slid his arm around her waist then whisked her down the hall to his room, trying to calm his overactive hormones. He slid the plastic card into the lock slot and pulled it out, but he did it too quickly and the light flashed red. She smiled and took the card from his fingers, then repeated the process. As soon as the light flickered green, she pressed down on the door latch, then pushed the door open.

"Oh, what a lovely room," she said as she stepped inside.

Her gaze traveled over the burgundy and gold decor enhanced by the dark-stained cherry wood furniture.

"Wait until you see the view." He strode past her to the window and pulled open the drapes to reveal the fabulous skyline of the city below, the stunning old architecture of the Chateau Laurier across the canal, and the reflection of lights twinkling on the water.

She stepped closer to the window, the swaying of her hips sending his pulse into overdrive. She glanced out appreciatively, but he couldn't drag his gaze from her.

"Mmm. Lovely."

She turned around and her gaze came to rest on the large four-poster king-sized bed, cozy-looking with its burgundy velvet covering. The bed had been turned back to reveal satin sheets of the same color. A gold foil–covered chocolate mint sat on the pillow.

She shifted close to him. He could feel the heat of her body. She smiled seductively.

"So what do two strangers who are wildly attracted to each other do now?" she asked.

He knew what he wanted to do now, but instead he said, "Well, I could order up some champagne and strawberries or—"

"Or we could do this."

Heat surged through him at the seductive timbre of her voice. She stroked his cheek, the light touch of her fingertips an amazing treat to his senses. He wanted to drag her into a passionate embrace, capturing her lips with wild hunger, but he waited for her to make the first move. Her fingertips trailed across his lips, lighting a fire inside him, then she clasped her hands around his neck and drew him closer. One hand moved to his cheek as she drew his face to hers. The first delicate touch of her mouth sent his heartbeat into overdrive. His lips tingled, sending streams of sensation through his entire jaw as her soft mouth moved under his. An explosion of sizzling need blasted through him and his cock throbbed.

She drew back and stared at him, her eyes wide.

"That was amazing." Her voice, breathless and sexy, made his blood boil.

"My God, you must be the sexiest woman alive." He sucked in a deep breath, then plundered her lips again. The velvet feel of her mouth under his did strange and wonderful things to him. His pulse surged and his heart somersaulted. His erection pulsed against the confines of his wool pants.

"Mmm." She gazed up at him, her silver-blue eyes glittering like moonlight sparkling across a lake at sunset. "It feels like you want me."

Her breathless words assured him the desire was mutual.

"You noticed that, did you?"

He captured her lips again, reveling in the heat of her, the sweet smell of her, the soft responsiveness of her lips.

Her hand slid up between them and he realized she was unbuttoning his shirt. She had started at the top, so he fumbled with the bottom buttons, finally just ripping the shirt open, impatient to feel her hands on his naked skin. He was not disappointed as her fingertips stroked up his stomach, then teased across his nipples. She kissed his neck, then her lips wandered down his chest. His breath caught as she lapped her tongue over one nipple, then sucked it into her mouth.

She shifted back and smiled at him, then turned her back to him, hands on her waist.

"Do you mind?"

He stared at the back of her neck, then his gaze trailed down past her shoulder blades to the edge of her red dress. Finally, he realized she wanted him to release her zipper. He grabbed the tiny tab between his fingers and eased it down slowly, his breath becoming heavy and hard as the fabric parted to reveal her creamy skin. As much as he wanted to, he resisted the urge to touch the newly revealed skin, knowing if he did, he'd drag the dress from her body and take her right there on the floor.

She eased the dress down, her back still to him, revealing the curve of her slim waist. She slipped the garment over her hips and dropped it to the floor. He smiled appreciatively at the small red lace triangle, all that was visible of her very sexy thong, then his gaze traced her smooth, shapely, and quite bare derriere.

She turned around and his gaze caressed her soft womanly curves. The red lace strapless demi-bra, barely covering her nipples, seemed to offer her breasts to him. Her tiny panties accentuated the long, elegant flare of her hips. Her fingers slid up the line of her torso and she struck a sexy pose.

"You like what you see?"

He almost laughed at the slight cloud of uncertainty in her eyes. She had to be kidding.

He stroked his hands up her body as she had, reveling in the feel of her satin skin.

"Absolutely."

She smiled and reached around behind her.

He drew her close and kissed her temple, then whispered, "Let me help you with that."

He covered her busy fingers with his own. She'd managed to undo three of the four tight hooks anchoring her bra closed. He unlatched the final one and held it in place a moment longer while he stroked his fingers along the soft flesh beneath the elastic. He placed whisper-soft kisses along the upper edge of her bra, listening to her breath quicken.

He drew the elastic of the bra away from her skin, then stepped back while she peeled the cups from her body, revealing her full, round breasts. His erection strained against his zipper.

He started to shrug out of his jacket, but she grabbed his lapels and stepped into his arms again. She parted his shirt and her naked breasts brushed his abs, then crushed against him as she wrapped her arms around his neck and kissed him ardently. His arms slid around her, his hands stroking across her naked back.

"You like this, don't you?" he murmured into her ear, cued by her soft, needy whimpers. "Being naked, while I'm fully dressed." It certainly turned him on. Immensely.

"Mmm. I think it's sexy," she agreed.

"Let me see you," he urged, cupping her elbows and easing some distance between them.

She stepped back and twirled, her lips curling into an impish smile, revealing a lovely row of white teeth. She raised one arm straight up and tucked the other behind her head and sashayed back and forth, swaying her hips in an enticing fashion. She turned back to him, gliding her hands under her breasts as though holding them up.

"You want to see these?"

"Mmm. You bet."

Her eyes crinkled as she smiled more broadly, then she brushed her arm against the sleeve of his fine wool jacket, her skin soft and fair against the dark, charcoal color.

"You want to *touch* these?"

His hands itched to touch them. He had to stop himself from grabbing them and squeezing.

"Yes, I'd love to touch them." The serious tone in his voice surprised even him.

Her smile softened and her face almost glowed.

"You really do want me, don't you?"

The sound of awe in her voice surprised him. Was she so uncertain of her allure?

"I've never wanted a woman more." The words were absolutely true.

She took his hands and drew them to her breasts. The feel of her warm, round flesh filling his palms took his breath away. Reverently, he stroked her soft, white mounds, and her nipples hardened and extended.

"You are incredibly beautiful." He stroked the tips of her jutting nipples with his thumbs, her little gasping breaths accelerating his blood flow. He desperately wanted to strip off his pants and release his raging, painfully confined cock, but he wanted to indulge her more.

He leaned down and captured one taut nipple between his lips, then teased it with his teeth.

"Oh, yes," she murmured.

He used one hand to hold the weight of one magnificent, round breast as he teased the nub with his tongue, and his other hand slid down her ribs, around her waist, then cupped one alluring buttock.

"Mmm." Her fingers forked through his hair.

He shifted to the other breast and coaxed it to the same level of arousal as its mate. When both nipples stood huge and swollen, he kissed her ribs, then trailed downward, crouching in front of her. Her fingers tightened in his hair. He dabbed his tongue into her navel, then continued downward. Settling onto his knees, he tucked his fingers under the lacy hem of her thong and drew it down slowly, revealing her dark, silky curls.

He stroked the pink flesh between her legs. She glistened with slickness. He drew the folds of her labia apart with his thumbs until he could see the little button of her clit. He dabbed at it with the tip of his tongue.

"Ohhhh," she moaned.

He wrapped his hands around her, cupping both buttocks, and kissed her soft, intimate flesh, then sucked lightly.

"Oh, God. Come here." She pulled him up and kissed him fervently, shoving his jacket and shirt off his shoulders and dragging them down his arms.

Her urgent movements set his blood boiling. He tugged his arms free and wrapped them around her. Her fingers worked at his fly and his pants finally loosened, easing the crippling tightness on his erection. He shoved the pants down, impatient to feel his naked skin against hers. She had him so hot he could barely hold himself at bay.

She eased downward and tugged the waistband of his briefs forward. His cock sprang free. She shoved his underwear to the floor and he stepped out of them, kicking them to one side.

Her fingers wrapped around his rigid penis and she stroked

him. He almost ejaculated on the spot. He tugged her hand away and drew her to standing again.

"Baby, I'm way too hot for that."

He kissed her thoroughly.

"I'm hot, too," she said when he released her mouth. "And so wet." Her breathing came in short, panting gasps.

She licked his right nipple, sending urgent need pulsing through him.

"I want this to last," he murmured as she grabbed his cock again.

"It will." She pumped him. "Next time."

She leaned forward and nuzzled under his chin.

"I want you right now." She blew into his ear, then murmured, "I'm so wet you could slide right in."

Her words and her light breath swirling around his ear drove him insane with need. He backed her to the wall and cupped her butt, lifting her against him. She guided his rigid cock to her opening and he thrust inside her.

"Oh, God, yes!" she exclaimed as she wrapped her legs around his hips.

Her melting heat surrounded him. His groin became impossibly tight. She had brought him to the brink before he'd even slid inside her. He knew there was no way on Earth he was going to last, but he had to find a way. He intended to bring her to climax before he satisfied himself.

He drew out slowly, then just as slowly eased in again. She wriggled against him, almost sending him over the edge.

"Fast. And hard," she insisted.

"But—"

She tightened her legs around him and arched forward.

Oh, God, too late.

He thrust once, then again, and she wailed in pleasure. Thank God, he thought, before coherence left him completely. He continued to pump, erupting inside her.

JENNA DROPPED HER head to his shoulder and sighed, clinging to his broad shoulders. His tremendous cock twitched inside her and she squeezed affectionately.

"Sweetheart, that was incredible." His words rumbled against her neck.

He twitched again and she tightened her legs around him. She could feel him swelling inside her.

"I think you want me again," she murmured in his ear.

"I don't think I'll ever stop wanting you." The coarse tone of his words elated her. She'd never seen him express so much emotion.

He pivoted forward, pressing his growing cock deeper into her. She sucked in air. He pivoted back and forward again and she clutched him tight against her as the intense pleasure threatened to send her over the edge once more.

"Oh, God."

He thrust harder and her breath caught as waves of pleasure crashed over her. Again and again as he thrust and thrust. Coherent thought eroded like sand on a beach as she gave in to the sensuous delight. Another orgasm swept through her, sparking every cell to awareness.

Finally, she flopped her head onto his shoulder again, breathing in the musky male scent of him, enjoying the feel of his still-erect penis inside her. She eased her feet to the floor.

"Well, stud, it feels like you still have some strength left in you."

He pushed deeper and kissed her neck, finding the place that drove her wild with need, sending tingles through her whole body.

"I sure do. This time, I want to be able to touch those beautiful breasts of yours longer, and explore the rest of your body in detail."

She smiled. "Explore away, Magellan."

He drew back and she sighed as his penis slid from her depths.

He led her to the big, gorgeous bed and she stretched out, the feel of the burgundy velvet cover sinfully sensual against her back. His gaze traveled the length of her and he smiled in admiration.

"You are absolutely beautiful."

Jenna felt the heat of a blush cross her cheeks. He sat down beside her and stroked along her jawline, then trailed his finger downward, along her neck, down the center of her chest between her breasts, and around her navel.

"Absolutely beautiful."

She couldn't help staring at his broad, muscular chest, with the sprinkles of dark, curly hairs shadowing the hard planes. She stroked her hand across his chest, adoring the taut strength of him, and circled one nipple with her fingertip.

He cupped her breasts, then his fingertips found her nipples, which immediately thrust forward, hard and needy. He leaned forward and touched one with the tip of his tongue. He licked first the tip, then drew his tongue around the circumference; then he dabbed the tip again. She groaned at the exquisite torture.

It became impossibly hard, aching for him. He switched to the other nipple and brought it to the same level of need.

"Oh, God, that feels wonderful," she murmured.

It had been so long since he had touched her like this. In fact, he had never had quite this effect on her. Even though she'd already had two orgasms, she wanted him inside her again. Urgently.

But even more she needed his closeness.

"Kiss me." She opened her arms, inviting him closer.

He smiled and stretched out beside her, drawing her against him as she wrapped her arms around him. His lips met hers sweetly, a gentle pressure that sparked a deep need within her. Her tongue slid to meet his lips, then pressed inside his strong, masculine mouth. The tip of his tongue met hers, then stroked the length of it until they were entwined in an undulating dance. The inside of her mouth tingled, and those tingles rippled through her lips and jaw and quivered over the length of her entire body.

Her mouth moved on his while his tongue explored her depths. Her breathing and heartbeat accelerated. Her hand stroked down his chest, loving the feel of his coarse, curly hair caressing her palm. She slid over his navel and bumped against the head of his penis. Her finger trailed from the tip to the base. She loved the feel of his long rod springing up against her hand in excitement.

She cupped his fur-covered balls and closed her hand around them, gently pressing them together, then fondling them. He groaned into her mouth. Her other hand found one of his nipples and lightly pinched then teased it between her fingertips.

She drew her mouth from his and smiled, then shifted downward to suck on his nipple. He groaned and she sucked harder, then moved to the other and captured it in her busy mouth.

"Darling, you know just what I like." He kissed the back of her head.

"Which is amazing, since we're total strangers," she said, reminding him of the fantasy.

Making love with a stranger. How illicit. And ferociously exciting! She drew on him harder and he gasped.

"Oh, God, honey, you are something else." With that, he flipped her onto her back and prowled over her, pinning her hips between his knees.

He cupped her breasts with his hands and squeezed, then kneaded until her breathing became ragged. Never letting up, he captured one taut, pink nipple in his mouth. She almost cried out at the exquisite pleasure.

He cajoled with his tongue while he teased the other nipple between his fingertips. She reached out and grasped his long, hard cock, stroking from base to tip, then pumping him, wanting him to feel as invigorated and incredibly hot as she did.

He grabbed her hands and pinned them above her head.

"Honey, I don't want to be rushed." He sucked one of her nipples deep into his mouth until she groaned out loud, arching against him, then he squeezed the other between his tongue and the roof of his mouth. He smiled down at her.

"If you rush me, you'll miss this."

He released her and slid his hands down her thighs, easing them wider apart, then he leaned forward and thrust his tongue into her navel. She kissed the top of his head as he slid farther, dragging his tongue along her belly. His fingers slid across her labia, stroking along the outer lips, then teasing the folds apart. When she felt his tongue touch her moist, hot flesh and lick the length of her slit, she gasped. Ryan rarely performed oral sex on her, yet here he was doing it twice in one night!

He licked again, sending burning need sizzling through her. Wow. This Jake persona had some definite advantages.

His fingers drew the lips of her labia apart and stroked across her clitoris.

"Ohhh," she moaned at the intense sensation.

The tip of his tongue replaced his fingertip and he cajoled her to dizzying heights of need. She clung to his shoulder.

"Oh, God, yes. That's wonderful. Oh, yes!"

He circled and dabbed, sucked and licked.

"Ohhhhhh. More. Please, more."

He slid his hands up her belly and stroked her breasts, all the while keeping that wonderful tongue of his busy on her clitoris, sending potent pleasure jagging through her.

"Ohhh my God, you're so good at that."

Her fingers spiked through his hair, then clenched. She almost broke into tears at the powerful pleasure surging through her. Her whole body seemed to swell, then explode in the most potent orgasm yet.

As she lay gasping, he kissed his way up her belly to her neck, then lay down beside her and nuzzled her ear.

"Wow! You are incredible." She drew in a deep breath. "This really is a fantasy come true."

He kissed her cheek. "You're going to give me a swelled head."

She smiled impishly.

"That's a great idea." She sat up and climbed over him.

Nudging his knees apart, she kneeled between his legs and stroked his rigid cock from base to tip, then wrapped her fingers around the shaft and stroked a couple of times, loving the feel of his hard flesh in her hands.

She leaned forward and dragged her tongue along the

length of his shaft, then circled the ridge at the base of the head, alternately licking and tapping. When she reached the place where the foreskin had once been attached, she lapped and teased, excited by his accelerated breathing.

She took the head into her mouth and twirled her lips around the ridge. He moaned as she continued to sweetly pleasure him. She felt the head swell slightly and she knew he would soon climax.

"Sweetheart, you better—"

She shook her head, continuing to twirl and tap.

"Oh, God. Too late."

She felt warm liquid spurt into her mouth. She continued to lick and twirl until he collapsed back onto the bed. She swallowed and smiled up at him.

"Your head definitely swelled."

"Oh, God, come here, you," he insisted.

As Jake pulled her to his side and kissed her, his lips dancing with passion, he wondered at his luck at finding such an incredibly sexy woman. His arms wrapped tightly around her and pulled her close against him. He then proceeded to bathe her breasts with warm, wet licks.

He sucked one nipple into his mouth, feeling it harden and pebble against his tongue. Her quick little catches of breath as he alternated between one nipple and the other sent his pulse rising. Even though he'd ejaculated in her hot, sexy mouth only moments before, his cock sprang into action, swelling and hardening against her belly.

His fingers moved to her warm, wet opening and slid inside. She felt like slippery velvet. He couldn't stand it any longer. He shifted and his impatient cock nudged at her entrance.

She wanted a fantasy lover and he intended to oblige her.

She pivoted forward and the head surged inside. At the feel of her velvet depths surrounding him, he thrust his rigid cock deep inside her.

"Ohhh, yes," she cried.

He pulled back, then thrust again. She tightened around him and he almost gasped. He pulsed forward and back, forward and back, his excitement accelerating at her rapidly increasing moans of pleasure.

"Oh, God, yes. Deeper."

He drove in, deep and hard.

"Yes!" she wailed. "Faster."

He increased his pace and she contracted her muscles around him in a pulsating rhythm, sending him over the edge. As he exploded inside her, her moans grew to enthusiastic cries of ecstasy, rising to a scream, long and loud, leaving him in no doubt she'd reached orgasm. Again and again!

She dropped back against the bed exhausted, her arms still around him.

"That was wonderful." She sounded totally sated. "You really are an incredible stud."

"Thank you." He shifted to his side, drawing her against his chest. "You're pretty incredible yourself."

She snuggled against him, giving in to the contented sleepiness overtaking her. Within moments, she'd fallen asleep.

CHAPTER 3

JENNA AWOKE WITH a start. It was dark and the surroundings seemed unfamiliar. Warm, strong arms held her fast against a muscular, definitely masculine chest. She glanced at the face inches from her own, his features illuminated by soft moonlight.

Ryan. Posing as a stranger to realize her fantasy. Her heart melted. She'd been totally blown away by his actions. She hadn't realized he'd even been paying attention when she'd told him about her fantasies. A part of her had started to believe he didn't care enough to listen to her at all anymore.

He had truly surprised her, and such a delightful surprise. In fact, she'd surprised herself. In their playacting, she'd found a side of herself she'd never known existed. She smiled at the memory of the brazen sex kitten she'd become. He had certainly liked that side of her.

She stroked his whiskered cheek. She couldn't believe how different he'd been last night. Almost like a true stranger. A wonderful, sinfully sexy stranger.

His eyes opened and her heart jolted at the loving look in his eyes.

"Hello." His throaty, sleepy voice sounded incredibly sexy.

"Hi, there."

His arm tightened around her, drawing her closer. As her breasts came in contact with his hair-roughened chest, her nipples hardened.

"Mmm. You feel so good," he murmured.

He nuzzled her neck and she felt her blood heat.

She nibbled his earlobe, but as her gaze flickered across his wavy hair, the blue digits of the clock flipped to the next minute, grabbing her attention.

Four fifty-two.

"Oh, no." Damn, she had to get home. She had volunteered to drive seniors to a pancake breakfast at the community center in the morning. She couldn't be late.

"I have to get home. I have an eight o'clock appointment." She still had to go home and shower and change.

She started to ease away, but he tightened his arm around her waist.

"Hold on." His lips brushed her forehead and the sweet contact weakened her muscles. "Surely, you have time for this."

His mouth covered hers and moved in sweet, silent persuasion, asking her to stay, asking her to forget about responsibilities and think only of him and the bliss she could find in his arms. When his tongue joined the urging by stroking inside her lips, she slumped against him. Her lips responded, moving against his, and her tongue joined the dance. Delicious sensations quivered through her body.

Some small, sane part of her glanced at the clock again. Four fifty-six.

"Mmm." Her voice was muffled as she struggled to part

her mouth from his. "I really can't be late." She put a little distance between them, then gave in to her weakness and kissed him again.

He kissed along her jawline and nuzzled the hollow at the base of her neck as he prowled over her.

"Are you sure you have to go right now?"

She nodded, pleading in her eyes. If he kept this up, she'd melt into a puddle on the bed and let him have his way with her.

He sighed deeply. "Okay, but I'm letting you go under protest."

She wrapped the sheet around herself and tried to stand up, but he tugged at the fabric.

"Hey, that's not fair," he complained. "If I can't make love to you, at least let me see you again."

She gazed at him uncertainly, her cheeks flushing. She wasn't one to parade around naked.

"Come on, sweetheart. You're not going to tell me you're shy. Not after last night."

He was right. She was being silly. She had loved parading around naked last night.

She stood up, letting the sheet fall from her body. At the look of darkening need in his eyes, however, she raced into the bathroom squealing in laughter as Ryan leaped up and raced after her, hot on her heels. He caught her and spun her around, kissing her like there was no tomorrow. He eased her into the shower stall and proceeded to soap every inch of her body. Twenty minutes later they emerged, squeaky clean and quite sated. For now.

Jenna gathered up her clothes and pulled on the tiny red thong. Ryan helped her hook her bra, then zipped up her dress once she had it in place.

He had never been quite so attentive and she loved it. She headed for the door.

"Wait a second, Aurora." He tugged on his pants. "I'll walk you to your car."

She smiled at his use of her play name, amazed he still wanted to keep the fantasy alive. She resolved not to ask him anything about the Toronto trip, or to do anything else to shatter the fantasy.

He pulled on his shirt, then his socks and shoes.

"Okay, let's go."

She grabbed her evening bag as he opened the door. At this time of the morning, the hotel corridor was empty. When they arrived at the elevator, he pushed the Down arrow button, which lit up. Seconds later, the light went out and the elevator doors whooshed open.

They stepped aboard and the doors closed behind them. She touched the *L* button for the lobby. His arms circled her waist from behind and he drew her back against his chest. His lips nuzzled her neck.

"It's too bad you have to go."

She melted against him and his hands skimmed up to her breasts.

"Mmm. I know."

As she watched the floor numbers illuminate one by one, she smiled. A quick glance at her watch told her she could afford another few minutes.

"You know, you did such a great job of realizing my fantasy of making love with a handsome stranger, I was thinking maybe you could help me out with another one."

His hands tightened on her breasts.

"Oh? And what might that be?"

"I've always wanted to make love with a stranger on an elevator."

He shifted forward and jammed the red Stop button. She felt his cock stiffen against her buttocks as the elevator came to a halt.

"I'd love to."

He stroked her thigh, then slid his hand up, pulling her skirt with it. The large volume of fabric swirled around her legs as he drew it upward, gathering it together. The bulk of it draped in front of her as he arranged it around the sides of her waist. She leaned forward, rested her hands against the mirrored side of the elevator, and smiled at her own reflection. He tugged on the elastic of her thong, pulling the fabric tightly into her slit. He teased her by tugging and releasing it. One of his fingers slid under the satin of her panties to her clit and he dabbed at it.

She watched the look of rapture on her own face reflected in the mirror as she lost herself in the pleasure. He slid two fingers inside her as he continued to stroke her clitoris, faster and faster, bringing her to the brink of orgasm, then slowing down.

He hooked his fingers under the elastic of her thong and eased it down. She stepped out of it and watched in the mirror as he unzipped his pants and pulled out his long, semi-erect cock.

"Wait." She turned to face him, then knelt in front of him, tucking the drapes of her skirt between her knees. She wanted that beautiful penis in her mouth. She wrapped her hands around it and drew it to her lips, then ran her tongue around the corona. She drew the large, purple head into her mouth and sucked hard, then circled her lips around him, hearing his breathing accelerate. She slid up and down on him, feeling his cock grow and harden in her mouth. He stroked her shoulders as she pleasured him.

She wrapped her hands around him, cupping his hard, muscular buttocks in her hands, and drew him deep into her throat, squeezing him within her mouth. His muscles tensed in her hands. She knew he wouldn't last much longer.

She squeezed and pulsed around his now fully erect cock, eliciting a deep, masculine groan. She tucked her hands underneath and fondled his testicles, then released his cock and licked his balls thoroughly.

"God, Aurora. I'm going to come any minute."

She sucked him deep into her mouth again, sliding up and down, faster and faster, tightening around him. He exploded inside her, his semen pulsing down her throat.

She released his flaccid member, thrilled at the power she had over him. She stood up and unzipped her dress, dropping it to the elevator floor.

"Oh, you've been a naughty boy, going all soft like that. Now I'll have to tend to these myself." She cupped her breasts and squeezed, then tucked the lace of her bra under them and trailed her fingers across the nipples. The throbbing hardness excited her.

As he watched, his eyes glazed, and his cock curved upward.

She ran her fingers down her belly, then slid over her very damp opening.

"Mmm. Wet."

He reached for her breasts and caressed one, then the other. His mouth captured her nipple and suckled greedily. Her excitement intensified. His hand teased the other to almost unbearable hardness. He reached around her and unfastened her bra, sliding the lace garment out of the way.

He sucked on her nipple, hard and fast. She moaned at the intense pleasure. She could almost come now. But she wanted him inside her.

She turned around, facing herself in the mirrored wall again. She leaned forward, thrusting her behind toward him. His hands circled her buttocks, stroking and teasing, closer to her hot slit. She groaned and finally his fingers slid along the slick opening. She felt the tip of his rigid cock brush against her pussy, then he eased inside her, the thick round head stretching her. She pushed backward and he thrust forward.

"Oh, yes," she cried.

He drew back, then thrust forward again, deeper this time.

"Oh, my God." She felt the start of an orgasm. "Harder."

He thrust harder and faster, surging into her again and again. She watched his face in the mirror, his features tense, concentrated. The pulsing need flooded through her, releasing ripples of pleasure, which grew to enormous waves of ecstatic delight.

"Oh God, oh God, oh God!" She bounced up and down, riding the intense waves, her breasts bobbing up and down. She looked thoroughly wanton. Her voice rose in intensity with the mounting pleasure, which exploded through her like a supernova.

His hands cupped her breasts, plucking at her nipples, intensifying the cataclysmic orgasm. She threw her head back and moaned loudly. He groaned and pulsed inside her.

Slowly, she became aware of his hands around her waist, easing her back toward him. She leaned against his broad chest, resting her head in the crook of his neck, squeezing his cock with internal muscles.

"Mmm. That was spectacular," she murmured.

He nuzzled her cheek.

"You got that right." His lips nibbled behind her ear and she giggled at the delicate sensations quivering through her.

"I've really got to go."

His cock eased out of her and he turned her around to face him. He gave her a deep, sound kiss, then held her close in his arms. She felt so loved. Once they parted, his gaze locked with hers, and he smiled.

"This has really been a pleasure, Aurora."

She smiled. "Yes. It certainly has . . . Jake."

He picked up her dress and undies from the elevator floor and handed them to her, then zipped up his pants and straightened his clothes.

"I'd really like to see you again." He helped her fasten her bra.

She pulled on her dress and smoothed it into place. He adjusted it so that the top lay straight over her breasts, the touch of his fingers sending tingles across her skin.

She pushed the elevator button and they progressed downward.

"But then, it wouldn't be a stranger fantasy, would it?"

The doors opened and she stepped into the lobby. The desk clerk glanced up, then his gaze returned to his computer screen.

"I'll walk you to your car." His arm slid around her waist.

They walked down a hallway then out a side door.

"Are you saying you won't see me again?" he asked as he followed her past the first row of cars.

She stopped at her small red Toyota Echo in the middle of the second row and unlocked the door.

"If I saw you again, then it wouldn't be a one-night stand with a stranger. Now, if you were a pirate . . ."

He grabbed her and dragged her into his arms for a passionate kiss.

"I can be a pirate."

"And you'd be a damned fine one, too," she responded breathlessly.

She glanced at her watch. Five forty-three.

"I've really got to go."

She reached for the door handle, but he clutched her hand. "Aurora, at least tell me your last name."

She laughed. "You're really into this, aren't you?" She cupped his cheeks and kissed him sweetly. "Thank you so much for tonight. You don't know what it means to me."

She climbed into her car and started the engine.

Jake watched her, feeling completely helpless. She didn't want to see him again. His gut twisted into a knot.

She glanced at her watch. "If I hurry, I won't be late. I hope your meeting in Toronto goes well."

As he watched her drive away, he committed her license plate to memory, then her words surfaced to his consciousness. How in hell did she know about his trip to Toronto?

SHE WAS LATE!

Jenna glanced at the calendar beside the fridge and counted again, knowing she wouldn't find any change in her calculation, but doing it anyway.

Damn, definitely late.

Jenna shoved her hair back from her face as she slumped onto the cream and beige stool in front of her kitchen island

and plunked her elbows on the oak countertop. She glanced at the clock over the doorway, counting the seconds to one minute, then she picked up the little blue wand sitting in the plastic stand beside her. She stared at it, blinking. A plus sign stared back at her.

She stuck the wand back onto the stand and dropped her face into her hands.

Oh, God, she was pregnant.

The phone rang and her back stiffened. She crossed to the desk by the fridge and plucked up the receiver.

"Hey, girl, how's it going?" At the sound of Cindy's cheerful voice Jenna broke into tears.

"Jenna, honey, what's wrong?"

"I'm pregnant." She sobbed.

"Pregnant? I thought you and Ryan weren't . . . oh, except for last Saturday."

"That's right. Saturday. And you know me. I'm regular as clockwork. When my period didn't start on Monday, I started to worry. I'm now four days overdue . . . and I'm never overdue." She sobbed again.

"Except that one time last year," Cindy reminded her.

Jenna started to pace. The spiral cord of the phone knocked over her pen mug, scattering pens across the desk. She set the black and gold cup upright and scooped up the spilled pens as she talked.

"Yeah, and I had that pregnancy test left over."

"I remember. You bought the double pack because it's cheaper that way and I said you wouldn't need another one."

"And you were wrong." Jenna tapped a pencil on the desktop.

"I did suggest you put the extra money into condoms," Cindy replied gently.

"I know. I got sloppy. But when you're as regular as I am, it's easy to believe it won't happen."

"That's what you said last time."

Jenna jabbed the pencil into the mug.

"And last time I was right," she snapped.

"Jenna, whatever made you take the chance?"

She sank onto the desk chair, scenes from that fabulous night skimming through her mind. She stared off into space.

"Cindy. Picture it. Five in the morning. Alone in an elevator with an incredibly hunky stranger."

"Mmm. Yeah, okay."

Jenna knew Cindy was imagining the scene, probably drooling. Jenna's own thoughts strayed back to the incredible experience and her insides quivered.

"We're still talking about Ryan here, right?" Cindy confirmed.

"Of course we are!" Jenna replied.

"Okay, good. Well, you two are in a committed relationship. He'll probably want to take it to the next level. Things are working out between you two again, aren't they?"

Jenna thought about the months of neglect, then thought about the amazing fantasy he'd given her.

"He really made an effort last week, but is it enough?" Her face fell to her hands. Oh, heavens, this couldn't be happening to her.

"Did he call you while he was away?"

"No." Jenna twirled the phone cord around her finger. "He called me when he got back yesterday."

"When are you seeing him again?"

"Tomorrow night." Jenna tugged her finger free from the cord and watched it spring back and forth. "We're having dinner together."

"Are you going to tell him then?"

"Yes."

"Will you marry him if he asks?"

Would she? Marriage didn't necessarily solve everything. If they got married but he still threw himself into his work, she might as well be on her own. Would he be emotionally and physically available to her, married or not?

"Jenna?"

She laid her hand on her stomach, imagining she could feel the stirrings of a new life inside her.

She wanted her baby to grow up with his father fully a part of his life. Not like hers. Her parents had divorced when she was only three and she remembered crying desperately, begging Daddy to stay. He'd held her and she remembered him shedding his own tears. Her older brother, Shane, had gone with their father. For a couple of years she saw them every weekend, but then Daddy's work required him to move to Vancouver, on the far side of the country. After that, she only saw them a couple of times a year.

The void that had left in her life still haunted her. She couldn't do that to her own child.

"Yes. I will."

CHAPTER 4

RYAN KNOCKED ON Jenna's apartment door, longing to see her face again. The face that filled his dreams every night, and his daydreams all day.

She opened the door and warmth flooded through him. Her eyes shone brightly and her face seemed to glow. He'd definitely been away from her too long. The problem was he never wanted to be away from her at all. If he did what his heart dictated, he'd be with her all the time, neglecting everything else, and if he did that his business would slide. All the success he'd worked so hard to achieve would dissolve.

She had become a dangerous obsession. Staring at her sweet glowing face right now, however, he almost didn't care.

And that scared him most of all.

"Hi." She seemed a little reserved as she stepped back from the door to let him in.

She closed the door behind him and stood silently watching him. The rich blue sweater and snug black jeans she wore accentuated her lovely curves. He couldn't believe such a beautiful woman chose to be with him. He took her hand and drew her toward him, then tipped up her chin and kissed her.

Her hands curled around his neck, her soft lips responsive under his.

The familiar stirrings rumbled within him but he stamped them down, not allowing them to overtake him. He'd had lots of practice over the past several months. If he gave in to them, he'd have her clothes off and her flat on her back within moments. He longed to claim her, fast and hard, but that wouldn't do justice to the feelings he had for her, and it wouldn't be fair to her. She deserved a long, languorous session of making love, where he would worship her body from top to bottom, where he would make her feel every bit a woman and very thoroughly pleasured.

He drew back and smiled down at her.

"How's my girl?"

"Fine," she replied, but he sensed tentativeness in her voice. Was she still upset about his breaking their date?

He drew her into his arms and hugged her, loving the feel of her against his body. It had been so long since he'd felt her body naked against his. His groin tightened at the thought. Tonight he would make love with her. Long and leisurely. He'd been holding back too much. Putting his work ahead of her too much. But only because he had to know he could. He had to know that loving her wouldn't totally destroy his way of life. He'd felt badly about missing the wedding. He'd done a lot of thinking while he'd been away and realized he wasn't being fair to her. He had to find a better balance in his life. He had to find a way to love her, while still having time to build his business to the success he wanted. At least to the success of Jake's company.

. . .

HE TOOK HER out to dinner. An intimate little restaurant with candlelight and Italian decor. Over dinner they talked about his trip, then he asked her how her project for Health and Welfare was going. She told him about the latest changes to the prototype system to handle DIN numbers for new drug releases, but generally she seemed a little distracted.

As dinner neared the end he found himself getting anxious to leave. Knowing what the night ahead held, he was eager to get her home and into bed.

Once back in her apartment, he followed her into the kitchen. He opened the top cupboard beside the stove where she kept the wine.

"Red or white?" he asked.

"Just pick whatever you'd like."

He chose a bottle of his favorite Riesling wine.

She opened the fridge and pulled out a bottle of mixed citrus and berry juice.

"Are you having sangria?"

If she had said so, he would have selected a red wine. She often took a glass of half wine and half juice—she liked this particular mix of fruit because it made a nice combination with wine—but she liked it only with red.

"No, I don't feel like wine tonight, but you go ahead."

He placed the bottle on the island and she handed him the corkscrew. As he pulled out the cork, she retrieved two tall, pale blue stemmed glasses from a cupboard and filled one with juice.

He filled his glass with white wine and followed her into the living room. He turned on the stereo, selecting a station with soft music, then sat beside her on the couch, sliding his arm around her shoulders.

She shifted slightly.

"Ryan, we need to talk."

His gut clenched immediately. In his experience, the only time a woman said those words was when she wanted to break up.

He stroked the hair back from her face.

"What is it, sweetheart?"

"You know, Suzie's wedding was really important to me. I don't think you understand how disappointed I was when you didn't come."

Oh, no. Here it comes.

"I know, sweetheart, and I'm really sorry, but—"

"But your business is important. I know that." She rested her hands on her chest, over her heart. "But I should be important, too."

The glimmer in her eyes, hinting at unshed tears, tore at his heart.

"You are. I—"

She waved her hand, cutting him off.

"Wait, I know you want to have your say—and I'll listen to whatever you have to say later—but please just listen right now. I need to get this out."

He took her hands, holding them between his own.

"Okay, go ahead, Jenna. I'm listening."

"When you didn't come, I was very upset. Hurt, really." Her eyes shone brighter, glistening in the lamplight.

His gut compressed. He'd never meant to hurt her. He'd never really thought about it like that.

She drew her hands away and shifted slightly. The result put a little distance between them.

"I . . . I had decided that . . . well, that we weren't working out."

Oh, God, she really was going to break up with him. He felt blackness closing in around him.

"There had just been too many times. Your work seemed more important than me and if we were really meant to be, that wouldn't be the case." She fiddled with her hands, not looking at him. "And you and I hadn't made love for over three months."

Three months, two weeks, and five days. But who was counting?

"But that night turned out to be the best night of my life. Living out my sexual fantasy was intensely exciting."

"Fantasy?" What the hell was she talking about?

Her eyes crinkled and she smiled impishly.

"Yes, having hot, wild sex with a complete stranger in his room. It was fabulous."

He stared at her, speechless. He couldn't be getting this right. Surely she hadn't allowed herself to be picked up by a stranger. Not his Jenna.

Her voice dropped in timbre.

"And then there was the elevator. Oh, God, that was . . . Wow."

His blood froze and numbness claimed his body.

Her hand crept over his and she squeezed his fingers. The gleam in her eyes absolutely tortured him.

He remembered her telling him about her sexual fantasies, though he didn't remember anything about an elevator—and he was sure he would remember. He'd had to hold himself tightly at bay, spending every ounce of discipline he had to stop himself from throwing her down and taking her in a wild bout of passion. He'd almost failed, so he'd finally made an excuse to leave early. He just couldn't allow himself to grab her and tear her clothes off. What if he hurt her in his semi-madness?

Damn it. Anger welled up at the thought she'd been untrue, but it couldn't drive away the desolation he felt at knowing he'd lost her. His relationship with Jenna was the most important thing in his life yet he had tried to control the relationship, to keep it locked up in one small compartment. He'd been so afraid his need to be with her would overwhelm everything else in his life, yet now that he had lost her, he knew nothing else was half as important as Jenna. He had neglected her so much she'd felt she had to go searching for love elsewhere. It was all his fault he had lost her.

"The thing is, after that, I decided I want to stay with you."

His head reeled. She wasn't dumping him? Emotions swirled through him, making him dizzy.

Here she was telling him she'd had sex with another man—a complete stranger—yet relief flooded through him that he hadn't lost her after all.

She leaned forward and kissed him, then wrapped her arms around him, resting her head against his chest. His arm circled her waist and he just allowed the sensations of her soft body pressing against his to flow through him. He should protest. Tell her how angry he was that she'd slept with another man. Instead, he tightened his arms around her and held her closer, never wanting to let go.

Good God, he'd almost lost her. That changed his perspective on everything.

"There's something else I have to tell you. Something important."

Something important? What the hell did she consider more important than deciding to dump him, then sleeping with another man?

She eased away from him and took both his hands in hers. She looked up at him and her eyes were filled with such trepidation he wanted to sweep her back into his arms and tell her everything would be okay, no matter what she had to tell him. He loved her that much. He needed her that much.

"Ryan, I'm . . ." She hesitated and shifted back and forth, glancing down at their linked hands. She stroked his knuckles with her thumbs.

The suspense was driving him over the edge.

"Just tell me, Jenna," he urged.

She raised her face to gaze into his eyes. "I'm pregnant."

Pregnant. Oh, God, and by another man. He felt his face drain of color.

She continued to stare at him, her eyes starting to shimmer. As he let the whole notion sink into his befuddled brain, he realized tears had started to flow from her eyes.

"Oh, God, Jenna." He dragged her against him and held her close, his arms tight around her. "Jenna, sweetheart."

He kissed the top of her head, soft strands of her hair a light wisp across his nose. She must be afraid he'd dump her after finding out she'd cheated on him. Apparently, he had done an excellent job hiding just how much he was in love with her. Since the father was some one-night stand, she was probably afraid she'd wind up raising the baby alone.

"What do you want to have happen now?" he asked.

"I . . . I want my baby to have a father."

Oh, God, was she going to try to find the stranger—the father of her baby? Or worse, did she hope to marry the guy?

Did she hope Ryan, with his expertise in computers, would help her to find the man?

But she'd said she wanted to stay with Ryan. Maybe she just wanted to share custody of the child with the father. The thought of another man sharing such an important and intimate thing as raising a child with Jenna tore through him. It might start out innocently enough, but sharing life-altering moments like watching their child be born, hearing its first words, watching its first steps . . . Ryan knew these things had a profound effect on parents. Not only that, she was obviously attracted to the guy. If they spent a lot of time together, she might just fall into his arms again. Hell, she'd barely spent any time at all with him before she'd jumped into the sack with him the first time.

The first time. Hell, he was already thinking of her as having a permanent relationship with the guy.

Jenna's fingers curled around his sleeve.

"I . . . I'm hoping you'll want to raise the baby with me. I'm hoping you'll want to make our relationship more permanent."

Relief washed though him and his heart swelled. He eased her to face him, staring deeply into her watery blue eyes.

"Jenna, are you telling me that if I ask you to marry me, you will?"

She glanced up at him and nodded, her expression uncertain.

He hugged her close, then released her and lowered himself to the floor. At least he could do this right. Settling on one knee, he took her right hand in his and kissed it.

"Jenna, darling." He gazed deeply into her eyes. "Will you marry me?"

Tears streamed freely down her face now. She nodded, then seemed to find her voice.

"Yes." She threw herself into his arms and he held her as close as he could. "Yes, I'll marry you." The soft words, whispered into his ear, trembled through him.

He held her for a long time, savoring their closeness. Finally, he drew her to his side and rested his hand on her stomach, thinking of the little spark of life growing inside her. Maybe this was another man's baby, but he would raise it as his own, and he would love it as much as he loved its mother. His beautiful Jenna.

And he would never give her reason to seek love in another man's arms again.

"Tomorrow, we'll go out and get you a ring. The most beautiful engagement ring we can find. We can set the wedding for next month so you won't be showing yet, and—"

Smiling at him, she eased back and touched her finger to his lips. The sensation sent tendrils of warmth curling through him.

"Okay, Mr. Organization, that all sounds great, but right now there's something I'd rather be doing than planning our wedding."

"Really? I thought planning her wedding was the biggest thrill of a woman's life," he teased.

"Well, there is something I find marginally more thrilling." She tugged on his collar, then slid her hands down his neck to the top button of his shirt and released it.

A fire ignited deep in his groin and his cock slowly inflated. He wanted to slide his hands over her soft blue sweater, to feel her even softer breasts through the fine wool. His fingers ached to push under the garment and caress her bare skin, to find her nipples and stroke them between his fingers and thumb until the soft nubs hardened and elongated.

"I wonder what that could be." He stroked her hair behind her ear, clamping down on the yearning inside him, keeping it to a manageable level.

She leaned forward and touched her lips to his collarbone. Her soft mouth sent his senses whirling. The inferno in his groin blazed hotly and his hard cock ached painfully in the confines of his cords. As she kissed up his neck, then nuzzled under his chin, a wave of need more powerful than a tsunami shattered his tightly held control. He grasped both sides of his shirt and tore it open, scattering buttons everywhere.

She gasped in surprise, then laughed.

"My goodness, Ryan, you're really learning to loosen up."

CHAPTER 5

HER MOUTH COVERED his nipple and he groaned at the sensation of her tongue teasing the tip. It grew as hard as a bead and his throat went dry. He ran his fingers through her long chestnut hair, the silken strands caressing his hands. She stroked her hands down his rib cage, then settled over his stomach. At the clinking sound, he realized she was unfastening his belt. The sound of the zipper sliding down shuddered through him. He had longed for her touch, and denied it to himself for too long.

He held his breath as her soft fingers slipped into his pants and encircled his rapidly growing cock. He expelled the air quickly at her delicate touch on his hard, masculine flesh. God, this was exquisite. He shoved the pants down, cords and boxers together, giving her free access.

"Mmm." She stroked him base to tip, then flicked her tongue over the tip.

He groaned as he felt her tongue touch the base of his shaft, then lick the length of him. She twirled her tongue under the ridge of the head, then tapped right where the foreskin would have been attached. The sensation shot through him, exciting every nerve ending. One of her hands slid up his torso to his nipple and her fingers tweaked and stroked it. He stroked her hair as she stroked his cock to rigid arousal with her lips. She drew him deep inside her mouth. He never understood how she did it, but she could take him right to the base, opening her throat wide.

As he felt his cock move deeper into her hot, wet throat, he had to hold back the need to thrust. He could come right now, could already feel the tightening of his balls. Only the desire he had to prolong this, to feel her hot, dripping pussy hugging his cock, allowed him to hold back.

She moved up and down on him for several long, sensual moments, bringing him to the height of arousal, then she twirled her tongue around the head.

She released his penis from her mouth, the air cooling him off a little, then she kissed the head. Her tongue lapped across the tip, dabbing at the small opening, then she slid down his cock. She licked his testicles, then sucked them into her mouth.

"Oh, God, Jenna."

She smiled up at him, licked his shaft like a popsicle, then covered him with her mouth again, swallowing him whole. Her mouth moved up and down enthusiastically.

"Baby, I'm going to come soon."

She shifted to the tip and swirled her tongue around and around, nudging under the ridge of the head, driving him insane. She stroked her hand up to meet her mouth, keeping him in the warmth of her hand. She released him for a moment.

"Show me, sweetheart," she said, then captured him in the warmth of her mouth again.

She sucked deeply while fondling his balls in her hand. His groin tightened and he felt the heat flood through him. His whole body tensed as the semen flooded his penis then shot out into her mouth. His breath caught on the ecstatic feeling of release, pulsing into her warmth. Finally, he slumped back on the couch and she burrowed in beside him.

Once he'd caught his breath, he stroked her hair, then started lifting the hem of her sweater.

"Now it's your turn."

She stood up and tugged the sweater over her head, dropping it into a puddle beside her. His gaze fixed on the swell of her breasts as she reached behind to unhook her lacy blue bra. She slid the straps off her shoulders and let go of the garment. It remained suspended by friction alone, teasing him, until finally she slowly peeled it away, revealing her full, round breasts. The areolas were tight and hard, each nipple a hard, round bead in the center. He licked his lips, longing to run his tongue over those hard nubs. She shoved off her jeans, revealing tiny blue lace and satin panties. She climbed on top of him, one long, shapely leg on each side of his thighs. When the satin of her panties, warmed by the heat of her body, came in contact with his sagging penis, it pulsed to life.

He covered her breasts with his hands, reveling in the feel of her hard nipples pushing into his palms. She leaned forward, one hand on either side of his head, offering her breasts for a feast. He took one in his mouth, loving the way the areola pebbled in his mouth, the feel of the hard nipple against his tongue a definite turn-on. He covered her other breast with his palm, then found her nipple and stroked it with the tip of his finger.

"Mmm. That feels so good," she crooned.

She shifted her hips up and down, stroking his growing penis with the heat of her womanhood. His erection grew rapidly and he realized this was moving too fast. He grasped her hips and stopped her movement.

"Honey, let's slow this down." He pulled her against his chest and kissed her. "Why don't we go into the bedroom?"

She smiled. "Sure."

She rolled off the couch and he followed her down the hall and into the tranquillity of her bedroom. While he snatched the three light moss green pillows from the bed and tossed them onto the easy chair by the window, she pushed her tiny blue panties down her legs, then kicked them aside. Smiling broadly, she stretched out on the green paisley duvet, positioning herself on one side, propping her head on her arm, her breasts pushed together, one leg bent, in a super sexy pose. He sat down on the bed beside her and stroked the soft, dark curls of her pubic hair, unable to resist, then covered her breasts with his hands. He leaned forward and, nuzzling the juncture between her neck and shoulder, found the place he knew drove her wild.

She moaned, sending tremors through him.

Jenna felt she must be in heaven. Ryan had asked her to marry him. He wanted the baby. And now he was making love to her. She moaned again as his hands claimed her breasts, then his mouth covered her nipple. Shafts of pleasure stabbed through her, straight to her vagina.

He laved his tongue across her nipple then twirled around it. Cold air stimulated it to more intense rigidity as he shifted his mouth to her other breast. One nipple cold, one hot. Oh, so hot. She arched her lower body, ready to be touched down there. Needing to be touched. She wanted to grab his hand and place it exactly where she wanted it, but she didn't. She'd wait, allowing him to move over her slowly, prolonging the pleasure. He would ensure every part of her was fully explored. She wrapped her hand around his erection, pumping it, just to increase his urgency a little.

His mouth wandered lower as his hands covered her breasts, keeping them warm and stimulated. He paused at her navel, teasing it with the tip of his tongue. One hand stroked downward, past his mouth, then teased the curls below her stomach. His hand stroked lower still, lightly caressing her labia, then down her thigh. He caressed upward again, lightly touching her folds on the way to her stomach. She raised her pelvis to meet his hand, but not soon enough. She groaned.

He chuckled, then stroked downward again. This time, he cupped her mound, then his fingers stroked over her damp slit and she moaned at the intense pleasure. His mouth moved south, pausing to blow on her curls. He used both hands to open her lips, then he touched the tight bud of her clitoris with one fingertip.

"Oh, yes," she murmured.

His tongue replaced his finger and he nudged and licked. Electrical currents tore through her. His fingers slid along her slit, then one delved inside her as his tongue busily prodded and pulsed against her. Waves of pleasure drifted over her. His finger stroked the wall of her vagina, then a second finger joined it. His tongue moved faster. Her breathing increased. The waves grew higher and stronger. A third finger joined the others and after a moment of the intense combination of sensations, she gasped, then moaned long and hard as she fell over the edge in an eruption of potent pleasure.

"You're so beautiful, Jenna." The words floated through her consciousness as if from far away as she drifted back to the here and now. When she opened her eyes, he was gazing down at her with a rapt expression on his face.

"So beautiful."

His smile dazzled her and the depth of feeling in his midnight blue eyes warmed her soul. She opened her arms and he lowered himself into them, sweeping her into a tight embrace. She snuggled against him, exquisitely happy at the thought of the tiny baby growing inside her, of being held in Ryan's arms. The father of her baby. Her soon-to-be husband.

"Make love to me, sweetheart," she murmured against his ear.

"Absolutely, my sweet angel."

He prowled over her. His cock, swollen with need, fell across her belly. The hot, heavy flesh singed her nerve endings. He grasped it and positioned it against the cradle of her womanhood. She opened her legs, welcoming him. He slid inside, until the head nudged open her flesh, then he leaned forward and kissed her. A sweet and loving kiss, yet so passionate it stirred her past mere excitement to an arousal beyond the measure of the soul.

"Oh, sweetheart, push it in, deep and hard."

Her words flitted into Ryan's ears, sending his eyebrows arching and his blood boiling.

"What did you say?" he asked as he eased forward, giving her a little of what she'd asked for.

She arched her lower body, trying to capture him deeper, but he teased her by pulling back.

"I said deep and hard," she insisted.

He dipped down and kissed her, then pushed in a little more. She wrapped her legs around his thighs and tried to pull him in all the way.

"Tell me more, sweetheart," he whispered against her ear. "What is it you want me to do?"

She smiled. "I want you to drive your big cock deep inside me."

Her words seared through Ryan. He couldn't believe how exciting it was to hear her saying these things. He wanted more.

"What kind of cock?"

She rolled her eyes and giggled.

"Okay, I want you to thrust your *enormous* cock into me, again and again."

Her words were very persuasive, triggering his body to send more blood to his engorged penis until it was as hard as rock.

"I want you to give it to me hard and fast," she insisted, getting into the spirit of their play.

He pushed in farther, his smile broad, his heart hammering with excitement.

"Jenna, I love it when you say things like that."

He rewarded her by plunging into her, right to the hilt. She groaned in appreciation, then he began thrusting in and out, deep and hard, just as she'd requested.

She grasped the vertical bars of the maple headboard and met his thrusts.

"You've never talked like that before."

"Except that one time. Ohhh." She tightened her legs around him, arching to take him in even deeper. "When you were Jake."

He lost rhythm for a moment, almost losing his hard-on, but then she squeezed him with intimate muscles and cried, "I'm going to come, Ryan. Give it to me hard and deep."

He felt his own orgasm pulse through him, then totally engulf him as he pumped into her in a steady, rapid pace. She screamed in a long wail of ecstasy.

He collapsed on her, then rolled to the side, pulling her close to his body. She nuzzled against his chest. He held her possessively, obsessing about the fact she'd said his brother's name. He'd never mentioned Jake to her. All his childhood and young adult life, people had confused him and Jake. Sometimes Ryan had felt he didn't have an identity of his own. When he'd met Jenna, he hadn't wanted her to meet Jake, hadn't wanted to take the chance she might confuse the two of them, even for a moment. He wanted to be unique and special to her.

He struggled with his desire to ask her why she had mentioned Jake's name, knowing he should be afraid of the answer, even though he had no idea what that answer might be. He stroked her hair, pushing aside his doubts and drawing in a deep breath.

"Jenna? Did you call me Jake earlier?"

"Hmm?" She sounded sleepy. "No, I called you Ryan."

She snuggled in closer. "I love you, Ryan."

The words reverberated through his soul. Jenna loved him. He tightened his arms around her. He must have heard wrong. He'd just asked the woman he loved to marry him. That had probably triggered his deepest insecurities. That his woman would leave him for his brother. It had happened several times when he and Jake were in their teens. Not that Jake intentionally stole Ryan's women. They just seemed to be attracted to Jake's more fun-loving nature.

Damn, the man made his fortune developing a computer role-playing game, for God's sake. He made a living having fun. How could Ryan compete with that? Ryan, the one everyone always described as the serious-minded one. The one who crossed every t and dotted every i. He could push those insecurities aside now. Jenna loved *him*. She had chosen to marry *him*.

Of course, she hadn't met Jake yet, and Ryan would make sure she didn't, at least until the wedding. He wouldn't even tell her he had a twin brother. Not that he wasn't confident in their relationship, he just believed in being cautious. Okay, maybe he was a little insecure about their relationship. She *was* carrying another man's baby. No sense tempting fate.

He relaxed, loving the feeling of being wrapped around her.

"Oh, Ryan, I'm so happy." She took his hand and moved it to her stomach. She flattened it palm down and rested her hand on top. "We're going to have a baby."

Another man's baby. The thought of some stranger making love to Jenna tore him apart. At least it hadn't been Jake. Damn it, if only he hadn't been such an idiot and neglected her for so long. He'd been such a fool.

He kissed the top of her head.

"Mmm. Nice." She snuggled closer.

He'd find a way to balance work and home and make sure she felt cherished. He would not lose her. To Jake or anyone else.

CHAPTER 6

JAKE CLUTCHED THE large sealed brown envelope in his hand as he stared across the panoramic view from his penthouse window. The lights of the city twinkled all around him.

He couldn't stop thinking about the incredible woman who'd provided him with sexual fantasies to last a lifetime.

Aurora.

His body tightened as he remembered her soft hands stroking down his chest, her eyes glittering with desire. He imagined her standing before him now, then leaning forward and wrapping her arms around him and kissing him. At the thought of her full lips on his, her luscious breasts pushing against his chest, her nipples hardening and pressing into him, his groin tightened. He smiled at the memory of her impish smile as she had slid down his body and unfastened his pants. His cock hardened as he remembered her deliciously sinful lips encircling his growing cock.

Damn, every time he thought about her, which seemed to be all the time, he fell into this same state. Wildly turned on and damnably frustrated.

He'd wanted to see her again, had become almost desperate

to see her again as the weeks passed after their night together. So much so that he'd finally given in and hired someone to track her down. He'd given a private investigator her license plate information. Ten minutes ago, a messenger had dropped off the report.

The report in the envelope he now held in his hand. He had impatiently waited for it, had dreamed of tearing it open and tugging out the contents, of opening the folder and revealing everything he needed to know to contact the woman of his dreams.

He stared at the envelope, his fingers running over the edge.

Yet, for some reason, now that he had it, he couldn't bring himself to open it. He tapped the envelope on his knee. This was crazy. He'd paid good money to get this report. More important, he throbbed painfully. He had never wanted a woman more in his life. The thought of never seeing her again ached in a way far deeper than just physical need. He grabbed the letter opener from his desk and jabbed it under the flap, then slit the edge. He needed to find her.

He tipped the envelope upside down and a manila file folder slipped out about an inch. He grasped it between his fingers and pulled it the rest of the way out ,then laid it on the desk before him. His hands glided over the top, savoring the moment. Once he opened this folder, he could pick up a phone and call her. The thought of hearing her voice again stirred his emotions. Better yet, he could hop in his plane and fly to Ottawa tonight. Show up at her door. See the look of surprise on her face.

He imagined Aurora opening her door to find Jake on the other side. She'd be surprised, of course, but what else? Annoyed? Angry? Maybe even frightened, thinking he was some kind of stalker?

He slammed his hand on the folder.

Damn.

She had told him she didn't want to see him again and, as much as he hated it, he had to respect her wishes. He shoved the folder back into the envelope and paced across the room, the report clutched in his hand. Finally, he dropped into his leather lounge chair by the fire.

He pounded his fist on the table again. Damn it! He didn't understand it. How could she not want to see him again? Had their night together meant so little to her?

He raked his hand through his hair. No, that wasn't fair. She had told him their time together had meant a lot to her, but she wanted to keep it in the realm of strangers passing in the night. She had only used him to fulfill a sexual fantasy, but she had been quite forthright about it. She had not led him on in the least.

His chest tightened.

That might be fine for her, but he was left with a longing that wouldn't be denied. His finger traced the ragged, open edge of the envelope. He thought about her night and day. His body ached for her. His soul yearned for her.

All he had to do was flip open this folder. Her secrets lay inside.

An image flashed into his head, of her stripping off the slinky red gown she'd worn, revealing her round, full breasts. His cock swelled, pushing tightly against the confines of his jeans. He remembered the feel of her silky breasts in his hands, of her moist, velvet pussy as he'd run his tongue along it, then found the button of her clit within the folds.

He leaned back in his chair and unzipped his fly as he remembered her doing. Her delicate fingers had stroked his shaft. He reached under his briefs and pulled out his cock, stroking as she had, but his large, coarse fingers didn't feel the same as hers. He wrapped his hand around it tightly and stroked back and forth as he remembered her warm lips sliding over his cock, then the heat of her mouth surrounding him. He pumped vigorously as he remembered the way she took him deep into her throat. The thought of sliding into her hot, wet vagina sent him spewing semen into his hand as he climaxed with a groan.

Oh, God, she'd been so sexy—and sweet. He remembered the feel of her curled up against him in bed, snuggling close. He remembered the pleasant smell of her hair. Strawberries and coconut. He remembered the delicate feel of her gentle lips on his skin.

His fists clenched. Obsessing. He was obsessing.

He grabbed a handful of tissues from the box on the side table and cleaned up, then tucked his limp penis into his pants and zipped up.

Damn it all. He had fallen in love with her.

He was a man who ran on instincts. It shouldn't be a surprise to him that he would fall in love at first sight. Or rather, first encounter of the extremely erotic kind. Not that the sex was why he knew he loved her. She had been spontaneous, sensual, fun-loving. She would be the kind of woman who would keep him on his toes, constantly surprised. Definitely his kind of woman. And he had sensed in her a deeply loving nature.

The fact that she played out her sexual fantasies told him she was comfortable with her sexuality and between them they would keep their sexual relationship exciting and always filled with new experiences. He would definitely ensure she would not go looking to strangers, or anyone else, for satisfaction of those fantasies. He would be the last stranger she ever fooled around with.

Maybe she didn't want to see him, but his feelings had to count for something. The fact that he'd fallen in love with her meant he had a right to talk to her again. Even if, after meeting with him, she decided not to give him another chance, he had the right to at least try to win her.

The phone bleeped. He strode to the desk and picked up the receiver.

"Hello."

"Hi, bro. How's it going?"

Ryan. Jake's gaze settled on the gray linen envelope from Ryan propped up against the family picture on his desk. He smiled as he realized he'd be in Ottawa this weekend for the wedding. He could look up Aurora then.

"Have you got Mom and Dad all squared away?" Ryan asked.

"Yes, I've got the tickets all arranged and I'll pick them up and take them to the airport."

They chatted about details of the weekend and transportation. His cat, Sam, leaped onto the desk and meowed, then ducked her head under his hand, insisting on being petted. As the conversation progressed, Jake realized it wouldn't be fair to think about contacting Aurora soon.

Ryan had finally gotten his life sorted out and found a woman to love. He'd been dating his fiancée for about a year and Jake had been wondering if he'd tie the knot this time or lose this one, too, like so many before her. Ryan tended to focus too much on work and not enough on love.

The irony didn't escape him. Here he was thinking about

Ryan's shortcomings in his romantic relationships, but at least Ryan hadn't had to hire a detective to find his one-night stand.

The conversation ended and he and Ryan said their good-byes.

Jake smiled as he hung up the phone. He picked up Sam and draped her over his shoulder, then petted her from head to tail in long, smooth strokes. His brother was getting married and Jake was happy for him. Right now, that's where Jake's focus should be. On his brother's wedding, not on his own shaky love life. Ryan deserved Jake's undivided attention and if Jake was dwelling on an upcoming meeting with Aurora, a meeting that put his entire future happiness on the line, he wouldn't exactly have his mind on his brother and the happiness he'd found.

Jake would wait until after the wedding. He stared at the brown envelope lying on his desk and tapped it with his index finger.

"But look out, Aurora, because the week after the wedding, I'm coming to find you."

He opened his desk drawer and tossed the envelope inside.

JENNA PARKED HER car on Nicholas Street around the corner from the hotel, then put a token in the parking meter. She pulled her collar up against the mild rain and raced for the light, avoiding the larger puddles. When the red hand switched to a green walking man, she crossed the busy road and walked west on Daly to the front of the Westerly Inn. As she approached the entrance a doorman opened the door for her and she stepped inside out of the rain. She shook her head, then fluffed up her hair, only slightly damp from the drizzle outside.

She crossed the grand lobby through the throng of guests on her way to the catering manager's office, her mood almost as gray as the weather. The wedding was in two days and she hadn't seen Ryan in three weeks. He should have been back from Paris three days ago, in plenty of time to help with all the last-minute details, but he'd been delayed and now wasn't due back until tomorrow.

Luckily, she'd finished her consulting contract for Health and Welfare early, so her days were free to handle what needed doing. She wouldn't start her next contract, developing a training course for a local software firm's new application tools, until after the honeymoon.

It was a great job. The firm, Quixote, knew her work since they had used her services several times before, and had agreed that she could work off-site, which meant at home. They didn't need the course for at least six months and she knew it would only take about two months to develop, so that would give her the chance to take it slow and take time off if she needed to. That definitely would keep the stress level down as she and Ryan adapted to living together and prepared for a new baby.

The clicking of her heels on the marble floor stopped as she turned off the lobby into the carpeted hallway at the left of the reception desk. As she approached the chestnut-stained oak door with the word CATERING on it in gold letters, a large, burly man with a dark mustache and curly hair turned into the hallway ahead of her. She recognized him as the catering manager, Mr. Deluse.

"Ah, Miss Kerry. Perfect timing." He shook her hand. "So

nice to see you again." He glanced past her. "Is Mr. Leigh meeting you here?"

"No, I'm afraid not. He's in Paris."

His bushy eyebrows bobbed upward.

"And he did not take you with him?"

"Don't I wish, but with our wedding only four days away . . ." She shrugged.

"Yes, of course." He gestured her toward one of the two burgundy leather chairs facing his desk and she sat down. "So many details. But it is too bad, yes?"

Yes, it was. She would have loved to go. Not even to see Paris. Just to be with Ryan again. He'd left two weeks ago, but he'd been gone longer than that.

As if that wasn't bad enough, with the pregnancy her body had been undergoing disconcerting changes. At first, she noticed that her nipples had become extremely sensitive. The mere brush of fabric across them made her horny as hell. One day at work, her breast had brushed against the edge of a binder as she'd reached for something on the top shelf of her bookcase. That had set off an intense tingling in her nipples and her hand had slipped under her jacket and caressed one hard nub as she'd imagined going down on Ryan as he lay sprawled across her desk right there in the office. Her face had flushed hotly when her coworker Sal had walked into the office and teased her about daydreaming. Luckily, Jenna had been facing away from the door so the woman couldn't see Jenna's hand stroking under her blazer. Since then, it had gotten worse. With the rush of hormones in her system, she seemed to be intensely horny all the time now.

As soon as Ryan got home, she intended to throw him down on the bed and screw him silly.

"Our pastry chef has a new dessert he would like you to try for your dessert table. He's sending a sample in a few moments."

Jenna shifted in her chair, willing the images of Ryan, lying flat on his back on her bed with Jenna surging up and down on his thick, hard cock, to go away. The imagined sensations of his steel rod sliding along her sensitive vaginal walls did not want to go.

Mr. Deluse opened the file folder on his desk, labeled Kerry–Leigh.

He glanced up at her.

"Are you alright, Ms. Kerry? Your face is flushed."

Her face burned hotter still at his words.

"I'm fine," she mumbled, his words acting like a splash of frigid water, allowing her to thrust away the sexual distractions in her head.

His gaze lingered a moment longer, his brown eyes dark with concern, then he glanced down at his papers again.

"I've arranged for the basket of flowers for your mother's room, as Mr. Leigh requested," he continued. "It will be there when she arrives this evening. Chef is putting together a nice gourmet fruit basket for your father's room for tomorrow. You have a very thoughtful fiancé to think of these things."

Ryan certainly was thoughtful—when he was around. Anger simmered through her that Ryan had abandoned her, leaving her so sexually frustrated.

Mr. Deluse rummaged in his file drawer for a moment, then turned to her, looking almost as harried as she felt.

"I'd like you to review the centerpiece designs but my assistant borrowed the folder. Excuse me one moment, please."

He stood up and hurried out of the office, leaving her to her thoughts.

Ryan had been so great the first few weeks after proposing. He had been extremely attentive and had spent every evening with her, as well as weekends. She had almost—but not quite—felt a little crowded. How could she when he was trying so hard? Then it became clear he'd been neglecting work at the office, and things had started escalating out of control.

His assistant had called one evening when Ryan had been out picking up pizza. Apparently, Ryan had been putting off trips to Toronto, where he needed to solidify plans for another software development project for Bryer Associates, and he had a thick binder full of reports he had to read and respond to in order to keep his staff working effectively. He also had some new endeavor that needed attention, requiring a trip to Paris. She didn't know all the details, but she knew something had to be done. When Ryan returned with dinner, she had told him he needed to see to his business. She didn't want everything falling apart because of her. That wouldn't do either of them any good.

Unfortunately, Ryan took that as permission to totally ignore her.

She stopped herself at that thought, knowing it wasn't really fair. He was trying to tie up a lot of loose ends and get the Paris thing going on its own momentum so that his assistant and senior staff could handle it. That way, it wouldn't take all his time and attention later, and he could focus on her and the baby.

The plan was, by their wedding date, he would be down to a reasonable workload and able to work a normal workday, leaving his evenings and weekends free to spend time with her and the baby, once he or she arrived.

Jenna just hoped that's what would really happen.

· · ·

JAKE TOOK THE key card folder the hotel reception clerk handed him and turned toward the elevators. He waved away the bellhop who offered to carry his bag. He had only his small carry-on with him. His luggage had been lost by the airline. A big reason he preferred to fly his own plane when he came to Ottawa, but this time he'd flown here with Mom and Dad. There's no way Mom would climb into his little aircraft, preferring the comfort and stability of the commercial jets.

Jake had the cab drop them off at Ryan's, then continued on to the hotel. Ryan was still in Paris, but Mom and Dad had a key. It was funny that Ryan hadn't suggested, as he usually did, that Jake stay there, too. Probably just prewedding jitters. It was really a moot point, given that Jake always politely declined and stayed in a hotel. It's not that he didn't love his brother, he just preferred to have his own space.

Anyway, with the folks there, they would drive them both nuts. Especially when Mom regaled Ryan with Jake's successes, which she was bound to do. Jake knew Ryan was sensitive about how well Jake had done with Finale Alley, the computer role-playing game Jake had created for fun but that had taken off in popularity, becoming the bestselling computer game in North America. Jake knew it was primarily luck that had landed him such extensive success, but Ryan seemed to believe Jake had some superior business expertise, or knowledge of markets, or some such. Jake knew he just had an instinct. An instinct he knew his brother also possessed. If only Ryan would stop trying to think everything to death and listen to his gut.

As Jake crossed the lobby to the elevators, he caught sight

of a young woman in a tailored blue suit, specifically her long shapely legs flashing from the slit in the center front of her long, straight skirt as she walked. He allowed his appreciative gaze to slide upward along the contour of her skirt, following the line of her tailored jacket in to her slender waist, then flaring out to her generous breasts.

Gorgeous. His gaze continued upward, past the soft drape of her shiny, dark brown hair at her shoulders to her face.

CHAPTER 7

JAKE'S HEART COMPRESSED and he almost stumbled.

"Aurora."

The woman's gaze flicked toward him and she stopped, her eyes widening.

"What are you doing here?" she asked.

His heart stopped. Would she storm away in anger? He relaxed when a slow, sweet smile spread across her lips.

She stepped toward him, closing the few yards between them, her smile glowing brightly. She leaned in close to him, resting her hand on his arm. Her delicate touch thrilled him. The scent of her hair and the heady heat of her body made him feel almost light-headed.

"You called me Aurora," she murmured close to his ear. "Does that mean what I think it does?" She raised her eyebrows.

Of course he'd called her Aurora. What else should he call her? Had she wanted him to call her sweetheart or honey? He couldn't very well call her sex kitten across a crowded lobby. Could he? With her and her fantasies, he couldn't quite be sure. My God, she had a way of keeping him off balance.

"Uh, what do you think it means?" he asked.

She glanced at his hand and her smile grew even broader as she tapped on the key card.

"Apparently, it means exactly what I think it means." She curled her right arm through his elbow and turned toward the elevator. "Hot sex for Aurora and Jake tonight."

His penis jumped to attention at her words.

She hugged his arm tightly as they walked, her warm breast brushing enticingly against him.

"This is so sweet. I really needed this."

She *needed* this. His heart soared, confident this meant he had a chance to convince her to start a relationship with him.

He squeezed her arm. "I'm glad."

He reached across in front of her and jabbed the elevator call button, praying. As he drew his arm back it brushed against the front of her breast. He could feel the nipple thrust forward as a low moan escaped her lips. He glanced at her face. Her eyes were half-closed and her cheeks stained crimson. She met his gaze and her eyes, dark and intense, oozed sexuality. Adrenaline rushed through him at the thought of what would happen once they got inside his room. He prayed the elevator would arrive soon.

She leaned in close and kissed his cheek as they waited.

The elevator arrived with a ding. They moved out of the way as five people exited. A woman with a teenage girl and a boy about ten in tow stepped into the elevator, followed by Aurora and Jake. A couple of businessmen joined them before the doors closed again.

Jake glanced at his key card folder and the number handwritten on it. Fifteen twenty-five. He pushed the appropriate floor button. The softness of her body against his side as she clung to him kept his desire burning. Only the fact that other people rode the elevator with them stopped him from dragging her into his arms and performing a repeat of their last elevator ride, though the memory of thrusting into her while watching her face contort in pleasure in the mirrored wall made it an uncomfortable ride as his throbbing cock sought escape. The elevator stopped at six and one man exited, then the family left at ten. At fifteen, as the door slid open, he tucked his arm around Aurora and they stepped off the elevator. The door whooshed closed behind them.

The suites were always at the end of the corridor, but there were two on each floor, one at either end, so he checked the sign attached to the wall facing the elevator to see which direction to go. Fifteen twenty-five was to the left.

As they headed down the hall, he pulled at his shirt collar, suddenly very hot. This time, he wanted to make sure he could see her again.

Her hand lay nestled in the crook of his elbow. He laid his hand over hers.

"There's something I need to talk to you about," he said.

She looked at him, the light in her eyes dwindling a little.

"Really? Is it something that could wait?" She stared up at him with wide blue eyes. "I've had a really tense few days and I would love to just enjoy each other for a little while, before we have to deal with any issues."

For the first time, he realized she looked tired. Her jaw seemed tense and there were dark smudges under her eyes. He wondered what was stressing her, but he resolved to keep his questions for later.

"Sure," he agreed.

They stopped in front of the door to his room.

"It's been so long since we've seen each other and I've

missed you so." She tucked her arm around his waist and leaned her head on his shoulder as he slid the key card into the slot.

Inside him a tornado flared, swirling his emotions around and around. She had missed him. His confidence that she would agree to continue their relationship jumped another notch. Hopefully for a long-term relationship.

Hopefully forever.

He pushed the door open.

As soon as they stepped inside and closed the door behind them, she threw her arms around him. He dropped his bag to the floor and held her close.

"I've missed you so much." She planted her hands on his cheeks and kissed him soundly, then snuggled against him.

He stood there holding her and stroking her back while she held on to him, her arms wrapped tightly around his waist.

"Is everything okay, honey?"

She gazed up at him, her eyes glistening as though tears threatened. She nodded. "I just love you so much."

His breath caught deep in his lungs. She loved him?

A broad smile claimed his face. The woman he loved, loved him back. Could life get any better?

He gathered her close, holding her so tight he suddenly feared he might crush her. He loosened his hold and gazed down at her sweet face. The face that had haunted his dreams.

"Sweetheart, I love you, too."

He wanted to blurt out that he wanted to marry her, that he wanted to be with her forever, but he held back. He had time now and he would spend it getting to know her, building a trusting, loving relationship that would be a foundation for their life together.

She eased back and he saw that tears streamed from her eyes. Were the tears because she'd had no way to find him? Had she thought she would never see him again? A sense of supreme satisfaction oozed through him as he thought that she must have been longing for him just as he'd longed for her.

He tugged out his handkerchief and dabbed at her wet cheeks, then handed it to her. She wiped her eyes.

"Sorry, I'm just a little emotional these days."

"That's okay." He stroked her cheek tenderly. "You're allowed."

Her hand covered his and the brilliance of her eyes as she stared into his took his breath away. She kissed him, a delicate brush of her lips, then her mouth turned up in a wicked smile. Her fingers shifted to the top button of her jacket and she released it, then the second, then the third and last. She grabbed his tie, right below the knot, and backed toward the bed, tugging him with her.

"Now, *Jake* . . ." She released his tie and dropped her jacket off her shoulders, then onto the floor. "Let's get on with the fun."

JENNA COULDN'T BELIEVE Ryan had surprised her by returning from Paris early. Just when she'd started to fear he was neglecting her again, he did something like this. And reviving the Jake persona. Delightful.

She unbuttoned the back of her skirt and slid it off, leaving it in a pile on the floor. Although "Jake" wasn't exactly a stranger anymore, he wasn't her usual guy, either, so she could be different. Wicked and wild.

She toyed with the top button of her blouse, then released it. She pulled the lapels apart to show a little cleavage, then spun around and swayed her hips. She leaned over to pick up her skirt, giving him a view of her bottom, then wiggled it enticingly.

He stepped up behind her and flattened his palms on her black lace–covered derriere, but she danced away, tossing her skirt onto the nearest chair. She turned to face him and unfastened the next button, then the next, watching his hungry expression intensify.

Finally, she slipped the silky blouse off her arms and spun it around before tossing it over his head. He tugged it slowly off his face, then drew it to his nose and breathed deeply.

"Smells wonderful. Like sweet, sexy woman."

He tossed it sideways, then moved toward her with a purposeful stride. His hands slid to her waist and he drew her near. The feel of his strong hands on her sides warmed her, inside and out. She leaned forward for the kiss he offered. Their lips touched and excitement flared between them. The kiss turned hot and passionate, nothing like the delicate, tender, almost-afraid-to-touch-her kisses he had given her ever since he'd found out she was pregnant.

Sex with him had become gentle and tender. Tame. Almost boring. She missed the raw, powerful sex they'd shared when he'd brought her fantasy to life. So much so that she'd worked up the nerve to ask her doctor whether they could get a little more . . . exuberant during sex. He'd chuckled and assured her that a wild, passionate ride would not only be fine, but would do her a world of good.

Which was great, because what she really wanted right now was hot, torrid, *dirty* sex. She wanted him to bury himself so deep she'd feel it into next week. She wanted him to thrust into her until her whole body quaked with an orgasm she would never forget.

Her hands stroked down his chest. Remembering the last really erotic sexual session they'd shared, she grasped the sides of his shirt and ripped it open, sprinkling buttons every which way. It had been so sexy when he'd done that last time.

He beamed. "Oh, baby, you're really into this."

"Mmm. You know it."

She nuzzled the base of his neck, then trailed kisses downward to his nipple. She teased it to beadlike hardness, rolling it around on her tongue. Her hands slid down his stomach then under the waistband of his pants. Hurriedly, he unbuttoned and unzipped around her hands as her fingers found his hardening flesh and wrapped around him. His belt buckle clinked as his pants hit the floor. She lapped her tongue over his other nipple, then slid her mouth down his body until she reached his rapidly growing penis, the head broad and purple. She licked around it, gliding her tongue under the ridge, then smiled at his groan. She slid her lips slowly down the head, until it was buried inside her mouth. She sucked, then pulsed a few times before sliding farther down the shaft, taking him deep into her throat.

"Oh, yes," he moaned. His hands stroked her hair lovingly.

She moved up and down on him, cupping her hands over his hard buttocks. Oh, God, she loved the feel of his muscles clenching under her hands. She sucked and pulled until he was ready to burst, then she released him. She wrapped her hands around his gorgeous cock and stroked while she dipped lower to kiss his hot, hard sacks. She drew them into her mouth, and licked them all over. He groaned loudly.

She released them, not wanting him to come just yet, and licked up his shaft, then gave a quick kiss on the tip of his cock. It twitched in response. She dragged her body up his stomach to his chest, crushing her breasts into him. Her nipples ached with painfully intense pleasure.

"Jake, I want you. Fast and hard."

He had told her many times how he loved hearing her talk this way and she found it made her feel very sexy.

"I want you to drive that *enormous* cock of yours deep inside me."

She flung off her panties and fell back on the bed, spreading her legs wide. Her hands traveled up her stomach then cupped her breasts, still covered with black lace. He fell to his knees on the floor in front of her. His hands stroked up her thighs, circling around her heated, dripping pussy, to her ribs. She flicked open the front-opening clasp of her bra and pulled it apart. Her fingers found her stridently erect nipples and plucked at them.

He watched in complete fascination.

"Oh, sweetheart, that is so sexy."

He kissed her stomach, never shifting his gaze from her busy fingertips, then thrust his tongue into her navel, jabbing it in and out as though fucking her with his tongue. She flushed at the thought. Oh, wow, she felt dirty and wild even thinking dirty words.

She dragged her fingers through her hair, abandoning her

breasts. His hands claimed them both, then he captured one nipple in his hot, moist mouth. Need seared through her.

"Oh, God, Jake." Desperation tinged her words. She was so turned on. "I want you to fuck me right now." She flushed hotter. She couldn't believe she'd said that out loud, but the words aroused her, heating her to unbearable need.

She grabbed his cock and pumped it rapidly. The soft, kid-leather skin glided over the steel beneath.

"I am so hot. Give it to me now, baby," she cried.

He seemed ready to salivate. He climbed on the bed, his knees between her widely spread thighs.

"How did you say you wanted it?"

"Deep and hard."

He kissed her neck, nuzzling her ear. She felt him guide the head of his erection to her soft folds.

"Actually, you said fast and hard, then you asked me to drive my enormous cock deep inside you."

His breath wisped against her ear, sending her insides trembling.

"Oh, yes." She arched upward, capturing a little of his head inside. "Do it."

He eased his cock away, then stroked her slit with his finger, delving a little inside.

"Don't worry, baby, I'm good and wet."

He smiled. "You really are being a dirty girl today, aren't you?" He nuzzled her again and murmured, "And I love it."

She grabbed his face and stared him straight in the eye.

"Then give me what I want."

He laughed.

"You bet."

She felt his cock nudge her dampness again, then she gasped as his hardness impaled her in one deep thrust.

"Oh . . . my . . . God."

He eased back and she could feel the ridge of his penis pulling on the wall of her vagina, deliciously stimulating her every inch of the way. He thrust again and she moaned as she arched up to meet him.

"Oh, God, give it to me fast."

He thrust again. "And hard."

He pumped into her. Again and again. Deeper and harder than she'd ever experienced before. Lighting a fire within her. Blazing. Raging out of control. It swept over her until she screamed in delight, her body pulsing with scorching pleasure. She seemed to explode in a flash of electrified sparks. Just as that orgasm waned, he thrust again, spiraling inside her, then pumping rapidly until she exploded again.

She sagged, the shimmering heat of her orgasms slowly ebbing.

JENNA LAY CURLED in his arms, savoring the feel of her man wrapped around her. He had cuddled her for quite a while, nuzzling and kissing, luxuriating in the afterglow; then he had fallen asleep. She loved listening to the deep, slow rhythm of his breathing. Finally, she eased away, sliding his arm from across her hips, managing to stand up without waking him.

She visited the bathroom, cleaning up and brushing her hair, then she gathered her clothes, pulling on appropriate pieces as she went. As she crept toward the door, she noticed a lovely fruit basket on the dresser, beside the TV. It looked just like the one Ryan had arranged for her father and his brother, who'd be coming in from Montreal today. She noticed a copy of the invitation to the rehearsal dinner attached to the ribbon, the side with the map facing upward. She flipped it over. Why would he have this here? She reached for the card, but at the sound of rustling bedclothes, she turned.

He sat on the side of the bed, his feet on the floor.

"What are you doing?" he asked.

"I've got to leave," she answered as she pulled on her shoes.

"No, wait. Don't run out on me." He stood up and stepped toward her, the lamplight glistening on his naked body. "We were going to talk."

Her eyebrows closed together.

"Oh, right. I forgot." She glanced at her watch. Six thirty-four. "I'm sorry, but I have to go right now. I'm picking up my mom at the airport. I promised to have dinner with her this evening."

"I see." He scratched his head. "Okay, well, may I see you tomorrow?"

She smiled. It was so cute how he managed to stay in character.

"Of course."

Unless he'd forgotten that the rehearsal dinner was tomorrow.

"How about dinner?" she hinted.

"Hmm. I have this rehearsal dinner for my brother tomorrow. He's getting married on Saturday."

Oh, he really was being so cute.

"Oh, really? Your brother?"

"I don't think he'd mind if I brought a date."

She stepped toward him, then ran her hand along his

naked chest, through the sprinkle of hair, then downward, enjoying the feel of his well-defined abs. There must have been some great gym at the hotel in Paris. She smiled. Maybe he'd worked out every day to ease the tension of not being with her.

"I'm sure no one will mind if you bring a date." She nipped his earlobe and murmured breathily, "In fact, I'm sure they'll expect it."

"Well, it certainly will make my mother happy."

She laughed. She'd yet to meet his mother. That would happen for the first time tomorrow at the rehearsal. She desperately hoped she'd make a good impression.

At that reminder of mothers, she kissed his cheek and rushed to the door.

"I've really got to go."

"Wait, I need your address so I can pick you up."

She laughed.

"No, that's okay. I'll be coming straight after a meeting." She pulled open the door. "I'll meet you here. The Autumn Ballroom. Six o'clock." She closed the door behind her.

JAKE STARED AT the closed door. How did she know? Then he noticed the basket she'd been looking at. He tugged the little envelope from the spike and pulled out the card.

Dear Jake,
  You won't stay at my place so here's something to make the room more homey. The invitation will remind you of the time and place for tomorrow.
  Ryan

He flicked the soft pink parchment card attached to the ribbon. That's how she'd figured it out. She'd seen the invitation. She was quick, that one.

He couldn't wait to introduce her to his mother. He was certain Mom would be thrilled.

CHAPTER 8

JENNA AND HER mother walked past the tall palm plants in the large atrium on the top floor of the Westerly Inn. She and Ryan had booked a room overlooking the river for this afternoon and had invited their parents, siblings, and the wedding party for a get-together before the rehearsal. A few people had already arrived, judging from the voices trickling from the room.

"Oh, it's beautiful, dear," Mom said as they stepped inside. Wall-to-wall windows displayed a magnificent view of the river and the mountains beyond. A string quartet played soft background music.

"Come outside and see the view," Jenna insisted. She led Mom to the double doors leading out to a balcony, knowing she'd love the flowering plants in large planters. Jenna didn't know what the large purple flowers were, but Mom definitely would.

As Jenna pulled the door open for her mother, she spotted Dad and Shane heading their way. From the way her mother clamped tight on Jenna's arm, she knew Mom had, too.

"I really don't want to talk to him right now."

"You know, you're bound to run into him sometime over the next couple of days. For instance, while we're doing the wedding photos."

"I know, dear. Just not now."

"Fine, I'll head him off."

Her mother went out to the balcony and Jenna closed the door behind her. She wished her mother would get over her discomfort around her father. Jenna knew that the breakup of their marriage had something to do with the fact that her mother had fallen in love with another man. Not that Mom had told her that, but it wasn't hard to figure out, since she started seeing a man shortly after the separation and was married within six months of the divorce. Jenna had learned to love her new stepfather, Henry. But ever since his death seven years ago, she had secretly hoped her parents would reconcile. She sighed, knowing she should face facts. Mom was sure that Dad would never forgive her for cheating on him. Maybe she was right. How could a relationship survive that kind of betrayal?

"Jenna." Her father stepped up to her with open arms.

She smiled and fell into them.

"Daddy, it's so nice to see you again." She hugged him tight. "How was your flight from Vancouver?"

"Long. As always."

"Gidday, sis."

She turned around to see Shane approaching them. She beamed and dashed into his arms. His bear hug nearly knocked the wind from her.

"Hey, big brother."

He'd been working in Australia for the past year and she'd missed him. He'd returned last week but, since he lived in Toronto, this was the first she'd seen him. She and Ryan had held off the wedding for a couple of weeks to coincide with his return. She was glad it had worked out so well. If it had been a couple of months later, she would have been showing. She gave him a big kiss, then linked her arm with his.

JAKE STEPPED INTO the room, glancing around to see if he spotted Ryan or their parents. He wanted to mention that he'd invited a date before Aurora arrived. His gaze swept across the room, past a dozen or so guests, then settled on three people by the balcony doors. An older man and a couple embracing. As the woman pulled back, he stiffened as he realized it was Aurora. The man slid his arm around her waist. Anger and jealousy swept through him as he watched, dumbfounded. How the hell did she know people here?

His fists clenched. Of course, this woman didn't need to know a man before she'd follow him back to his room and make love to him. Hadn't she gone off with Jake himself, a stranger, a mere two months ago?

"Hey, Ryan, how's it going?" The woman he'd seen Aurora with on the night they met stepped up to him. What the hell was she doing here? Why would Aurora invite her along?

"I'm not Ryan. I'm his brother, Jake."

"Jake? Yeah, right."

He ignored her odd tone and glared in Aurora's direction.

"Look, Cindy, is it?" He pointed to Aurora. "Who is that guy?"

Cindy glanced around and smiled.

"Oh, that's right. You've never met her family. That's her brother, Shane. The other is her dad."

Relief surged through him, followed by confusion at why Aurora would have brought family and a friend along on their date. He turned back to Cindy.

"So why are you here?" he asked, keeping his tone amiable.

"Well, I am the bride-to-be's best friend and her maid of honor. I wouldn't miss it."

His eyebrows raised at the odd coincidence.

"You know Jenna Kerry?"

She rapped him on the arm lightly with her fist.

"Ryan, you're just a barrel of laughs today, aren't you?"

"I told you, I'm not Ryan. I'm Jake. We're identical twins."

Cindy laughed but Jake's attention fixed on Aurora, who had spotted him and approached, the soft sway of her hips and her luminous smile mesmerizing him.

"Hi there." Her low, sexy murmur reminded him of warm sheets and naked skin. Her eyes, kitten-soft, shone warmly as she gazed at him.

"Hi." The tenderness of his voice clearly conveyed his love for her.

Cindy guffawed. "Yeah, and you're trying to tell me you aren't Ryan. Just look at the two of you all moon-eyed for each other."

Aurora gave her friend a sidelong glance, a bemused smile on her face. "What are you talking about, Cindy?"

"Your sweetie here has been trying to convince me his name is Jake." Cindy leaned in close to her. "I think he's trying to lure you away to relive that fantasy again."

Aurora giggled. "We already did."

Cindy gave Jake a speculative glance, then grinned like the Cheshire cat. "Well, girl, do tell me all about it."

Aurora bopped her on the arm. "Cindy, you're awful. Don't embarrass him."

She tucked her arm around his and drew him away from Cindy, laughing quietly.

"If you're trying to steal me away from the party," she said, "I think you should wait until the festivities are over."

He slid his arm around her waist. "I'll certainly try to hold off that long." He took both her arms and drew her close to him. "But I can't wait for this."

A soft murmur of approval surged through the small crowd as he slid his arms around her and dragged her close, capturing her lips with all the passion in his heart. She melted against him. Her lips moved under his, soft and sweet. As his blood simmered, he realized waiting would be harder than he'd thought.

Aurora's friend, Cindy, gasped behind him.

"Oh, my God," she said. "Uh, hello Mrs. Leigh, Mr. Leigh. Have a nice trip here?" Cindy asked.

Jenna stiffened a little, nervous about meeting Ryan's parents, and now having to face them after this uncharacteristic public show of affection. She tried to ease away, but Ryan held her firm.

"Very nice, dear," an older woman, probably Ryan's mother, said. "Uh, Ryan, why is your brother kissing your wife-to-be?"

Ryan stiffened in her embrace, then his arms loosened around her and his hands shifted to her shoulders as he drew back. Jenna gazed up at an ashen-faced Ryan staring at her as if he'd never seen her before.

"Ryan, what's wrong?" she murmured.

"Jenna?" he whispered hoarsely.

"Yes?" She felt her stomach clench. What was wrong with him?

He shook his head. "I'm not Ryan."

She just stared at him. His words made no sense to her.

Then her blood turned cold. His mother's comment, a comment that had made no sense, trickled through her consciousness. *Why is your brother kissing your wife-to-be?* The meaning of those words danced in and out of her mind, ultimately eluding her. Somehow, the consequences seemed too threatening, too frightening even to consider.

Slowly, she turned sideways, toward the voices. An elegant elderly woman stared at her with intense gray-blue eyes full of curiosity. Holding her elbow was a very irate-looking Ryan.

Ryan!

A sick feeling bubbled through her stomach and she felt as if she was going to throw up. She turned her head back to face the man she'd just been kissing.

Ryan. Jake?

"Oh, God." The words trickled from her in a very small, tight voice. Her fingers clamped down, clutching the fine wool fabric of his suit sleeves.

She glanced from one Ryan to the other, feeling faint. Suddenly, the whole situation became clear. The man who held her in his arms, who'd just kissed her with such passion—whom she'd just kissed with such passion—was not her beloved fiancé, but a complete stranger.

"Oh, God," she uttered again, as she remembered her fantasy lover. *A complete stranger.*

Tears prickled at her eyes. The air around her felt thick and heavy, almost impossible to breathe. The light seemed to fade and her knees turned to rubber. She felt arms tighten around her as consciousness fled into the waiting darkness.

JAKE'S HEART SANK and a numbness claimed his body as he slipped his arm under her legs and lifted the unconscious woman into his arms. Her head fell against his shoulder.

He couldn't believe it. Aurora was actually Jenna. Ryan's wife-to-be.

Cindy rushed toward him. She took Jenna's hand and patted it frantically.

"Oh, no, she's fainted." Cindy's hand clamped around Jake's arm. "Let's get her somewhere she can lie down."

She led him forward but Ryan stepped in front of them. His hands planted firmly on his hips, he leaned toward them slightly.

"What the hell did you think you were doing?" Ryan demanded. Fierce anger stormed in his eyes.

Jake faced his brother's barely contained rage, suppressing a little anger of his own. Jake had fallen in love with Aurora—Jenna, he reminded himself—only to find out she was going to marry his brother. How could he not be angry at the man responsible for stealing his happiness?

"Ryan, I didn't know she was your fiancée," he said through gritted teeth. "Do you really think I would have kissed her if I'd known?" Impatience shimmered in his words.

Cindy planted a hand on each of their shoulders and held the distance between them.

"Look, you two," she scolded. "Right now you need to think about Jenna. Deal with your own issues later."

Ryan glared at his brother and forked out his arms. "She's my fiancée. I'll carry her."

Reluctantly, Jake placed Aurora—Jenna—in his brother's arms. Her head lolled to the side, resting against Ryan's chest. A shock of jealousy burned through Jake at the sight.

A large, burly man in a tuxedo appeared, wringing his hands together.

"Is Miss Kerry alright?" The concern in his accented voice was clear.

Cindy drew the man through the gathering crowd of people surrounding them.

"Ryan, you remember Mr. Deluse, the catering manager?"

Ryan nodded his head, barely turning his glare from his brother. Cindy turned back to Mr. Deluse.

"Do you have somewhere we can take her?"

"Yes, of course." He gestured toward the door. "Gentlemen, please follow me."

He led them toward the elevators, then past them through a door to a service elevator. He inserted a key, then summoned the elevator. Ryan tapped his foot as they waited. Finally, the door slid open and they stepped inside. Mr. Deluse took them down to the lobby level, then led them down another hallway. He unlocked a door, flicked on a light switch, and ushered them inside.

"This is my office. There's a couch over there." The older gentleman led them to the couch and watched as Ryan settled Jenna on the burgundy leather sofa. "I'll get some water. Would you like me to call an ambulance?"

Ryan's face drained of blood, leaving it a ghostly white.

"No, Mr. Deluse," Cindy jumped in. She rested her hand on Ryan's arm. "She'll be fine."

She said it more to Ryan than to the other man, her tone reassuring. Ryan looked at her like a drowning man might at a lifeline thrown his way. She nodded, then turned back to Mr. Deluse.

"We just need to get her away from the excitement for a bit. Please just bring the water, and maybe a couple of drinks for Ryan and Jake."

"Of course." He rushed out the door, closing it behind him.

Ryan turned back to Jake, the storm flaring in his eyes again.

"Why in hell were you kissing my woman?" Ryan demanded.

Jake almost snapped back that he loved her and she loved him and he had every right to kiss her, but he stopped himself. Remembering their first time together and how she had told him her fantasy was to have sex with a stranger, he realized that she had believed he was Ryan all along. When she'd told him she loved him yesterday, she'd thought she'd been saying it to Ryan.

Jake's heart broke right on the spot, and the devastating pain seared every nerve in his body. He drew in a deep breath, then sighed.

"I told you. I didn't know she was your fiancée." He kept his voice calm and steady, even though he felt anything but. "I thought she was a woman I've been . . . seeing."

Cindy stared from one man to the other, her green eyes wide.

Ryan scoffed. "You're trying to tell me Jenna has an exact double in Montreal and you just happen to be dating her?"

"No, I met her here."

Ryan stopped in his tracks. His eyes narrowed as he stared intently at his brother. "When, exactly?"

"Two months ago. The day I flew down to meet with you before the meeting with Bryer Associates."

Cindy made a choking noise. She'd obviously figured it out.

Ryan's expression turned as dark as a thunderstorm. Jake fully expected lightning to flash from his eyes.

Jake raked his hand through his hair. Damn, this was a total mess. The woman he wanted to marry more than anything in the world actually loved his brother, and would be marrying him tomorrow. The fact that Jake was brokenhearted didn't mean his brother should suffer.

Good God, how can I tell Ryan I slept with his fiancée? Their relationship might never recover from this.

"Where did you meet her?"

"In this hotel. She was at a wedding." He nodded toward Aurora's—Jenna's—friend. "She was with Cindy here."

Cindy's eyes widened even more and her head shook back and forth.

"How many times have you seen her?" Ryan demanded.

"Just that one time . . . and again yesterday."

"Yesterday?" Ryan roared.

Cindy pressed her fist to her mouth, as though watching a disaster in action.

"I told you, I didn't know—"

"What the hell difference does that make?" Ryan bellowed.

Cindy grasped Ryan's wrist. "Calm down. This isn't helping anything." She stroked his arm in a soothing manner. "Look, Ryan, why don't you go to housekeeping and get a towel or something so we can put a damp cloth on her forehead?"

He sucked in a deep breath, then nodded. "You're right. That's a good idea."

Jake stared at the unconscious woman lying on the couch. The woman he loved. His brother's fiancée.

She looked so fragile and pale lying there against the dark burgundy leather. This whole situation had certainly been a shock to all of them, but Jenna didn't strike him as the fainting type.

"I wonder why she fainted," Jake mused.

"Probably because she's—" Cindy's sentence ended abruptly. Jake glanced up in time to see Ryan shooting her a withering glare.

"Stress," Ryan answered between clenched teeth. "Cindy, come with me to housekeeping."

He grasped her elbow and led her to the door.

COOLNESS ON HER forehead lured Jenna from the darkness.

"Jenna." A deep voice said her name. "Jenna, are you alright?"

Ryan's voice.

Confusion swirled around her, like a dark gray curtain on a stormy night, but she struggled against it.

She opened her eyes. Ryan's concerned face stared down at her, his sensuous lips pinched in a straight line.

Cindy's head bobbed into view.

"Her eyes are open," Cindy said to someone behind her. She smiled down at Jenna and through the numbness Jenna felt Cindy's fingers curl around her own. "How you doing, honey?"

Cindy squeezed Jenna's hand and Jenna squeezed back, allowing the firm grip to draw her farther into consciousness.

Her eyes drifted closed again as she drew in a deep breath. Someone put a glass to her lips.

"Take a sip, Jenna," Cindy said.

Cool, flavorless liquid trickled into Jenna's mouth and down her throat. She opened her eyes, intent on the glass, wrapping her hands around it. She leaned forward and tipped more of the water into her mouth. Cindy kept her hands around the glass, guiding it forward, then took it away when Jenna urged it back. When Jenna glanced up again, she saw two Ryans staring down at her.

"Oh, God, I'm seeing double." The inside of her head started to swirl. A pounding started in her temple.

One of the Ryans took her hand. "No, sweetheart, you're not. This is . . ."

His lips continued moving, but the words were drowned out by the increased drumming in her ears. His face was tight with concern, but she couldn't follow what he was saying. She blinked a couple of times, trying to clear the fog closing in on her, but then she fell into the wonderful, cushioned blackness again.

ANGER STORMED THROUGH Cindy and she batted Ryan on the arm.

"You idiots. What are you trying to do? Scare her witless? It's a really bad idea to upset her in her—" at Ryan's murderous glare, she bit back the word *condition,* "—situation," she finished.

"What situation is that?" Jake asked, eyebrows pinched together.

Pregnant, she wanted to scream, but Ryan had dragged

her aside earlier and forbade her to let Jake know anything about the baby. Not that she agreed with him, in the longer term anyway, but she realized that adding that complication to an already tense situation wasn't a good idea. Ryan was ready to wring his brother's neck as it was, and if Jake found out about the pregnancy and put two and two together . . .

She wanted to shake some sense into them. The two of them were jockeying for position, readying for a head-butting contest. Men and their egos.

"The situation is that she's getting married," Ryan said through gritted teeth. "Or had you forgotten?"

Cindy's fists clenched.

"Guys, get over it. Right now your only concern should be Jenna. If she wakes up and sees the two of you again, the shock will probably send her into a coma, so I suggest one of you leave."

Ryan settled deeper into his chair. "She's my fiancée. I'm staying right here." He dipped the cloth in the spare glass of water and wrung it out, then placed it on Jenna's forehead again, turning his back to Cindy and Jake.

Jake crossed his arms over his chest, his eyes narrowing.

Cindy glanced from one to the other, then walked to Ryan's brother's side and wrapped her hand securely around his arm.

Jake. Jenna's fantasy man.

"I really think you should go," she said gently, using her most persuasive tone. "Just until we get her up and around again."

Jake's tension eased. He glanced at Jenna's slack form and he dragged his hand through his hair. Long, wavy brown hair. A surge of heat went through Cindy. She couldn't help thinking that whichever one of these fine hunks Jenna discarded, she'd be doing a great favor to single women everywhere.

Jake nodded.

"Yeah, okay." He pulled a card out of an inside pocket of his suit jacket and handed it to her. "I won't be far. Call me on my cell as soon as she's awake. I want to talk to her."

Cindy took the card and ushered him to the door. "I will. I promise."

She felt for Jake right now. This must be a terrible shock. She couldn't imagine what he must be thinking.

She thought back to when Jenna had told her about Ryan playing out her fantasy. Jenna had been so excited that her cheeks had glowed with happiness. But the fantasy stranger had not actually been Ryan. Chills rippled through Cindy. She imagined herself in Jenna's shoes and a stream of butterflies twirled through her stomach. She couldn't help thinking how terribly exciting and illicit that made the whole situation.

Of course, Jake might not share her view, and Ryan definitely wouldn't.

Cindy's eyes strayed back to Jenna, lying there totally oblivious to the whole situation. No wonder she didn't want to wake up.

Good heavens, Cindy hadn't experienced this much excitement since the time . . . Her thought trailed off. She dug back deep into her memory. Actually, she had never experienced this much excitement.

CHAPTER 9

RYAN PATTED JENNA'S cheeks. She felt so cold.

His heart wobbled at seeing her so fragile.

"Jenna?" He pushed her hair behind her ears then patted her cheeks some more. "Jenn, wake up, sweetheart."

"Mmm." Her eyelids slowly lifted. "Ryan?"

She ran her hand across her forehead, then wrapped it around the damp cloth and dragged it away. Ryan drew the cloth from her fingers and set it on the tray on the table beside the couch.

"What happened?" She raised her hands to her temples and rubbed.

"You fainted." He stroked her cheek and smiled down at her.

"Don't be silly, I don't faint." She glanced around. "Where am I?"

"We're in the catering manager's office." He took her hand and patted it. "It's okay, it's just the two of us here." The sound of a clearing voice interrupted him, reminding him that Jenna's friend sat behind him. "And Cindy."

"Cindy?" Jenna glanced past him.

"I'm here, Jenna." Cindy moved beside Ryan and peered

at Jenna from over his shoulder. "You're fine, honey. You just had a bit of a shock."

Cindy gave Ryan a quick stare and nudged her head toward Jenna. She mouthed some words to him. *Tell her.*

"Jenna, I've never told you much about my brother."

Jenna's hand tightened in his.

"Jake," Jenna said weakly and her eyes started to glaze.

Cindy pushed past him, kneeling beside the couch, taking Jenna's hand from Ryan. "No, Jenna, stay with us, honey." She grabbed the cloth and patted Jenna's cheek with it. "Sweetie, it's okay. Ryan has a brother. His name is Jake."

Cindy patted Jenna's hand. Ryan watched helplessly, his gut twisting at the thought of Jenna in his brother's arms. It killed him knowing she'd had sex with Jake, knowing the baby was *Jake's* baby.

"Listen to me, Jenna. Jake is Ryan's brother. His twin brother. But it's okay." Cindy enunciated each syllable clearly. She sent Ryan a quick follow-my-lead-or-else stare. "Jenna, are you still with me?"

She didn't answer.

"Jenna," Cindy said sharply.

"Yes," Jenna responded weakly.

"Everything's okay, because Ryan understands. He knows you thought Jake was really Ryan. Right, Ryan?" She nodded as she stared at Ryan, daring him to contradict her.

"Of course I do, Jenna." He stroked her shoulder. "I know you thought it was me. I don't blame you for anything."

He leaned in close, waiting until her eyes focused on him. "I don't blame you for anything."

And he didn't. This was all Jake's fault, not his sweet, innocent Jenna's.

Jenna shook her head. "Really?" she asked weakly.

"Really," he stated firmly.

Jenna burst into tears.

"WHAT THE HELL'S going on?" Jake demanded as he stormed into the room. The sight of the woman he loved sobbing uncontrollably on the couch dragged out all his protective instincts.

"Jake, it's okay." Cindy stepped toward him, placing her body in front of his to stop his forward momentum. "She's just letting out her tension. This has been a terrible shock for her."

"Join the club," he grumbled, watching his brother hold Jenna in his arms. A deep longing to shove Ryan out of the way and drag her into his own arms burned through him. "Look, I want to talk to her."

"Now isn't the best time," Ryan commented tightly. Jenna pulled back, staring down at her hands. Ryan handed her a tissue and she blew her nose.

She leaned close to Ryan, her hand resting lightly on his shoulder, and murmured something Jake couldn't hear. He hated the easy intimacy they shared.

"I really don't think it's a good idea, Jenna. Not right now," Ryan responded. She murmured something more. "Are you sure?"

She nodded, staring down at her hands again. "Just give me a minute." She pulled another tissue from the box on the table beside her and wiped her eyes, then took a few calming breaths. Finally, she glanced toward Jake. When her gaze hit his, she quavered a little and it ricocheted away, but slowly she brought it back.

"Jake, I'd like to talk to you, too."

"Thank you, Jenna." He smiled reassuringly, despite the twisting of his stomach at the way she looked at him. Like a complete stranger.

Ryan leaned in close to her and whispered in her ear. She glanced up at him sharply.

"But I don't think—"

He leaned in and whispered some more. She nodded.

Ryan stood up and strode to the door, giving Jake a warning glance on the way by. Cindy patted Jake on the arm, then followed Ryan out the door and closed it behind her with a gentle thump.

Jake stepped toward the couch, noticing the look of panic on her face as he approached. He held out his hand.

"Hi, my name's Jake. I'm Ryan's twin brother."

She stared at his hand, as though afraid to touch it. Finally, she reached out her own hand, tentatively, and laid it in his. He shook hands with her, gently but firmly.

"How do you do?" he asked.

"I've been better."

He sat down beside her, folding his hands between his knees. Now that he had his audience with her, he didn't know what to say. *Why not run off with me and get married?* seemed totally out of the question.

"So, you're going to marry my brother tomorrow."

"That was the plan," she agreed.

Why had she said "was?" Could it be she was reconsidering? Could it be she loved him more than Ryan? His heart filled with hope, then crashed as he asked himself if he could really run off with his brother's bride.

"Look, I need to know something." She glanced up at him, then fiddled with her fingers. "That kiss . . . in the ballroom just now . . . Was that the first time?"

"The first time? What do you mean?"

"Did I . . . when I kissed you like that, did I just catch you by surprise? Did you just sort of get caught up in it?"

"So let me get this straight. You think it's possible that we met for the first time this evening and when you kissed me—mistaking me for Ryan, of course—that I joined into that red-hot kiss, even though I knew you were my sister-in-law-to-be and thus totally off-limits?"

She glanced up at him hopefully.

"No, Jenna. This was not the first time. I met you over two months ago, in this hotel, when you led me up to my room and made love with me. Though back then I thought your name was Aurora. A fascinating woman very much into sexual fantasies."

Her face turned bright red.

He was still a little ticked that she would suggest such a thing, so he decided to turn the tables on her.

"Okay, now tell me something. Be honest. Did you really mistake me for Ryan that night we met or were you actually looking for a stranger to fulfill your fantasy? Did finding your brother's twin become a thrill for you, so much so that you or-chestrated our whole affair knowing I wouldn't jeopardize my relationship with my brother over a woman?"

She flinched at the word "affair," but her head lifted in indignation.

"Of course not. I wouldn't do such a thing."

"Well, neither would I."

Her indignation drained away. "I'm sorry. I shouldn't have asked that." Her tiny fists clenched in her lap. "I just want it not to be true."

"But it is true, Jenna," he said gently. "Our meeting in the lobby yesterday and our first meeting, where you wanted me to fulfill your fantasy of having sex with a stranger. And the elevator."

"The elevator," she wailed. She dropped her face into her palms. "Oh God, this is so embarrassing. I don't even know you."

His lips turned up in a half-smile. "That was rather the point, wasn't it?"

She looked close to tears again. He rested his hand on her shoulder and his heart clenched when she stiffened under his touch.

"Look, Jenna, it happened. There's nothing we can do about it now. And as much as I hate it, you're going to marry my brother tomorrow."

He felt a stabbing pain through his chest, but as much as it hurt, he couldn't stand in the way of his brother's happiness. After all, when Jenna had said she loved him, she'd been saying it to Ryan. The tightness in his chest threatened to topple him over, but instead he smiled.

"Honey, we'll just have to put this behind us."

She shook her head. "It's not that simple."

"What do you mean?"

She grabbed a new tissue and blew her nose again, then released a crumpled mass of tissues from her fist onto the table. She took a sip of water, then set the glass down firmly.

"I have to tell you something. Ryan asked me not to, he said it would make things too complicated right now . . . but things are already complicated enough, so . . . I have to tell you."

"What is it?"

She drew in a deep breath, then settled her gaze on him, keeping it steady this time. She reached for his hand, clasping it gently. The feel of her fingers in his, the awareness that she'd taken his hand knowing he was Jake, not Ryan, sent wildly erratic emotions storming through him.

"Tell me what?"

She squeezed his hand gently.

"Jake, I'm pregnant."

His heart flopped over.

"Oh . . . I see." He drew his hand from her grasp, instantly missing her warmth, but needing space from her. "Congratulations."

She laid her hand on his sleeve. "No, you don't understand. When I mistook you for Ryan that first time, when we . . . uh . . . when you and I . . ."

"Lived out your fantasy?" A vague feeling of uneasiness grew within him.

She nodded. "Right. Ryan and I weren't . . . we hadn't been . . . intimate in several months."

He froze.

"My God. Are you trying to tell me . . . ?" His voice trailed off, his thoughts in turmoil, not quite allowing himself to frame the words.

She nodded.

"Yes, Jake." She stared down at her hands as she wrung them together. "You're going to be a father."

A father. Good God. His brother's fiancée, the woman

Jake loved, was carrying his child. Elation swirled through him, chased by raging consternation.

He was going to be a father. All else drained away at the wonderful thought that the woman he loved carried his child.

He took her hands in his.

"My baby?" A note of awe tinged the words.

Her gaze met his and she nodded.

He grabbed her and hugged her tightly.

"My baby." His smile split his face from ear to ear.

She frowned. "I don't think you're fully understanding this situation. I'm supposed to marry your brother tomorrow and he thinks . . ." Her eyes grew wide. "Oh, God."

"He thinks what?"

Her eyes glazed over and she stared into nothingness.

"Jenna?" Was she going to faint again? Suddenly, he realized that's why she'd been fainting, because she was pregnant.

"Jenna. Do you want me to get you a drink? Wait, no alcohol. Do you want some water?" He took her hand and squeezed it. "Jenna, can you hear me?"

"What?" Her eyes focused on him.

"Ryan thinks what?"

"Don't you understand?" She shook her head. "I thought he thought it was his baby . . . Because *I* thought it was his baby. But he knew it wasn't his baby all along." Tears welled up in her eyes. "And that means . . . Oh, God." She dropped her face to her hands.

"Are you saying he's known it was my baby right from the beginning?"

"No," she wailed. "He thought I'd slept with a stranger." She moaned. "He actually believed I'd gone out and had a one-night stand with a stranger . . . and got pregnant." She grabbed Jake's lapels, scrunching the fabric tightly in her fists. "And he asked me to marry him anyway." Tears rolled down her cheeks and her voice lowered to a mere whisper. "He must really love me."

"You got that right."

Jenna's gaze darted to the door at the sound of Ryan's voice. He stood just inside the room, his hands in his pants pockets, his tie hanging loose.

"How long . . ." Jenna took a shaky breath. "How long have you been standing there?"

"Long enough to know you've figured it all out." He walked toward her and kneeled by the couch, pushing past Jake. Ryan took her hands in his. "I know you, Jenna. You're reconsidering the wedding tomorrow. You want to postpone or maybe even cancel. But don't do it."

Guilt crept through her. He knew her so well.

He kissed her palms, the gentle touch of his lips on her hands sending tender feelings of love quivering through her. She rested her hand on his cheek and stared deep into his eyes.

"Ryan, you're so sweet, so caring. I can't believe you wanted to marry me believing I'd cheated on you." Horror washed through her and her hand skittered away from him. "Oh, God, I *did* cheat on you."

He took her hand and held her palm to his lips.

"What else could I do? I didn't want to lose you." He placed his hand under her chin and brought her gaze to his. "Jenna. Marry me tomorrow. Pretend none of this ever happened. Pretend the baby is mine. Walk down the aisle with me and become Mrs. *Ryan* Leigh."

Moisture pooled in her eyes, then flooded over and trickled slowly down her cheeks.

She shook her head back and forth as though on ball bearings and brought her hand to her mouth.

"No," she said weakly. She stroked his cheek. "I can't. I have to have time to think about this. I have to have time to talk to Jake, to see what he wants to do. It's his baby, too."

Ryan's mouth compressed. "Damn it, I know it's his baby. Don't you think that's tearing me up inside?"

She drew back, startled at his sharp tone, her hands falling into fists in her lap.

The hard lines of his expression softened.

"I'm sorry, baby." He stroked her cheek tenderly. "Look, Jake can still be involved with the baby. He can visit whenever he wants. When the child is older he or she can visit him for vacations. If Jake wants to be involved at all."

"Of course I want to be involved. Do you guys remember I'm still in the room?"

Ryan glared at Jake, now sitting in one of the chairs across from the couch.

"Why *are* you still here?" Ryan challenged.

"I have a right to be here."

"The hell you do. You've caused enough trouble as it is."

"Stop it," Jenna pleaded. "Please." She rested her hand on Ryan's sleeve. "Ryan, I'm sorry. I can't marry you tomorrow. I need time to work all this out. We all do."

Ryan turned back to her, a tender expression on his face. "I don't have anything to work out. I want to marry you no matter whose child you're carrying." The warmth of his words curled through her. He leaned closer. "Jenna, I love you."

She placed her hand on his arm.

"Then you should be willing to wait for me. To let me

make whatever decisions I have to for me and the baby. And the baby's father."

His face tightened until she thought it might crack.

"Damn it, Jenna. I don't mean to be harsh, but you were just a fling to Jake. A stranger he had sex with. It's not like Jake wants to marry you. Right, Jake?"

Silence followed his outburst.

Ryan and Jenna both turned to look at Jake.

"Right, Jake?" Ryan prompted tightly.

Jake leaned forward, his hands linked between his spread knees.

"Ryan," he said quietly, "I think you should listen to the lady and give her some time."

The blood drained from Ryan's face, leaving him absolutely white.

CINDY HOVERED IN the corridor as Ryan and Jake led Jenna out the door. Cindy put her arm protectively around Jenna's shoulders.

"I'm going to take you home, honey. Don't worry about the party. I explained to everyone that you aren't feeling well."

"Mom's going to be worried."

"I told her it was a headache. With the stress you've been under organizing the wedding, and the embarrassment of kissing Ryan's brother and all, she understood."

Jenna nodded and allowed Cindy to lead her to the elevator. Cindy pushed the Down button to go to the parking garage. The men hovered beside them.

"I'll walk you to the car," Ryan said.

"No, you two stay here. She needs some space." Cindy pushed the Up button for the two men. "And anyway, Ryan, you need to get to that party and see to your guests."

Jake stepped closer toward Jenna. "Okay, then I'll—"

"No, you go talk to your parents while Ryan talks to the other guests."

An elevator arrived with a ding. The doors slid open and Cindy led Jenna inside.

"I'll call you tomorrow, Jenna, and we'll talk," Ryan called after them.

"We'll all talk," Jake added.

As the door closed, Cindy watched as the two men stared at each other, their arms folded as they waited for the next elevator.

JAKE SLAMMED HIS hand on the receiver and ripped it from its cradle to stop the incessant buzzing.

The digits on the clock read 10:54. Oh, man, he'd had a few too many drinks last night and now his head ached like crazy.

"Yeah, what is it?"

"Jake?" a feminine voice said. Not Jenna's.

"Who is this?"

"This is Cindy. Jenna's friend."

Jake shot straight up, the sheets tangling around his legs.

"What is it? Is Jenna okay?"

"Yeah, she's fine. I spent the night with her last night. I . . . uh . . . I'd like to talk to you, though. About all the stuff that's happened. Would you meet me for lunch?"

"Sure. Not at the hotel, though. The place is crawling with friends and family."

He grabbed his watch from the bedside table and pushed his hand through the metal band, then snapped the clasp closed.

"Okay. Do you know the Blue Moon restaurant over on Nepean Street near Bank? Most out-of-towners will stay near the hotel or over in the market area."

He grabbed the pen and notepad from the drawer in the bedside table and jotted down the information.

"I'll find it. How about one o'clock so we miss the lunch rush?"

"Okay, I'll see you there."

At five to one Jake arrived at the bistro-style restaurant with small round tables, wrought-iron chairs, and lots of plants. He ordered a coffee, which arrived five minutes later just as Cindy stepped in the door.

"You found it okay, I see."

She asked a passing waitress for a soft drink then glanced at the menu. A different waitress brought Cindy's drink, then Jake and Cindy ordered sandwiches.

"Jake, I don't want you to misconstrue what I'm going to say here. I'm not taking sides, or rooting for one of you over the other. I'm here to help Jenna."

He raised his eyebrows. "Does Jenna need help?"

"She needs to make a big decision that will affect the rest of her life, and her baby's, not to mention you and Ryan. She wants to make the best decision for everyone. You may be the baby's father, but Ryan loves her."

"I love her, too." He sipped his coffee.

She leaned forward, her clasped hands resting on the table. "Really? Or are you just saying that because of the baby?"

He pushed his coffee cup aside and leaned toward her.

"I fell in love with her that first night. I didn't realize it until later, but it was love alright."

She narrowed her eyes skeptically. "And you're sure it wasn't just because she slept with you?"

"Are you kidding? That's the perfect situation for most men. A woman who wants one night of wild sex, then never to see you again. No strings, no heartache. As Aurora, she made it clear it was a one-night thing—all part of her fantasy."

"Maybe you wanted her because you couldn't have her."

"Cindy, you know Jenna. You know how easy she is to love. Believe me when I say I want to spend my life with her."

Cindy nodded. "But you're holding back because you have trouble with the idea of taking your brother's bride."

He gripped the edge of the table. "No kidding."

She propped her chin on her hand. "Okay, then. There are some things you should know."

CHAPTER 10

JAKE PACED BACK and forth across his hotel suite, waiting for his brother to arrive, still seething from the revelations Cindy had shared with him. When the knock came, he swung open the door.

"There are a few things you neglected to tell me the other night about you and Jenna."

Ryan sent his brother an impassive glance as he closed the door behind him.

"Like what?"

"Like the fact that as of the night I met Jenna, your relationship with her was over."

Ryan crossed to the bar fridge and pulled out a tiny bottle of scotch.

"Did Jenna tell you that?" He flipped over one of the glasses on the counter and plucked several ice cubes from the bucket Jake had filled about an hour ago. The cubes clinked as they tumbled into the glass.

"Is it true?" Jake demanded.

"No." Ryan poured the amber liquid over the cubes. They cracked loudly.

"Don't lie to me, Ryan." Jake leaned back against the dresser and stared at his brother.

Ryan met Jake's gaze squarely.

"I'm not lying." Ryan's voice remained calm and steady.

"She was going to break up with you." Jake crossed his arms.

According to Cindy, that's what she and Jenna had been talking about when he'd first seen her standing outside the banquet room that night. That's why she'd looked so unhappy. His inconsiderate brother had been neglecting her, just like he'd neglected every other woman with whom he'd had a romantic relationship. As far as Jake was concerned, if Ryan was too stupid to understand what he had with Jenna, he didn't deserve to keep her.

"*Was* is the key word. She didn't break up with me." Ryan sat on the arm of the couch and sipped his drink.

"Yeah, because she thought I was you. The fact that she met me that night saved your butt. If I hadn't shown up, you two wouldn't still be together today."

"You seem to have missed something, brother." Ryan twirled his glass, staring at the swirling liquid. "We aren't exactly together. That fact is also thanks to you."

"Don't try to sidetrack me. She was going to break up with you, wasn't she?"

Ryan sighed. "Yes." He set his glass on the coffee table, then walked to the window and stared out at the view.

"Because you were neglecting her." Jake strolled to the couch and grabbed his drink from the end table. He took a gulp, the rye burning as it slid down his throat.

"I wasn't spending as much time with her as I should have."

"You were neglecting her."

Ryan turned to face Jake again. "Fine. So what?" He strolled back to pick up his drink. "That's all changed now."

"Right. And how much have you been with her over the past three weeks? Paris for two weeks. Before that a trip to Toronto for several days. And her pregnant and pulling together a wedding alone."

"I was trying to get loose ends tied up specifically so I could delegate more work to my staff and spend more time with her. Is that all?"

"No. What about the fact that you didn't ask her to marry you until *after* you knew she was pregnant."

Ryan froze.

"So?"

"So maybe you never would have asked her if she hadn't gotten pregnant."

Ryan's jaw tightened. "It wasn't even my baby."

"Great, so you were being noble. That doesn't mean you love her." Jake settled onto the couch.

For the first time in this conversation, Ryan showed a hint of anger, his nostrils flaring and eyes turning dark and stormy.

"Don't question my love for Jenna."

Jake leaned forward. "You love her so much you were willing to cheat and lie to get her."

"What are you talking about?" Ryan glared at Jake.

"I'm talking about the fact that you told Jenna not to tell me about the baby. Were you going to hide it from me forever? Raise it as your own? It's not like anyone would ask questions if it looked like me."

"She was under a lot of stress." Ryan paced back and forth. "I didn't want to complicate things."

"So you would have told me later?"

Ryan had the good grace to look guilty.

"I didn't think so. Listen, if you really love her, you'll help her make the right decision for *her*. You'll let her get all the information she needs."

Ryan halted. "Meaning?"

"She already knows you. She's been dating you for over a year. She knows what it's like to be with you every day. You need to give her the same chance to get to know me, to know what it's like to be with *me* every day. Then she can make an informed decision."

Ryan's eyes narrowed. "What exactly are you suggesting?"

"I'm suggesting she come and stay with me for a few months in Montreal. Without you. That way she and I can get to know each other."

"I'd be crazy to agree to that," Ryan growled, his fists clenched at his sides.

"Yeah, crazy in love. She'll count that in your favor."

RYAN RAKED HIS hand through his hair as he drove along Highway 417 on his way to Jenna's place. What the hell had happened? Yesterday, he'd been anticipating his wedding to the woman he loved, expecting to watch her walk down the aisle in a long, white dress today—his wedding day—but everything had fallen apart.

Because of Jake.

Now he had to sit still while Jake invited Jenna to stay with him for a month. At least Ryan had negotiated his brother down from his original proposal of several months. Knowing Jenna, she would agree. She would want to give

Jake, the father of her baby—Ryan's gut clenched at that thought—every chance. She would go to Montreal and Jake would have her all to himself for an entire month, influencing her, convincing her he was the better man for her.

Oh, God, Ryan just might lose her.

Yet to fight Jake on this would mean loosing. Jake would present the idea to her with or without Ryan's agreement. If Ryan made his feelings clear about not wanting her to go, it would work against him. Jake had pointed out that if Jenna really loved Ryan, a month with Jake wouldn't change her feelings. Ryan knew, deep down in his soul, that he loved Jenna, and that his love would survive anything.

Ryan parked in the visitor's parking of Jenna's apartment building, then let himself in the front door with the key she'd given him. He rode the elevator to her floor, strolled to her apartment door, then knocked. A moment later, the door was pulled open to reveal her mother's uncertain face.

"Oh, hello . . . uh . . ."

"I need to see Jenna," he said.

She nodded and pulled the door open.

"Come in." She turned and called, "Jenna. There's someone here to see you."

Clearly, she wasn't sure if he was Ryan or Jake.

Jenna appeared at the kitchen door.

"Hello, Jenna."

"Ryan." She rushed forward. Discreetly, her mother disappeared down the hall.

Jenna flung her arms around his waist and rested her head against his chest. The feel of her tucked in close as he wrapped his arms around her sent warmth flooding through his system. The warmth of being home. The warmth of being with the one person in the world he loved above all others. His Jenna. He closed his eyes as he soaked up that love.

"How did you know it was me?" he asked.

She drew away a fraction, her gaze meeting his. Her fingers stroked across his temple. "Your hair. It's shorter than your brother's."

"Oh." Disappointment seeped through him that her only way to tell them apart was as superficial as a hairstyle.

Her hand stroked down the lapel of his light wool suit jacket.

"And I helped you pick out this suit." She lifted his tie, letting it slip through her fingers. "Along with the tie to match."

He remembered when they'd gone shopping together that day. Afterward, they'd gone to a small restaurant overlooking the canal and laughed as they'd shared the sunshine, the view, and a great lunch together, savoring the newness of their relationship. That night, they'd made love for the third time ever. His heart ached to think he might never be able to touch her like that again.

"But mostly your voice," she continued.

"My voice?" Everyone said his and Jake voices sounded exactly alike.

He glanced down at her eyes, dewy with the sheen of unshed tears.

"You mean because Jake called you something else?" *Aurora,* he thought it was.

She shook her head. "That has nothing to do with it." She flattened her hand on his chest and her warmth stirred his heart. "When you say my name, there's a tenderness and familiarity that just isn't there when a stranger says it. Your brother is a stranger."

She rested her head against his chest and tightened her arms around him. "Oh, Ryan, I'm so sorry. I never meant to hurt you. When he and I . . ." She sighed softly. "I thought it was you . . . acting like a stranger."

Acting like a stranger. So she did notice a difference between him and Jake.

He held her close, stroking the top of her head. "It's okay, sweetheart," he murmured.

He drew her closer, their lips meeting in a tender, loving kiss. He could feel her heart beating next to his, filling him with an indescribable feeling of completeness. This is where she belonged. In his arms. In his life.

The buzzer rang.

"That'll be Jake."

She glanced nervously at the door. "Jake? Why is he here?"

"We have to talk to you about something."

JAKE'S HEART TURNED cold as Jenna stood at the door, staring at him like a stranger.

"Hello, Jake."

He hated how stiff his name sounded on her lips. She stepped back to let him in.

Ryan already stood inside. She stepped to his side, her arm brushing his, an intimate air about them. Jealousy surged through Jake at the easy closeness his brother shared with her. Their year and a half of shared experience and building a loving relationship showed.

As Jake explained his idea to Jenna, that she stay with him in Montreal for a month to get to know him, she glanced at Ryan, gauging his reaction, looking to him for support.

Jake didn't kid himself. It was going to be tough to convince her she belonged with him—probably impossible—but he had to try. He loved her too much. It's not that he wanted to hurt his brother—Jake would do anything to make this not be what it was—but it wouldn't be good for any of them if Jenna married the wrong man. As much as Jake loved Jenna, he had to believe she truly loved him, too.

JENNA CLUNG TO her purse as she watched the tall, dense trees pass by as Jake drove along the narrow private road.

What a mess. Although she and Ryan had been in a committed relationship for the past year and a half and she had accepted his proposal of marriage, she now had to deal with the fact that she was carrying Jake's child. She was going to spend a month with Jake to consider the possibility of spending the rest of her life with him. A virtual stranger.

She had almost broken up with Ryan two months ago, and the event that had caused their relationship to turn around had turned out to be a case of mistaken identity. Now, Jenna realized she had to reevaluate her whole relationship with Ryan. She hoped that this month would give her some perspective, rather than add to her confusion.

Jake pulled into a clearing and parked in front of a cozy-looking cedar home with a huge set of windows across the front. A lovely garden bright with pink and purple tulips and tall mauve and yellow irises curved around the front lawn.

This lovely, secluded hideaway would be her home for the next month.

The thought of spending an entire month alone with Jake

made her a little uncomfortable. Sure they had chemistry, but did they have enough in common to make a life together?

Of course, that's exactly what this month was supposed to help them figure out.

Jake opened the heavy oak door and waited for her to proceed inside. When they entered the house, they stepped right into the kitchen, a lovely, large room with maple cupboards and a long counter overlooking a spacious living area with a couple of couches and an easy chair. The whole place was filled with sunlight. Cozy.

A tortoiseshell cat with a white ring around the end of its tail trotted up to Jake and rubbed against his legs. He picked it up and scratched behind its ears. The cat showed its pleasure by purring loudly.

"This is Sam."

Jenna smiled widely. "Well, hello, Sam." She petted the cat. "What a good boy."

The cat's golden eyes drifted closed and its head rested on Jake's shoulder.

"Actually, she's a girl. Sam's short for Samantha."

"Samantha?"

"Well, when she showed up at my door, wet and alone, I didn't know if she was a he or a she, so I figured Sam would work either way."

He put Sam down and she trotted along behind them as they walked through the kitchen doorway to the living room.

"You live here all the time?"

"Actually, I have a penthouse in the city, but I spend a lot of time here in the summer, and several weekends in the winter. The cross-country skiing is spectacular."

He led her into the living room and pointed toward patio doors on the right. "There's a heated pool out back."

Through the glass, she could see a lovely kidney-shaped pool glittering in the sunlight.

"Come on, I'll show you your room."

She followed him down a hall to a bedroom on the right.

"My room?" she asked. She'd been worried he'd try to convince her to stay in his room.

"Yes, your room. Don't get me wrong. I'd love you to move right into my room, and my bed, but I didn't think you'd be comfortable with that idea." He pointed to the end of the hall. "That's my room. Anytime you want to join me, come right on in. Or, if you want me to come to you, just say the word. You call the shots here, Jenna. Whatever you want or need, you've got it."

She stepped into the room he'd indicated was hers. A queen-sized bed filled the center of the room, covered with a duvet in a teal and sapphire abstract print with fuchsia as an accent.

Ryan placed her suitcases beside the tall light maple armoire. She sat down on the bed, stroking the tightly woven cotton bed covering, amazed at the silky feel of it.

"You know, this is quite weird. I really don't know you at all. You and I are strangers, yet we've essentially moved in together."

He leaned against the edge of the dresser. "We're not exactly strangers, Jenna. We've shared some very intimate hours together."

"Yes, but I thought you were . . ."

Ryan.

She turned away, not wanting to think about Ryan and the

pain she'd caused him. Her finger toyed with the piping along the edge of the tailored pillow sham.

"You know what I thought. The point is I only met you for real on Thursday. Now, it's Sunday and . . ." She gestured around her. "Here I am."

"That's why I don't want you to feel pressure to do anything more than spend time with me, and I don't want to overwhelm you with that, either, so I'll still be going in to the office every weekday. That'll give you time to yourself." He smiled. "Now, if you find you want to spend more time with me, just say so and I'll arrange to be here full-time."

Jenna couldn't believe the difference between the two brothers. Ryan could barely find the time to spend with her, and here Jake had only known her a short time and he was willing to take time off work, and on short notice, to be with her.

"Thank you," she said.

He smiled. "My pleasure." He stood up. "Would you like help unpacking?"

The thought of him helping her sift through her clothing, including her lingerie, made her uncomfortable.

"No, I'll manage."

He lifted her large suitcase onto a lovely big armchair by the window.

"I'll let you get settled in then." He started to leave but paused at the door. "Jenna, I just want to warn you." He turned back to face her, his expression serious. "Although I don't want to pressure you, I am a man, and I do want you."

He stepped toward the bed and sat down beside her. His spicy, masculine scent surrounded her.

"Maybe we only met officially on Thursday, but I feel like I've known you a lifetime. And the reality is we have been intimate, more intimate than many couples who've been together for years." He smiled. "After all, you shared your deepest sexual fantasies with me."

She felt her cheeks flush.

He tipped up her chin and she gazed into his intense, deep blue eyes.

Heat flashed though her. Partly due to hormones, which she had in abundance with the pregnancy, but largely because of being so close to this strong, sexy man.

"Jenna, imagine acting out your stranger fantasy with me now." He stroked his hands lightly up her arms, sending tingling awareness dancing along her nerve endings. "Imagine how much more real it would be since, as you say, I really am a stranger."

Her eyes widened as she imagined his strong, masculine hands unzipping her dress, his fingers parting the fabric and stroking across her skin as he revealed her swelling breasts. Her nipples puckered as she imagined his lips encircling each one and dabbing it with the tip of his tongue. A *real* stranger touching her so intimately.

It would be incredibly sexy. Oh, God, she couldn't believe how turned on she was at the thought of having sex with Jake. Of knowing he was Jake, a stranger, while he touched her, pleasured her, brought her to orgasm.

She wanted to stand up and tear off her clothes right now.

He kissed her hand, sending tingles up her arm, then he stood up.

"I'll leave you with that thought." He turned and left the room.

Heat continued to sear through her. Although he was a stranger, she knew from direct experience he would pleasure her beyond compare. He would be tender, adventurous, thorough in his lovemaking, and wildly passionate. Some part of her longed to feel his hands skimming over her. Actually, every part of her wanted that, except her head.

With her body thrumming the way it was right now, how would she resist her desire for a sexual encounter with him? She remembered the elevator and how his hands had grasped her hips, how he had thrust into her. The image of his face in the elevator's mirrored wall, contorted in pleasure as he climaxed inside her, after catapulting her into her own powerful orgasm.

Just how long would she last?

CHAPTER 11

JENNA SPENT A night of exquisite torture dreaming of
Jake. Yearning for Jake. The fact that she was constantly
horny because of her blazing hormones didn't help.

Jake prepared a great ham and cheese omelet for breakfast, and served it with herbal tea. All through the meal, she
stole longing glances at him. Watching him raise his fork to
his mouth, then close his full lips over the food and slide them
along the metal prongs, sent her senses into a whirl. When he
caught her looking at him, he smiled, his midnight blue eyes
glittering.

"So, Jenna, why don't you tell me a little about yourself?"

She glanced at him over her tea as she sipped, then placed
the red stoneware mug on the table.

"Well, I'm self-employed . . . a computer consultant. I specialize in creating courses for software companies who have a
product to sell and need to train their clients."

She hesitated, not wanting to bore him with plain old
Jenna. She was a far cry from the Aurora persona he knew.

He smiled. "And what do you like to do for fun? Other
than dream up sexual fantasies, of course."

She felt her cheeks stain crimson. "Well, I . . . like to read." *Boring.* "And . . . I like to dance."

Oops. That scared off a lot of guys. Most men hated to dance.

"Sometimes I knit and crochet." *Oh, yeah, like that's more interesting.* What the heck was she thinking?

"That'll come in handy with the baby on the way."

The insecurity she felt at revealing the everyday Jenna to Jake washed away as she remembered she was carrying a baby. *Jake's* baby. His eyes glowed with warmth as he smiled at her, as though reading her thoughts.

"Maybe tomorrow I'll take you out shopping so we can pick out some yarn together."

"Really?"

She could never imagine walking through a quaint little knitting store with Ryan by her side, perusing the shelves of brightly colored yarns together. Yet she could imagine it with Jake for some reason, and it felt so . . . domestic.

"Then we could come back here and sit by the fire together. Maybe watch a movie."

Very domestic. And she liked the feeling. But Jake was a virtual stranger.

She shifted in her chair. She should be having these feelings about Ryan, the man she'd been in love with for more than a year. The man she'd agreed to marry.

"Jake, why didn't Ryan tell me about you?"

"What do you mean?"

"He never really talked about his family but . . . well, you're twins. I would have thought he'd have said something about you. I thought twins were usually very close."

Jake nodded. "Ryan and I do share a close bond, but my brother has a very competitive nature."

She rolled her eyes. "Tell me about it."

Jenna had certainly seen that in Ryan's approach to business and in the way he drove himself to succeed, but she saw it in other aspects of his character, too. Like the time they played mini golf with Cindy and her date. Ryan kept coaching Jenna on every hole to ensure she played her best, determined they would win.

"He always competed with me when we were kids," Jake continued. "For grades, in sports . . . for girls."

Her eyebrows shot up. "He stole your girlfriends?"

"No, the other way around, actually."

"You stole his girlfriends?" she asked in amazement. That would explain why Ryan had kept her and Jake apart.

"Not really. They just . . . gravitated to me. Not that Ryan isn't a great guy. It's just that his intensity put a lot of girls off. They just wanted to have fun."

"And you're the fun one," she surmised.

Jake shrugged. "That made him a little insecure, I think. Later, when the popularity of my first computer game accelerated, making my company a great success, he threw himself into his business with a vengeance. I told him I was just lucky—coming up with the right idea at the right time—but he took it as a personal challenge. The way he drives himself, I'm surprised he ever found the time to ask you out." He smiled. "But then, I'm sure he found you as irresistible as I do."

She blushed at his compliment and toyed with her spoon.

"How did the two of you meet?" Jake asked.

"At a conference. Actually, on the plane—we were seated

next to each other on the flight to San Diego. Later, we ran into each other picking up our baggage. When we realized we were going to the same hotel, we shared a cab."

"Was that the conference on Web site development techniques?"

She nodded.

"Man, I almost went to that conference. If I had, maybe you and I would have met back then instead."

"But you and I live in different cities. I probably still would have wound up with Ryan."

He took her hand. "Jenna, I would never allow something as trivial as distance to keep us apart."

She felt a tremor down her spine. If only Ryan felt that strongly about her. He lived in the same city as she did and yet she hardly ever saw him these days.

"What about you? I know you have a brother. Do you have any other siblings?" Jake asked.

"No, just Shane. I didn't see him much while I was growing up, though. My parents divorced when I was very young and Shane went with Dad."

Jake squeezed Jenna's hand and she welcomed the warmth.

"I'm sorry. That must have been very hard on you."

She nodded. "It was. I missed Shane a lot. And I missed Daddy." She'd missed being a family. Her heart ached at the unwelcome emotions welling up inside her.

Jake leaned close to her. "And you want to make sure that your baby doesn't suffer that same fate. Not having a father."

She nodded, unable to speak.

Jake slid his arm around her shoulders. "Jenna, I will always be there for our child. Always. I promise."

. . .

AFTER BREAKFAST, THEY carried their plates into the kitchen. Jake put the dishes in the dishwasher but Jenna insisted on washing up the skillet. Finally, he agreed and disappeared for a few minutes. He returned as she was wiping the counter.

"All finished, I see. Good. I have a surprise for you."

She dried her hands on the towel that hung on the oven handle. "What kind of surprise?"

"Come on. I'll show you."

He took her hand, enclosing it in the warmth of his, and led her into the living room.

A package sat on the couch, wrapped in gold foil with a bright red ribbon, a bow, and a small card labeled JENNA taped to the top.

She picked it up.

"Go ahead and open it."

She pulled off the ribbon and unwrapped the shiny paper. Inside, she found a long, thin box with a cellophane window. Her gaze traveled the length of the translucent purple, vaguely cylindrical shape of the item inside. It had a bulge on one side.

"What is it?" she asked just as her gaze followed the short curve outward then sharp change in direction over the mushroom-shaped end. Like the head of a man's penis.

"It's a vibrator."

It slipped from her fingers, then landed on the couch and bounced to the floor. Her face burned hotly.

He chuckled.

"It's okay, Jenna. I'm not suggesting anything kinky. I just wanted to let you know I'm serious about not pressuring you to have sex with me. I don't want you coming to me because you're sexually frustrated. You should only come to me because you want to be with me."

He leaned over and picked up the box from the floor. The *vibrator.*

She stared at it, not quite knowing whether to take it from his hand or wait until he put it down. Something about touching it at the same time as he was touching it felt a little too intimate, especially considering what she would do with it. What he knew she would do with it. What he probably imagined her doing with it.

Her face flamed hotter.

"I've . . . never actually used one."

"Really? A woman with such lively sexual fantasies? Well, let me show you."

"No!" she yelped, jerking back slightly.

"I don't mean actually . . ." He laughed. "I'll just show you what the buttons do." He opened the package, then slid the thing out. He discarded the thin clear molded plastic packaging surrounding it and held up the purple device. "This part is obvious," he said, indicating the penis shape that made up the bulk of the apparatus. He tapped the bulgy thing that curved out along one side. His finger moved along it, to where it narrowed to a small, delicate-looking tip. He tapped the end. "This is for clitoral stimulation. Here, give me your hand."

She drew back a little as he reached for her right hand, then realized she was being silly and allowed him to take it and rest her finger on the tip. It was soft and pliant.

"Stay there for a second," he said and pressed a button near the base. A whirring sound started and she felt a vibration against her finger. Light, delicate. She could imagine it brushing lightly against her clitoris. Heat washed through her womb and her nipples hardened, pushing against the confines of her lace bra.

He indicated the column of four buttons and pointed to the second button from the top. "This one changes the vibration." He pushed it and the vibration increased, thrumming through her finger and up her arm. He shifted her finger to the tip of the penis. Oh, God, she'd started to think of the thing as a penis. Embarrassment encouraged her to pull away, but fascination kept her planted to the spot, allowing him to touch her finger to the long, purple penis, designed exclusively for a woman's pleasure. Her damnable nipples thrust harder as though trying to escape their lace prison.

"You see, you can feel the vibration in the shaft, too."

She sucked in a breath as she imagined that long pleasure-shaft deep inside her, vibrating the length of her vagina.

His eyes glittered in amusement at her obvious enthrallment.

"Now, watch this." He pushed the third button and the shaft started to spiral around in circles. She snatched her finger away, but her gaze stayed fixed on it, moving around and around. "It's designed to hit the G-spot. The woman at the Secluded Hideaway said it gives quite an intense orgasm."

"Secluded Hideaway?"

"It's a store." He turned off the vibrator. The spiraling motion stopped. "They specialize in women's sexual items."

He'd actually discussed this device with a woman in a store? Jenna would never do such a thing. She rather admired that about him. If only she were so relaxed about sexuality.

"They have a full line of sex toys, lingerie, even women's

erotica. I bought a couple of books so you could try them out. On the side table."

She noticed three books on the table beside the couch. She picked up the top one. *"Virtual Love?"*

"You work with computers so I thought you'd like the virtual reality theme." He smiled. "And in the first scene the woman is captured by a pirate. I remember you mentioned something about a pirate that first day."

Oh, man, this stranger knew way too much about her. More even than Ryan, at least in this area.

"I figure you can read the book to get interested, then use this while I'm at work and I'll never know." He winked. "Unless you tell me about it."

"For not wanting to pressure me into sex, you certainly want me to keep thinking about it."

"Jenna, sex is healthy. I want you to have an outlet for sexual release. I can certainly be that outlet, but, as I said, I don't want you coming to me just for that reason. If you and I make love, I want it to be because you want to make love with me. Do you understand?"

She nodded.

"Don't you realize that if I wanted to hurry you into my bed . . ." He picked up the device as he talked and waved it in front of her. "I wouldn't provide something like this. I'd give you the books and hope you'd get all hot and bothered, letting it build up good and strong, with no other way to release it.

"Now, that said . . ." He stepped closer to her. "I am a man and I do want you, so don't let embarrassment keep you away."

. . .

AFTER JAKE LEFT for work, Jenna put the books and the *thing* in the drawer in her bedside table and forgot about it.

Actually, she tried to forget about it, but over the next few days, she opened the drawer and just stared at it several times a day. She actually pulled it out once and considered trying it, but what if Jake came home early for some reason? She'd be too embarrassed if he came in while she was using it, even if her door was closed. He'd probably be able to hear it.

Five days after arriving at Jake's, she sat on the living room side of the eating counter, her elbow on the counter and her face resting on her hand as she watched Jake prepare a fabulous dinner.

Oh, man, he was sooo sexy in his gray shirt with the top three buttons open, revealing the slight sprinkling of hair across well-defined pecs. He'd discarded his tie within moments of entering the house after his day at work. His pleated charcoal dress pants accentuated his trim waist.

He wouldn't let her help prepare dinner, using her pregnancy as an excuse to make her sit down and relax, though he did let her sip cranberry cocktail from a wineglass and watch.

Over the past few days, she'd found herself staring at him often, a stranger with a familiar face. Now, however, she found herself noticing the differences between Jake and Ryan rather than the similarities. Ryan hated to cook and when he did, he followed a recipe to the letter, or prepared something from a box. Jake seemed to fling in spices at random with a quick sprinkle or two from various hand-labeled bottles. He had a stand in the kitchen window with a variety of fresh herbs growing in small pots.

Jake glanced up at her as she stared at the plants.

"Do you like to cook, Jenna?"

She grimaced, her gaze gliding around his gourmet kitchen, with the brass-bottomed pots hanging from the ceiling, the complicated-looking appliances on the marble countertop, and the fancy utensils in a ceramic stand by the six-burner stove and double oven.

"Not like you obviously do. I cook because I have to eat, that's all. I love to bake, but the results are too tempting, so I don't do it very often. Just for the holidays."

Baking Christmas cookies was one of the rare childhood traditions she remembered that included Shane. Whenever he had visited Jenna and their mom over the holidays, the three of them baked fancy-shaped cookies and decorated them with colorful sugar, icing, and sprinkles. Shane had particularly liked the silver balls made of sugar and Jenna had loved the glittery red and green sugar.

Jake smiled, his eyes twinkling. "I can just see you in this kitchen, your face smudged with flour, as you help our son or daughter cut shapes out of cookie dough."

Her hand slid to her stomach. She sensed the life growing inside her and maternal warmth washed through her. She longed for that day.

"And what would you be doing?" she asked.

"Basting the turkey, of course."

She grew misty at the lovely family image that triggered in her mind. Their child laughing as flour plumed in the air after the bag dropped to the floor. Jake laughing as he swept the little one into his arms and twirled him around. Just like her daddy had done with her—before he'd left.

A happy family. Christmastime together.

Her heart ached. She wanted that so much. From every-thing she knew of Jake, she was sure he'd be a fabulous father.

And a wonderful husband.

"Why don't you pick a movie for us to watch after dinner?" he suggested.

"Okay." She shifted off the stool and strolled to the shelves along the wall beside the huge high-def TV on the main wall. She dragged her finger along the spines of the DVD cases.

Judging from his collection, he liked different movies than Ryan, or rather a wider variety. Ryan liked sci-fi thrillers and movies with military espionage as the theme. Jake seemed to like those, too, but he also had comedies, mysteries, fantasy, drama, and some offbeat flicks. Her finger stopped on *Run, Lola, Run,* a fast-paced character-driven German film where a young woman repeated the same forty-five minutes trying to save her boyfriend's life several times, allowing her to learn more about herself and the people around her. She skimmed along farther and stopped at the old movie *Bell, Book, and Candle* with Kim Novak and James Stewart, a movie about a witch in New York who casts a spell on a man but accidentally falls in love with him, losing her powers. It was one of her absolute favorites.

Also among his collection was *Paternity* with Burt Reynolds. Her cheeks heated as she remembered that this movie was the one that had given her the idea of wanting to act out the fantasy of having sex with a stranger. There was a funny scene in the movie where Burt Reynolds did exactly that with the heroine to make sex between them more exciting.

Jenna's fantasy had never been about having sex with an actual stranger, but about spicing up her sex life with Ryan by pretending to be strangers.

She pulled out the movie and stared at the back, not really

seeing it. Now she thought about sex with an actual stranger. A stranger who was becoming very familiar.

Well, why not? Jake had explained to her that Ryan was giving her this chance to get to know Jake. Ryan knew there was a high probability of Jenna having sex with Jake. She knew that because she'd drilled Ryan on the question. He had been reluctant, but had agreed when she'd said to be fair she should be able to explore that side of her and Jake's relationship.

She hadn't really intended to do it. After all, she and Jake already knew they were compatible sexually.

As she stared at the movie in her hand, she thought about the fact that she was already getting to know Jake. Soon, he wouldn't be a stranger at all. That was good, but a little devil voice inside her screamed that her opportunity to try sex with a real stranger, in the only way she would ever consider it, was fast slipping away.

"How did I know you'd be a fan of that movie?"

Jenna's gaze slashed to Jake, standing in the doorway from the kitchen with a steaming casserole dish in his oven mitt–covered hands. God, how did the man manage to look so sexy in kitchen attire? She jabbed the movie back onto the shelf. He raised an eyebrow and smiled knowingly.

The beef stroganoff he'd made was absolutely delicious. After the meal, they settled on the couch to watch a comedy she quickly selected from the shelf, not paying much attention to anything about it except that it wasn't *Paternity*. Sam curled up on the couch beside her.

Unfortunately, she'd selected *American Pie 2,* which she'd vaguely mistaken for *American Beauty.* The movie turned out to be a sexy teen movie about college friends looking for sex.

During the scene where two young women pretended to be

lesbians to tease the guys, Jenna found herself surreptitiously glancing in Jake's direction, wondering if this was one of his fantasies. Didn't all men want girl-on-girl action? Certainly the moviemaker seemed to think so; one character hiding at the window accidentally transmitted his description of what he saw across the radio waves and every man in the county seemed to be drooling over the situation the main characters found themselves in.

Although there was no actual sex during the movie, by the end, Jenna found herself thinking about sex. A lot. Her body thrummed with need, her aching nipples pushed outward.

She really wanted sex. She wanted sex with Jake. She wanted to experience sex with a stranger, but a safe stranger like Jake. Damn, she wanted sex with Jake, stranger or not. She sucked in a breath, trying to reel in her hormones.

As the closing credits rolled by, Jake grabbed the remote control and turned off the DVD, then turned on a Diana Krall CD. The sultry jazz curled around her. She took her last sip of cranberry and orange juice and settled back into the cushions of the couch, distractedly petting Sam, who purred happily.

"Here, let me refresh that for you."

"Just water this time, please."

Jake retrieved her stemmed glass and headed for the kitchen. She picked up her knitting and inspected the three inches of soft turquoise yarn worked into a delicate lace pattern. Jake and she had chosen the yarn and pattern yesterday and she'd begun the sweater this morning. She couldn't see any obvious mistakes, so she read the next instruction and began knitting again. Jake returned a moment later with a tall icy glass of water and a dark fizzy soft drink. He sat down beside her.

"Jake, you know a lot more about me than I know about you."

He tucked his hands behind his head. "What would you like to know? What I do for a living? Where I went to school?" He took a sip of his soft drink.

"I'd like to know about your sexual fantasies."

He almost choked on his drink. He set his glass on the table in front of them and twisted to face her. "My sexual fantasies?"

She finished the row of knitting and placed her project on the side table. "Well, sure. You know mine. Some of them, anyway."

He raised an eyebrow and his lips turned up in a heart-stopping grin. "You have others? What are they?"

"You first."

"Well, there's this one on an elevator I'm quite partial to."

She smiled. "Yeah, I like that one, too." She leaned closer to him. "But I'm serious. What kind of guy fantasies do you have? For instance, I bet you'd like to have two women."

He gazed at her with a warmth she found unnerving.

"Only if they were both you."

"Oh, come on. You're just sucking up."

"Yes, sucking would have something to do with it. So would coming."

She batted his shoulder. "You're terrible." She leaned forward, resting her elbows on her knees. "Are you trying to tell me if two gorgeous women with boobs out to here—" she gestured six inches in front of her chest "—got naked in front of you and started kissing and stroking each other's breasts, you wouldn't get turned on."

"Of course I would. I'm not dead. What about you?"

"Would I get turned on watching two women?" She blushed. "I don't know."

"I bet you would, but that's not what I meant. Would you get turned on with two guys?"

"You mean watching them . . ." She flicked her finger back and forth. "Together?"

"No, I mean, with you. Touching you. Kissing your breasts, one on each. Or one stroking here . . ." His hand slid up her stomach and circled around her breast. Her already hard nipples tightened even more. His other hand slid down her stomach and cupped her mound. ". . . while the other performs oral sex on you."

Her lower muscles pulsed, longing for him to touch her inside.

"Well, that sounds pretty exciting." She took the hand from her lower region and placed it on the side of her waist. He now leaned over her, looking down into her face. "But you're avoiding telling me about your fantasy."

He tipped down and brushed his lips against hers. The gentle contact triggered a wild rush of sensations through her.

"My one and only fantasy is when a beautiful woman named Jenna, a woman I care for very deeply, gazes into my eyes and says, 'Jake, I want you to make love with me.'" He removed his hand from her breast to stroke her cheek with the tip of his finger. "And this woman would assure me she knows I'm not someone else playacting. She would know it's me."

His lips found hers again and he caressed her mouth with his own. Tingles rippled through her. Her breasts swelled, demanding his touch again, but more thoroughly this time.

"Jake, I . . ."

"Jenna, I'm not my brother. We're two totally different people."

"Yes, I know." She stroked the side of his face, loving the feel of his wavy hair sliding between her fingers, loving the depth of longing in his eyes. "I knew that the first time we were together, though I thought it was an act then. Now I know that it was because you are a very different and very exciting man."

She tipped up her mouth for a kiss. His lips brushed hers sweetly.

"Jake, I want you to make love to me."

His eyes smoldered and he tucked his hands under her legs and lifted her off the couch with him. As he carried her down the hall toward his bedroom, her nerves started to jitter.

"Jake, I hope . . ." She hesitated.

"What is it, sweetheart?"

"I hope you won't be disappointed with me."

He stopped dead in his tracks.

"What are you talking about? How could you even suggest I might be disappointed with you?"

"I was playing the part of a stranger, too. That's not what I'm really like."

He smiled. "I bet that's more like you than you think. In fact, I bet that's the real you when you let down your barriers."

"But if it's not?"

He kissed her, a delicate pressure on her lips that built to a hard, insistent urging. His tongue swept inside her mouth and joined with hers in a pulsing dance. He drew back, leaving her breathless.

"You could never disappoint me. In fact, why don't you just lie back and let me do all the work."

CHAPTER 12

JAKE CARRIED HER into his bedroom. The king-sized sleigh bed made of dark-stained oak dominated the masculine navy and burgundy room. He laid her down and sat on the edge of the bed beside her, gazing down at her with a tender smile. She reached for the buttons of his shirt, but he wrapped his hand around her fingers and drew her hands away.

"I told you I want you to lie back and let me do all the work."

He stood up and unfastened his top button, then the second. He ran his fingers upward, parting the edges of the fabric, revealing the hard angles of his chest. Moving downward again, he unfastened another, then another, moving with painful slowness, the shirt parting, revealing his washboard abs a little at a time. He started to rock his hips from side to side. He unfastened his belt and tugged it from the belt loops, then tossed it aside.

"Have you ever had a man strip for you, Jenna?"

"Uh, well . . ."

He grinned. "Why, you naughty girl."

"It wasn't for me, exactly. It was for the bride-to-be. And we were at a club." Not in an intimate setting like Jake's bedroom.

"Well, sweetheart, this is all for you." He dropped his pants, then kicked them aside. He discarded his socks, then turned around and lifted his shirttail to expose his gyrating butt. The muscles, tensing and releasing, formed the hardest, firmest ass she'd ever seen. She itched to walk up behind him and wrap her hands around his buttocks, to feel the movement of those hard muscles against her palms.

But he'd told her to lie back, so that's what she was doing.

He turned around again and dropped his shirt off one shoulder, then the other. He pulled back one side, revealing half of his long, lean torso. Her gaze drifted to his nipple, which she longed to take into her mouth. He pulled back the other side of his shirt, then shrugged it off entirely. Holding the right sleeve with one hand in front of him and the other sleeve behind him, he drew the shirt between his legs and pulled it back and forth so that it rubbed over his crotch, and his growing cock, while thrusting his pelvis forward and back.

Her own crotch had become uncomfortably tight. She wanted to touch him. Even more, she wanted him to touch her. He tossed the shirt to the floor. It landed on Sam, who had been sitting on the floor watching Jake. The cat murmured a complaint and stalked off.

Jake stepped close to the bed and leaned in to kiss her. Her tongue flashed out, wanting to be inside his mouth. He allowed her one taste, then drew back and turned around. He reached down to pick up his shirt, giving her a great view of his tight butt only inches away. She reached out and touched the firm muscle. After permitting one brief squeeze, he stepped forward, out of reach, then glanced back at her with a devilish grin. He reached behind and drew down one side of his briefs, exposing half of one butt cheek, tantalizing her, then he drew down the other side. She licked her lips. Suddenly, he shoved his briefs all the way down to his ankles. He stayed bent over for a second or two while he stepped out of them, allowing her an eyeful of his tight, hard flesh. He stood up and turned slowly with his hands tucked in front, his briefs blocking her view of his cock. He stepped close to the bed.

"What do you want me to do now, Jenna?"

"I, uh . . ."

Her gaze stayed riveted on his groin as he shifted the briefs up a little, exposing a glimpse of his balls, then down a little, so the tip of the head peeked out before he quickly hid it again.

"I want you to make love—"

"Yes, I know that and I will, but what do you want me to do right now."

His right hand disappeared behind the briefs and she could see his wrist moving up and down.

"I want to see . . . uh . . ."

"You want to see what, sweetheart?" He lifted the briefs a little, exposing his fur-covered balls. His hidden hand came back into view as he slid it under his testicles and lifted them up. "You want to see these."

She nodded.

"Is that all? Is there anything else you want to see?"

"I want to see all of you. Naked."

His fingers moved over his balls, fondling them.

"What specifically do you want to see? Tell me," he urged.

"I want to see . . ." She licked her lips. "I want to see your . . . penis?"

He grinned. "I remember you had another name for it."

She flushed and giggled a little.

"Your cock. I want to see your cock."

His smile broadened.

"Man, you're gorgeous when you say dirty words."

He dropped the briefs and she sucked in her breath. His cock was long and hard, the head purple with wanting her.

"Here it is, sweetheart. What do you want me to do with it now?"

"Bring it over here." Her words were deep and throaty with need.

He sat on the bed beside her and she stroked down his stomach, reveling in the hard ripples of his muscles under her fingertips. Her fingers glided through his pubic hair and slid around his erection. She ran her fingertips lightly around the ridge below the head. After a moment, she leaned forward and licked the tip of him, then drew the head into her mouth. She swirled her tongue around him a few times before he groaned.

"No, Jenna. Stop." His hands grasped her shoulders gently and he eased her back.

She drew her mouth away and gazed up at him.

"What's wrong?" Her voice was as shaky as she felt, her confidence dropping to her ankles.

She glanced down at her hands, now folded in her lap. She'd been afraid that plain, old Jenna wouldn't be able to please him. He tucked his hand under her chin and lifted it so she faced him again.

"Don't look like that, sweetheart. I loved what you were doing." His penis bobbed up and down in agreement. "It's just that I want to concentrate on pleasing you."

"But touching you does please me."

He smiled. "I'm glad." He kissed her tenderly. "I tell you

what. How about you touch all you want, but not before you ask me to do something for you?"

Excitement skittered through her. He did want her touch and he wanted to please her.

"Okay, I guess I'd like you to undress me."

He stroked his finger down the placket of her blouse.

"Be more specific."

"I . . . I want you to take off my blouse."

His fingers moved to the neckline of her top. The brush of his fingers against her skin as he released the first button sent electricity coursing through her. He dragged his fingertip along her skin to the second button, and released that one. By the time he released the last one, below her belly button, her skin was on fire. He slid the blouse over her shoulders and slipped it off her arms. Goose bumps quivered along her exposed flesh. His gaze fell to her breasts, swelling over the top of her black underwire bra.

He looked but he didn't touch . . . and she wanted him to touch. Desperately.

She leaned forward and kissed him, stroking her hands over his temples.

"What now, Jenna?" His voice, low and sexy, rumbled through her.

"I want you to touch my breasts," she murmured, her voice full of need.

His fingertips stroked the white flesh above her bra. His other hand cupped underneath, warming her in his palm. She wanted the lace out of the way, wanted to feel his hands on her naked skin.

She nuzzled against his ear, then blew gently and whispered, "Take off my bra."

He slid his arms around her and unfastened her bra, then drew it slowly from her body.

"Jenna, you have the most beautiful breasts." He stroked over both of them, caressed the nipples with his fingertips. They rewarded him by hardening and extending, reaching out for him.

She wanted more.

"I want you to . . ." She licked her lips.

"Yes?" he encouraged.

"I want you to kiss them."

He kissed the right breast, over the top, then in a circle around the nipple, teasing the areola with his lips, then centered his lips over the nipple, kissing the tip. Then he moved to the other breast, doing the same. But just kissing.

She wanted more.

"Lick them, then take them into your mouth."

His tongue lapped across one nipple and she moaned at the delicious stimulation. Then he took it into his mouth, his tongue lapping constantly.

She sucked in a sharp breath. "Oh, yes, that feels good."

The other nipple received the same treatment.

"Now suck on it."

Immediately he sucked, drawing her deep into his hot, wet mouth. She moaned at the exquisite pleasure.

"Oh, yes," she said breathlessly. "Oh, that's so good."

He moved from side to side, kissing, licking, sucking. Suddenly, it occurred to her that this man—Jake, not Ryan—a man she hardly knew, was sitting on the bed beside her, totally naked and sucking on her bare breasts. Not only that, he had her telling him what to do to her. He had put her in control of the situation yet at the same time had forced her to push herself sexually by having to state out loud what she wanted. It was such a turn-on.

Her breasts ached with pleasure. Her vagina ached with need.

"Jake, take off my pants."

He unfastened the button, then slid down the zipper. She arched her hips upward so he could slide her pants down over them. He flung the pants away and ran his hands up her legs, but stopped at mid-thigh.

"I want you to touch me . . ." She couldn't think of an appropriate word so she took hold of his hand and guided it to the crotch of her panties. "Here. I want you to stroke me here."

He cupped her mound for a moment, then slid his finger along her slit, over the silk of her panties. Moisture drenched the fabric.

He leaned close and kissed her on the mouth, his fingers still working up and down. He nuzzled against her ear.

"May I lick you, Jenna?" he murmured.

"Oh . . . yes, I'd like that."

He moved downward and she felt his tongue glide the length of her. Over her panties. He licked the length of her several times, then he dabbed into the front, nuzzling at her clit. The wet fabric pressed firmly against her as his hot tongue churned.

"Oh, God, get rid of the panties."

He stripped them off in one swift movement and when his tongue touched her naked flesh, dabbing at the sensitive button, she almost jumped.

He licked and pulsed, pulling the folds of her labia wide to gain better access.

"Oh, Jake. Oh, yes." She whimpered as the first wave of pleasure stormed over her.

He lifted her legs over his shoulders, spreading her wider.

His tongue quivered impossibly fast against her, sending her spinning into an intense orgasm. She clung to his head, pulling it against her.

"Oh, God, Jake. Oh, yes."

He suckled, then dabbed, then suckled. The waves of bliss pummeled over her, then swept her away.

Once her moans subsided, Jake's tongue stilled and he smiled up at her. He stretched out beside her.

"It sounds like you enjoyed that."

She smiled broadly. "I did."

She reached for his erection and stroked lightly up and down, using only her fingertips.

"Do you like this?"

"I do."

She pushed him flat on the bed and climbed over him. "Good, I'm going to take my turn to play now."

She wrapped her hands around his rock-hard cock and lifted it straight up, perpendicular to his body. It twitched in her hands. Her lips brushed the tip and she dabbed at the tiny hole with her tongue. She stroked his shaft with a single fingertip, then spiraled around the tip. His cock was so gorgeous with its kid-leather skin, the bulbous mushroom-shaped head, and its long, *long,* shaft. She yearned to suck and squeeze it in her mouth, but this game he'd started appealed to her. He'd told her to let him do all the work.

She licked again, then released him and lay back on the bed. He glanced at her, eyebrows raised.

She shrugged. "You told me to let you do all the work." She glanced at his cock then his face. "So, go ahead."

He smiled and wrapped a big hand around his erection. His purple cock head peered out the top of his hand.

"You mean like this?" His hand glided toward his body, then forward again.

She nodded, watching intently as his hand moved forward and back in long, smooth strokes. She could imagine that beautiful shaft stroking the walls of her vagina as he thrust into her. Her nipples ached. She curled a finger over one and stroked.

He pivoted toward her, his hand moving faster, his eyes glazing as he watched her intently. She smiled and stroked her other nipple, plucking both hard nubs at the same time.

"Jenna, you're driving me wild."

She slid one hand down her belly, then between her legs, into the slick moistness.

"Oh, sweetheart, I . . ." Suddenly, he jerked and white liquid spewed from his cock, splattering across her chest.

She sucked in a breath. The hot semen spurted again and again.

He laughed, then pushed himself up on his elbow.

"You get me so damned hot." He dragged a finger through the white gobs, then slid it downward. "That should have gone here."

He pressed his fingertip to her opening. She moaned as he slid his finger inside and swirled around.

"Oh, yeah. That's a good place for it."

He stroked over her clit. The dripping moisture between her legs told her it was time to make another request.

"Mmm. I need something from you but I'm not sure you're ready."

Staring at his cock, she licked her lips and opened her legs wider. His wilted member twitched to life.

His mouth turned up in a wicked grin. "Baby, I'm ready if you are."

"I want you to come here. Then I want you to lick and suck my breasts until the nipples are so hard I can't stand it."

"Whatever you say, Jenna."

He prowled over her, then sucked one breast into his mouth so hard she gasped.

"That's one down," she responded shakily.

He smiled, then licked the second one and sucked slowly but mercilessly. Within ten seconds he had her gasping for air.

He grinned down at her, his eyes twinkling.

"Okay, now what?"

She smiled. "Now, I want you to thrust your *enormous* cock deep inside me."

His eyes darkened with potent sexual need. He pressed the tip of his cock against her moist opening and slowly eased it forward.

"No, drive it in fast and hard."

"God, Jenna, I love it when you talk this way."

He lunged forward, stretching the length of her vagina in one sudden thrust. She moaned loudly. He pulled back, the head of his penis dragging along her vagina, then he thrust again. She wrapped her legs around his body, crossing her ankles behind him, pulling him even deeper.

He pumped into her. Her breathing accelerated as the pleasure escalated. Swells of pure bliss pulsed through her, spinning her through a vortex of incredible sensations.

"Jenna, come for me. Let me hear you scream in pleasure."

"Oh, yes. You're making me come." She moaned as the orgasm crashed over her. His body tensed and she felt liquid heat flood her insides. Still he pumped into her. As she continued to ride his cock, his fingers edged between them and he stroked her clit. The ebbing climax flared again and she moaned against his ear.

He continued to stimulate her clitoris and thrust his rigid rod into her. The orgasm seemed to last forever. When it finally tapered off, she clung to him.

"That was fabulous." She nuzzled close against his chest, suddenly very tired. "The best ever."

She yawned, then kissed the base of his neck. "Going to sleep now." She stroked across his stomach. "Night, Ryan."

JAKE STARED AT the sleeping Jenna, his chest wrapped with iron bands of pain. The sex had been fantastic. His ploy to help her past her nervousness had worked beautifully. She had opened up and eventually reveled in sex talk. Then she had brought him to the brink of climax several times, then held him back, building his energy to finally burst out in an incredible release.

It's too bad she had forgotten who he was.

She'd called him Ryan.

A numbness settled deep in his belly. Now he knew how his brother had felt, and he didn't like it one bit. In fact, the pain was almost unbearable.

He stroked her hair behind her ear. He loved her so much his whole body throbbed with it. She had agreed to stay here with him this month, to give herself a chance to fall in love with the father of her baby—his baby—but now he wondered if that would even be possible.

Could it be that his lovely Jenna was actually in love with his brother after all?

THE NEXT MORNING, Jenna woke up in Jake's bed alone, but the glow from last night's lovemaking still warmed her. She pushed back the covers and checked the ensuite bathroom to see if Jake was in the shower, but all she found was a damp bath towel hanging on a heated towel rack.

She pulled a dry towel from the shelves beside the large Jacuzzi bathtub. Ten minutes later, she stepped out of the stall dripping wet. She towel-dried her hair, ran a comb through it, then shrugged into the fleece robe she found hanging on a hook beside the shower. It was baggy on her, the arms hanging over her hands, but she tied the belt tightly and rolled up the sleeves. She loved the smell of Jake surrounding her as the robe enfolded her in warmth.

As she stepped back into the bedroom, she glanced at the clock beside the bed. Five after eight. Jake didn't leave for work until eight fifteen. Maybe he was in the kitchen having breakfast. She headed down the hallway, trying not to run, wanting to feel his arms around her again before he left. Sam lay on the carpet by the living room window, stretched out in a patch of sunlight.

Jenna pushed open the kitchen door and smiled when she saw Jake sitting on a stool at the eating counter, sipping coffee and reading a report. Suddenly, she felt shy and nervous.

"Good morning," she said.

He glanced up.

"Hi. The kettle's full of hot water if you want to make some herbal tea. I didn't know when you'd be up so I didn't make it."

"That's okay." She felt awkward. He hadn't smiled and his tone was polite but distant. Had she done something wrong?

She sat on the stool beside him, deciding she was just being paranoid, and rested her hand on his thigh, needing some kind of physical contact with him.

"How did you sleep?" she asked tentatively.

"Fine," he answered and said no more. He continued reading from the papers in front of him.

Her heart clenched. He was shutting her out and she didn't know why.

"Jake?"

"Hmm?" He didn't look up.

Jake wished he'd left before Jenna had gotten up, but now he couldn't just jump up and leave. Damn it, he didn't want to talk to her right now. His feelings were still a little too tender.

He could still hear her kitten-soft words. *Night, Ryan.* His heart clenched. And the feel of her hand on his thigh was pure torture. He didn't intend to throw it in her face. She hadn't done it to hurt him. In fact, he was sure she didn't even realize she had done it.

"Jake, is there something wrong?"

He glanced at her.

"No, of course not." He stood up, putting some needed distance between them. "I've got to leave for work."

He could feel her staring at him as he grabbed his briefcase and headed for the kitchen door. Something compelled him to look back at her before he pushed through the doorway. Tears welled in her eyes.

Oh, damn. He dropped the case and strode to her side, then gathered her in his arms. "Sweetheart, what is it?"

"I . . . don't . . . know. Last . . . night . . . we . . ." Her words were punctuated by sobs, then trailed off into heavy-duty sniffling.

Hell, he hadn't meant to upset her. In fact, he'd wanted to escape before she even sensed something was wrong.

He grabbed a tissue from the box on the counter and handed it to her. "Here," he said in a gentle tone. "Blow your nose and take a deep breath."

She did what he suggested and tried again.

"Last night, we were so close and then this morning . . ." Another sob broke loose. "This morning, you don't even want to be near me." The words rushed out, then she sobbed again.

He wrapped his arms around her and pulled her against his body, feeling more than a little guilty.

"I'm sorry, honey. I just had something on my mind." He kissed the top of her head. "I didn't mean to make you feel bad."

The only response she made was a sniffle. He cupped her chin and lifted her face. It broke his heart to see her large blue eyes rimmed with tears.

"I told you, sweetie. Nothing's wrong."

"You're sure?"

He kissed the tip of her nose. "Absolutely."

She dashed fresh tears from her eyes.

"I'm sorry, I guess it's just the hormones." She clutched the lapels of the robe. A tenuous, trembling smile curved her lips. "If I keep acting like this, you really won't want to be around me."

His heart swelled at the reminder that she carried his baby. He hugged her tightly against him.

"It'll never happen, sweetheart. There's nothing you could ever do that would stop me from loving you."

Even if she didn't love him back.

JENNA WATCHED JAKE drive away. She wrapped her arms around herself, loving the feel of his fleecy robe around her, loving the scent of him enveloping her.

Still, she was disturbed by the conversation they'd just had.

Jake had told her he loved her. She opened the refrigerator and pulled out the orange juice, then poured herself a glass. In fact, remembering back, he had told her that before, the night before the rehearsal dinner, but it hadn't sunk in because at the time she'd thought he was Ryan.

My God, Jake loves me. How could that be? He had known her for only two days when he'd said it. Could he really have fallen in love with her so quickly? It had taken Ryan eight months to utter the words.

She watched two blue jays dipping into the birdbath out front, throwing the water over their backs and flapping their wings, splashing water every which way.

She knew Jake had brought her here to convince her to marry him, but she thought it was only because she was going to bear his child. Now, Jake said he loved her.

It was all so confusing. What did she really know about love? What did Ryan and Jake know about love?

Ryan said he loved her, but if it was true, why did he avoid being with her?

She dragged her finger along the glass windowpane.

Jake said he loved her, and she was starting to fall in love with him, too. Then he had shut her out. He'd said he had something on his mind, but that sounded more like Ryan than the Jake she thought she knew.

Sam wandered into the kitchen and peered at Jenna. She picked up the cat and cuddled her close.

Maybe he'd just convinced himself he loved her because of the baby and now he'd drift away, too.

AFTER A QUIET dinner that evening, Jake invited her to play video games with him in his den. He had a great setup, with two networked computers, high-resolution monitors, and state-of-the-art CPUs for game play. She preferred games of skill to role-playing games so they played a new online golf game. After one game of eighteen holes, she decided to call it a night.

They had spent the whole evening together but at different desks with virtually no real interaction between them. Jenna climbed into bed feeling lonely.

She had started to convince herself that she had real feelings for Jake, but it was far more likely that she saw in Jake what she wanted to see in Ryan.

She loved Ryan. Sure, they had a few problems to work out, but when she was with him, she never doubted his feelings for her. It was only when he was away from her. If only he wasn't away so often. If only he wasn't away now.

In fact, it wasn't he who was away, it was she.

She glanced at the silver phone in its stand on her bedside table. Maybe Ryan wasn't here, but that didn't mean they couldn't connect. She pushed herself up in bed and plumped up two pillows behind her, then picked up the phone and dialed Ryan's number. She glanced at the clock. Eleven thirty. It was a little late—Ryan had probably turned in about an hour ago—but she hoped he wouldn't mind.

It rang three times. Four.

"Hello?"

At the sound of Ryan's voice, hoarse from sleep, the tremors of uneasiness inside her slipped away.

"Ryan. It's—"

"Jenna." His voice sharpened. "Is everything okay?"

"Yes, I . . ." She paused, overwhelmed with feelings. The concern in his voice, the fierce protectiveness emanating from him, made her feel safe and loved. It was a wonderful feeling and one she knew came from a deep relationship built over time. One of trust and mutual respect. And love.

"Jenna? Are you still there?"

She realized her mind had wandered.

"I . . . just wanted to hear your voice." A tear slipped from her eye.

"Sweetheart, are you sure everything's okay?"

"I miss you, that's all."

"Honey, I miss you, too. You know, you can come home anytime you want. You don't have to stay—"

"No." She shook her head, trying to convince herself as much as Ryan. "I promised I'd give Jake a month."

"But, if you're unhappy . . ."

"I'm not unhappy . . ." She snuffled, belying her words. "It's just hormones. Jake's been wonderful. He's made me feel right at home. He's been a real sweetheart."

Silence on the other end made her sorry for the words.

"I just mean . . ." She wasn't sure what she meant anymore.

"Yeah."

She could imagine the tight set of his face and the frown

compressing his lips. He must hate having her so far away, leaving him no opportunity to influence her decision. That would make him feel powerless and he was a man used to exerting control over his environment.

"But, Ryan, I'm calling *you*." She filled her voice with warmth. "Because I miss you."

"Yeah." This time, the word came out as a smile.

Wistfully, she remembered his smile, remembered kissing those full, sexy lips of his, remembered the firm pressure against hers as he held her in his arms. Her hormones flipped into high gear.

"You know, I'm just sitting here in my bed . . . all alone . . ." She trailed off, waiting to see if he would take the bait.

"Really? What are you wearing?"

Nothing. The word almost slipped from her mouth, but that was way too cliché. She wondered if he was up for something a little more exciting.

"I'm wearing a skimpy little harem costume—you know, with the bra that barely covers anything and a skirt that sits well below my navel."

"Hmm. I like that."

She smiled.

"The swell of my breasts is pushing against the tight velvet fabric. You are a wealthy sheik and you acquired me at the casbah today."

"You mean the slave market?"

She grinned. Attention to detail was so typical of Ryan, but during phone sex?

"Sure. Now you've taken me to your room."

"You mean tent?"

She plucked at the sheets. "Ryan, do you want to be accurate, or sexy?"

"Right. We're in my room. Are you tied up?"

"Umm. Yes, my hands are bound."

She remained silent for a moment, but he said nothing, clearly waiting for her to continue.

"I'm just standing here, waiting to see what you'll do to me," she prompted.

"Ahh. I look at you, my eyes raking over your body, settling on your shapely breasts."

Her nipples tightened at his words, as she imagined him looking at her, wanting her. Her hand slid over one hard bud, need twining through her.

"I step toward you," he said.

"And I step back." She could feel it, the excitement of a handsome sheik—her Ryan—closing in on her, his coal black eyes boring into her. Heat sizzled through her.

"I grab you and drag you into my arms."

She almost gasped at the image.

"I kiss you. Long and hard," he continued.

"Mmm." The sound slipped from her as she imagined his strong arms around her, forcing from her what she wanted to give him but couldn't. Not as a slave. Not with the physical distance between them.

"You like it, I can tell," he murmured.

Her fingers stroked lightly over one nipple, then the other. They pushed up, the soft cotton of her nightgown conforming to the pebbled outlines.

"Yes, but I don't want you to know, so I resist," she responded.

"But as I kiss you harder, you succumb and kiss me back."

"Oh, yes." She ran her fingers over her lips, feeling the tingle as she imagined his mouth moving on hers.

God, she wanted him. If only he was here in the room with her. She would tear off her clothes and throw herself at him. She wanted to see him. To strip off his clothes and touch him.

"I drag my hand down your hard, strong chest. I feel your rippling muscles under my fingertips. You are my master and I want to deny you, but I can't help myself. I want you."

She could hear his accelerated breathing on the other end of the line.

"My hand slips over your hard stomach, then inside your pants and . . ." She paused, imagining her fingers touching his hard cock, then sliding over it.

"Ohhhh," she moaned.

"Jenna?"

"It's so big and hard."

At the awe in Jenna's voice, Ryan felt his erection push painfully at his jeans. He stroked his hand over it, wishing it was Jenna's sweet, delicate hand.

"I pull it out and stroke it gently," she continued.

He lowered his zipper. His cock pushed free, hard as a rock. This wasn't going to last.

"Hey, I thought you were tied up." He imagined her in the flimsy little costume she'd described, her breasts pushing out the top, her torso naked to her hips, her legs peeking from the sheer fabric of her skirt.

"Oh, yeah. I'm not now," she said.

"But I want you to be," he responded in a low, sexy growl. "You snatch your hand away because you realize you're being drawn into the passion and you refuse to succumb. I push you onto the bed and tie you up, your arms and legs spread wide."

"Oh, yes. I mean . . . Oh, no. Please let me free."

Her words sent need thundering through him.

"No, slave. You're mine and I plan to prove it to you."

He imagined her, spread-eagled on his bed, staring up at him with wide, passion-filled eyes. He would prove to her she was his in every way. His heart swelled as he realized she was giving him this opportunity to do just that. That meant he still had a real chance.

"What are you doing now?" she asked.

"I'm looking at you. You're breathing hard, so I'm watching the rise and fall of your breasts." He could hear her accelerated breathing. "You've been struggling, so the sheer fabric of your skirt has fallen back. Your legs are totally bare."

"Is that all that's bare?" she asked, her tone sultry.

"As you squirm, I can see the crotch of your panties."

Jenna felt the crotch of her panties becoming wet.

"Are you still just staring at me?"

"No," he murmured, his voice like hot silk wisping in her ear. "Now I'm sitting on the bed beside you, my leg brushing against your rib cage. I stroke your cheek . . ."

A quiver raced through her at the thought of his gentle touch, a contrast from the domineering persona he played. That was how this slave girl knew he really loved her, this forceful sheik of hers, even if she didn't acknowledge it. That's how she knew, deep down, she was safe with him.

"I continue down your neck then . . . over the swell of your breast."

Her fingers followed the path he described, then she cupped her right breast.

"The bra opens at the front," she pointed out.

"So it does. My finger slips under the clasp. I squeeze."

"I turn my head away."

"Oh, yeah. Your bra just popped open. I can see your naked breasts. Your nipples are hard. Standing straight up."

"Yes." She found the hem of her nightshirt and pushed it out of the way. Her finger toyed with first one nipple, then the other, sending tingles shimmering through her body.

"I stare at them, mesmerized by their beauty."

She drew in a deep breath, immensely turned on by the wonder in his voice, by the reminder that he loved looking at her body.

"I stroke them, covering them with my hands. They are so soft and warm."

"I love the feel of your hands on me." Oh, how she wished his hands were really on her.

"I lick your left nipple."

"Oh, yes." She licked her fingers, then slid them over her left nipple. "Oh, I like that, but I'm trying not to show it."

"But I can tell. Your face is flushed. Your breathing is fast. I lick the other nipple, then suck it into my mouth."

"Mmmmm." She squeezed and plucked her hard nub, wishing she really filled his hot, wet mouth.

"It's so hard in my mouth."

"And is that the only thing that's hard? Are you hard?" she asked.

"Oh, God, yes, I'm hard. I stand up and drop my pants, showing you what you have to look forward to."

She imagined him standing before her, his long, rigid cock twitching, aching to drive into her.

"Oh, it's so big."

"And all for you. Soon, I'm going to show you what it feels like to have it thrust inside you."

Her vagina clenched tightly around nothing. A fierce ache shot through her. Her hand traveled down to her panties, then slid inside and stroked over her wet slit.

"When?"

"Soon. Very soon."

"Are you stroking it now?"

"I wrap my fingers around it and stroke it a couple of times, to show it off to you."

She could imagine his hand stroking up and down on it. In real life, she was sure he was doing just that. Because he wanted her, and that thought excited her even more.

"Your stroking has made me wet. Oh, so wet."

Ryan groaned as he imagined Jenna, not a slave girl on his bed, but the real Jenna, lying on a bed and thinking of him, growing wet because of his words and the images he evoked. He stroked his throbbing cock, so close to release.

"I'm impatient to see your wet pussy, so I tear off your skirt. Your panties, too. Now you're lying completely naked."

"Oh, yes."

"My fingers slide between your legs and tease over you." He laughed. "Yes, you are wet. I can feel it."

"Oh."

"Can you feel me feeling you, Jenna?" he murmured.

Yes, she could. Jenna could feel his strong finger sliding over her soft, wet flesh.

"I'm pushing inside you now."

"Oh, yes." Her eyelids fell closed as she pushed her own fingers inside.

"My thumb strokes over your clit."

She stroked over her clit.

"Can you feel that, my love?"

She writhed on the bed.

"Oh. Yes." Her clipped words told Ryan she felt what he described.

Man, he knew she was using her own fingers to slide inside herself and the thought of her touching herself almost sent him to the brink. He had to hold off, to bring her there, too.

"My tongue is touching your clit now."

"Oh, yes, your tongue."

"You're getting close."

He wasn't kidding. Heat surged through Jenna as she imagined his tongue dancing on her clit. She pushed two more fingers inside herself while her thumb flicked over her clit, acting as his tongue.

"What about your cock? Is it still hard?"

"Hard. And long."

"Ohhh . . ."

Ryan tightened his hand around his rod as he pumped.

"I'm climbing over you now."

"Yeah?" Her short, whimpered word sounded so needy.

"I'm pressing it against you—"

"Ohhh . . ."

". . . and . . . Oh, baby, I'm thrusting forward."

"Oh, yes. Drive it into me."

"I'm driving it into you."

"Oh, God, I'm . . . I'm . . ." Her panting, then gasps, swirled into his ear and his breath caught. "I'm coming," she wailed between moans.

He pumped two more times and spewed, his hand clamping around the shaft as the hot liquid spurted onto his chest. Her sweet moans serenaded him through his intense climax.

Jenna arched and moaned as she rode the glittering orgasm, imagining Ryan's face contorted in pleasure as he pumped into her.

She could hear his breathing on the other end of the line. Slowing. She sighed against her pillow.

"I've released your bonds and now I'm wrapping my arms around you and cuddling you close."

She could almost feel the warmth of his arms around her and his strong, broad chest against her cheek.

"Mmmm, and I'm cuddling you back."

"No resistance?"

"Nope. You've won me over."

RYAN HUNG UP the phone. Maybe he had won Jenna over . . . tonight, but Jake had the advantage of proximity. Jenna had a strong interest in sex at the best of times. Now pregnant, with her hormones raging . . . With Jake in the same house, would she succumb to desire and go to him? Had she already?

Ryan raked his hand through his hair and glanced at the clock beside the bed. Twelve forty-eight. He yawned. He changed the alarm to eight o'clock to give himself an extra hour of sleep. He'd been working late every night, grabbing dinner at a restaurant on the way home, then dropping into bed as soon as he got there. He needed to keep busy. Not for the good of the business. For the good of his sanity. He had to keep his mind off Jenna and how much he missed her.

And feared losing her.

He picked up the phone again, realizing he hadn't checked his messages that evening. The interrupted pattern of the dial tone told him there were messages waiting. He dialed star-ninety-eight and then typed in his password code at the prompt. Two messages. He pressed one to listen to them.

"Hello, Ryan, this is Hannah." The voice of his assistant reminded him about a meeting at ten tomorrow morning.

He deleted the message and waited for the next.

"Hello, Mr. Leigh, this is Dr. Morgan's office."

At the pleasant female voice, Ryan pushed himself forward, his gut tensing. He and Jenna had gone to Dr. Morgan together when she'd had some tests to ensure the pregnancy was going well. Jenna had authorized their office to contact Ryan while she was away in case there were any problems with her tests or if they needed her to return to the office.

"Would you please call the office tomorrow at your earliest convenience? The number is . . ."

CHAPTER 13

JENNA FINISHED HER herbal tea and put the mug in the dishwasher, then strolled into the living room. The late-afternoon sun filled the room with warmth. Sam lay sprawled across the carpet, seemingly oblivious to Jenna's presence.

Last night, the phone sex with Ryan had been fabulous and it had helped her feel more connected with Ryan and more secure. Loved. It had not, however, satisfied her deeper physical need.

She glanced outside at the sunshine glistening on the trees. She felt very confused. On the one hand, she loved the deep sense of security and commitment she felt with Ryan. On the other, she loved the excitement and newness of her relationship with Jake. The two men were different, but still very much alike. She knew if she spent enough time with Jake, she could fall in love with him.

She'd spent most of the night tossing and turning, images of the incredible lovemaking she and Jake had shared two nights ago dancing through her head. The insistent need still prodded her insides. Oh, man, right now she wanted Jake inside her.

She decided she would finally try one of Jake's gifts. She trotted into the bedroom and selected one of the books Jake had picked out for her. She returned to the living room and sank onto the couch, then settled against the cushions, getting all cozy under a soft, plush blanket.

The book began on a pirate ship, where the sexy pirate captain threw the heroine over his shoulder and dragged her back to his cabin. When he tossed her onto his bunk and tore open her top, laying bare her glistening wet breasts heaving up and down, Jenna found her fingers sliding to her own breasts. As he pinned the heroine's wrists over her head, Jenna slid her hand over her soft curve, then cupped her hand around it, holding the weight of her breast in her palm. As the story progressed, she slipped off her bra and dabbed at her nipples, swirling around lightly during the most erotic parts, leaving them hungry when she stopped to turn a page.

Oh, man, she was getting hot. She turned another page. When the hero swiveled his hips forward and his rigid strength filled his captive, she remembered Jake's rock-hard penis gliding into her. Jenna's fingers swirled faster, then she flicked one nipple then the other, her breathing accelerating. A stroke of masculine hardness shattered the heroine's last crumbling barrier of control and the woman could no longer deny herself.

Damn, Jenna could no longer deny her need for a penis deep inside her. Oh, God, she wanted a man driving inside her. She wanted *Jake* driving inside her. She remembered his rigid cock thrusting into her, sending her to a thrilling orgasm. The hero pulled back and surged forward again. A sharply rising cry tore from the heroine's throat as the hero took her to a frenzied, exhilarating release. Jenna groaned in frustration.

She nibbled on her thumbnail as she thought about the throbbing heat in her vagina and the wet pool of need collected there. Thoughts of the purple passion machine, or whatever the label on the box had called it, shifted into her brain. She chewed harder.

She glanced at the time displayed on the DVD player. Four eleven. Jake wouldn't be home for another couple of hours.

She dropped the book on the floor, scurried into her bedroom, and ran straight to the bedside table, tugging open the drawer and grabbing the box with the long, purple penis in it. She licked her lips. Her own personal penis.

She trotted back out to the couch, shedding her jeans, then snuggling into the blanket. She pushed the top button, as Jake had shown her. The machine started to whir. She touched the little curved bit along the side, imagining it quivering against her clitoris. She felt more moisture drip between her legs. She shoved down her panties and tried to touch the gadget to her sensitive flesh, but it curved toward the shaft of the purple penis, so she couldn't get it to touch her there.

Damn, she'd just have to slide it inside to try it.

She placed the head of the thing against her damp slit. Oh, wow, the vibration felt wildly erotic. She pushed it in a little, then drew it out again. Gee, she could learn to like this thing. She pushed deeper, then out, then deeper still.

Well, here goes nothing. She slid it all the way in. She positioned the little quivering bit against the folds around her clit. It massaged lightly, stimulating her in a delightful way. Her head dropped back against the arm of the couch as she enjoyed the full feeling of the device inside her, the little flicker teasing her clit. Tension built inside her, an orgasm on the horizon. She waited, but it came no closer. She pumped the penis in and out, but that took the little flicker away, so she pushed it back in. She tried swiveling it around, hoping to coax the orgasm closer. No luck.

Then she remembered the other buttons. Jake had made the end spin around in a circle. She licked her lips. That sounded pretty good right now. With her fingers, she found the column of buttons on the end of the shaft, then pushed the second button. The whirring sound grew louder as the vibration surged to a higher level.

Yikes. It was too strong, too stimulating. She jabbed at the same button, but must have hit the third because the noise jumped a level and she could feel the shaft moving in erotic circles inside her, stroking her vaginal walls in an intensely arousing motion. Oh, God, it felt fabulous, but the vibration was drilling through her and the sound frazzled her nerves. She jabbed at the buttons again, but only managed to turn up the pace of the gyrating penis. The sensations and the noise rattled her, driving her looming orgasm far, far away. She jabbed at the buttons frantically.

She heard a car door close. Oh, God. Jake must be home.

She slid the machine from inside her and jabbed the first button; the noise and the movements ceased. Thank God. But the quivering need inside her remained. Well, hell, she had a man within reach. She dropped the machine on the blanket and covered it up, then kicked her panties under the couch. She could sneak the embarrassing evidence of her experiment away later, wrapped in the blanket. Right now, she'd keep Jake so busy, he wouldn't even notice.

She tugged her shirt down as she ran to the kitchen. The hem covered her naked lower body. She peered out the large window as she rushed through the kitchen and saw Jake approach the door. She flung it open.

"Jenna?"

She grabbed his hand and tugged him in, shoving the door closed behind him. She threw her arms around him, capturing his mouth with hers. He dragged his mouth away.

"Jenna, do you know—?"

She locked his lips with hers, moving persuasively.

"I know I want you." She grasped his hands and laid them firmly on her breasts, arching her back to press them deep into his palms.

She kissed him again. Explosive. Needy. Demanding.

His lips stopped protesting and started moving over hers.

"Oh, baby. You don't know how much I've missed you."

It had been thirty-eight long hours since they'd made love and she'd missed him, too.

She tugged his shirt free from his pants, then slid her hands up underneath, over his rippled abs to his hard nipples, tweaking and toying as he ravaged her lips. His hand slid down her back, over the curved hem of her shirt. His hands slid over the warmth of bare skin. The curve of her butt.

"My God, Jenna, you're not wearing underwear."

She found the snap on his jeans and tugged it open, then slid the zipper down. "You won't be soon, either."

She nibbled across his collarbone with her lips, then kissed down the V opening of his shirt. With one hand she released buttons on the way down, with the other she reached inside his fly and captured his growing erection. She slid it through the slit opening in his boxers. She kissed past his navel, then her lips slipped over the dark red head of his cock.

"Sweetheart." He sucked in a deep breath. "Oh, yes."

His hands stroked over her head.

"Sweetie, I really need to tell you . . ."

She slid her mouth fully over him, taking his cock down her throat, then sucked sharply.

He groaned.

JAKE OPENED THE door and froze in his tracks. There, in the middle of his kitchen, was Jenna, sucking his brother's cock deep into her mouth, his brother's face contorting in intense pleasure.

Anger surged through him, but then, as he remembered the warm feel of Jenna's sweet mouth moving on his own organ, the blood totally drained from his brain and flooded his cock, which twitched to life.

He watched her head bob up and down, Ryan moaning, Jake's cock growing. It pressed tightly against his zipper. He closed the door quietly, then stroked his hand over his erection. Jenna opened her mouth and licked Ryan from base to tip, then swirled her tongue around the corona. Jake almost groaned in time with Ryan as he watched the erotic scene.

Oh, man, he knew he should be angry but his raging hormones and his desire to thrust inside Jenna's sweet opening overrode every other emotion. Jenna wrapped her hands around Ryan's ass and squeezed, no doubt taking him deeper into her throat.

She shifted positions, pushing herself from one knee to the other; her shirt rode up and her bare ass peeked out. As she leaned into Ryan, Jake could see a few dark curls peeking out from between her legs.

His heartbeat leaped and a strangled sound escaped before he could choke it back. Ryan, in the throes of pleasure, didn't hear, but Jenna's gaze shifted, and caught on his.

JENNA COULD FEEL Jake's groin tighten and she pumped harder, squeezing him between her tongue and the roof of her mouth. She shifted slightly, and heard a slight moan from across the room. Her gaze lanced sideways, and locked onto Ryan, watching her from the doorway while stroking an impressive bulge in his pants.

She stopped for a split second, then felt Jake swell in her mouth. She proceeded to squeeze and slide on his erection, her gaze still locked with Ryan's. Warmth spurted from the hard cock within her mouth, hot and salty. She continued to pump, watching Ryan's eyes haze over, until Jake finished ejaculating. Slowly, she released Jake, then stood up and turned her gaze to Ryan.

"Jenna, that was so good, but—" the man in front of her said. She turned back to face him.

"Jake, Ryan's here," she said.

"I can see that."

Her blood ran cold as she realized it was the man at the door who'd responded. Her head spun around to face him.

She spun back again to face the man she'd thought was Jake.

"You're Ryan?"

The jeans and casual shirt. Not the clothes Jake wore when he left for the office this morning. She glanced back to Jake, who wore the dark gray slacks, white shirt with red patterned tie, and charcoal sports jacket.

"I tried to tell you, but you didn't give me much of a chance. I'm sorry."

He tucked his flaccid penis back into his pants and zipped up, then turned to Jake. "I didn't mean to trick anyone here."

Jake waved his words away. "Forget it. I could get mad, but I've been on the other end of this. Just tell me why you're here."

"I need to talk to Jenna. Something's come up."

"But we agreed—"

"I know, but it's important and it can't wait." He turned back to face Jenna.

"Jenna, it's something I have to discuss with you alone. You can tell Jake once we've had a chance to discuss it. Can we talk over dinner tonight?"

"I, uh—"

A mechanical grinding sound, followed by a cat's hiss and a thunk, snatched her attention to the living room. Oh, no, it couldn't be. A loud whirring sounded from the couch.

"What was that?" Jake asked as he headed to the living room.

"Oh, I'm sure it's nothing," she said as she tried to scurry ahead of him, but with his long-legged stride he reached the living room doorway before her.

He stared toward the couch, a big smile claiming his lips. She poked her head through and saw Sam sitting with one paw on the base of the purple penis, batting with her other paw at the head of the shaft as it moved in circles.

Jenna felt Ryan beside her.

"What in the world is that?"

"I'll give you one guess," Jake answered. "Jenna, I see you were enjoying my little gift."

Ryan waved his hands in front of him as if he could wipe away the image of what he'd just seen.

"Okay, I'm out of here." He turned and headed toward the door. "Jenna, I'll check in to a hotel and call you in an hour."

Jenna raced into the living room, sending the cat running, and snatched up the purple penis. She jabbed the Off button and the wild gyrations and noise stopped. She dropped it in the blanket and flipped over a corner, covering up the device.

Jake chuckled.

She perched on the end of the couch.

"Jake, are you mad?"

"I should be, I suppose, but truth to tell, the sight of you giving my brother head was a pretty heavy turn-on."

She flushed hotly. "I really thought it was you."

He smiled. "I believe you. I can picture the whole thing now. You were using the vibrator when Ryan showed up at the door. You weren't exactly thinking straight. Turned on as thoroughly as the gizmo, you jumped his bones. The only thing I can't figure out is why you thought I'd knock on the door."

"He didn't knock."

"He walked right in?"

"No, I heard the car door and I raced to the door to jump *your* bones. I was frustrated because I couldn't get that thing to work."

He grinned. "The cat got it to work."

She rolled her eyes in remembered frustration.

"Oh, it functioned all right, it just didn't work for me. I couldn't get it to do the right things at the right time and . . ." She trailed off, shrugging.

"I see. So you were plenty frustrated when he arrived."

"I still am. All I did with Ryan was . . . what you saw."

Jake's grin broadened. "So am I to understand you could use a little attention?"

She groaned. "I could use a lot of attention."

He moved toward her, his eyes growing ravenous. Almost as hungry as she felt.

He dragged her into his arms and kissed her. Hot and hungry.

She welcomed him, pressing her body against him, loving the feel of his hardness against her softness.

"Jenna, I'm not going to turn back now, but I want to know . . ."

She kissed him again. "Know what, Jake?"

"Did you really want me or did you just want to satisfy your craving?"

"I wanted to satisfy my craving . . ." She grasped his hands in hers and gazed deeply into his eyes, seeing the deep disappointment there. ". . . for *you.*"

She captured his mouth with hers and thrust her tongue inside. She stroked, then swirled around the inside of his lips.

"I want *you,* Jake." A smile spread across his face as his hands stroked down her back, then over her bare buttocks, then pulled her into his groin.

She groaned at the welcome contact, the bulge in his pants cradled against her hot center.

His lips captured hers and she wrapped her arms around his shoulders, her eyelids drifting closed, as she gave herself over to the kiss. His hot tongue darted in and out of her mouth. She stroked it while moving her lips ravenously on his. His hands clasped around her waist and he lifted her up. She wrapped her legs around him as she felt herself being carried backward. Into the kitchen.

She felt stone-cold marble under her bare butt and shivered in excitement. She was far too hot to be cooled off by a little cold stone beneath her. Jake released her waist and unfastened the buttons of her shirt, watching the fabric part as he moved down. She'd shed her bra earlier while reading the sexy book he'd given her. Now, seeing the delight in his eyes, she was glad she had.

His hands stroked over her breasts lightly; then he leaned down and drew one into his mouth. He sucked voraciously, sending her already lust-filled body into high gear. When he sucked the other nipple, she grasped his head to her, making tiny whimpering sounds deep in her throat.

Jake eased back and stood gazing up and down her body.

Here she sat, butt-naked on the kitchen counter, legs spread wide, with Jake fully dressed. She felt her insides melt and her pussy grew hot and slick. Jake studied every inch of her with his sultry gaze. Goose bumps flared across her skin.

Neither of them moved, mesmerized by the incredible, sexy moment. Her nipples extended into long, hard nubs and the moisture pooling in her pussy began to drip down her thighs.

Jake finally moved. Undoing his belt, he held her gaze with his smoldering, ravenous eyes. He released the button on his fly, then the sound of the zipper sliding down, an exceptionally sexy sound, sent shivers down her spine. He dropped his pants and they hit the floor with a clunk, thanks to the leather belt and buckle.

He started to undo his shirt but she stilled his hands.

She licked her lips.

"Leave it on."

She hooked her index finger under the waistband of his briefs.

"Leave these on, too."

She pulled on the waistband and tugged the elastic down, then tucked it under his balls, exposing all of him. She wrapped her hands around his huge erection.

A laugh rumbled deep in his throat.

"I sense another fantasy."

She smiled, stroking her free hand up his tie, then grasping it tightly under the knot and tugging him closer.

"No, just taking advantage of an incredibly sexy situation when it presents itself."

"Mmm." He kissed her throat, sending tingles down her neck and straight to the tips of her nipples. "My dirty girl wants to be taken advantage of by the powerful businessman who wants to have his way with her?"

He captured one nipple in his mouth and she groaned.

"Something like that."

She pumped his cock, suddenly impatient to have it inside her.

She leaned back against the cupboard and lifted her legs to hook her heels on the edge of the counter, which opened her legs wider, exposing her wet pussy to his view. She felt wanton. A dirty girl.

And she wanted to be a very *good* dirty girl.

"Do you like what you see, Mr. Leigh?"

Her hands stroked down her belly and over the damp folds between her legs.

"Oh, yeah." His eyes darkened and glazed a little as he watched her finger stroke up and down. She slipped the finger inside. His breathing accelerated.

"This is what I want you to do to me," she said as she slid

the finger in and out. She moved it faster as she grasped his cock. "But with this."

She removed her finger and shifted her hips back a little. His gaze remained locked on her pussy. He grasped her wrist and raised her hand to his lips, then sucked her damp finger into his mouth. The feel of his hot mouth pulsing against her finger, knowing he tasted her juices, made her drip all the more.

"Mmm. Very nice." He laid his finger on her hot, moist flesh and stroked, feeling her wetness. "But I have a different idea for my very dirty, very *wet* girl." His grin was pure mischief as he leaned forward and gave her a peck on the mouth. "Don't move."

She watched in amazement as he walked away, leaving her naked, legs spread wide open, on the kitchen counter.

A moment later, he returned, the purple penis sex toy in his hand.

"Oh, no." She waved her hands back and forth. "That thing doesn't work for me."

Grinning, he held it up and pressed one of the buttons. The penis began its rotation.

"I bet I can get it to work." He pressed another button and the little flicky thing near the base began to vibrate.

"I doubt it, I—" She felt a light vibration against her clit. "Ohhh." She watched him hold the tiny clitoral stimulator against her button as tremors of pleasure rippled through her. How had he managed to do that when she had failed so miserably?

He drew it away and she whimpered. He turned off the rotating shaft, then nudged it against her opening.

"I don't think—" Her halfhearted protest died on her lips as the purple erection glided into her. Her vagina clenched around the firm cock inside her.

"Sweetheart . . ." He leaned forward and nuzzled her neck. His breath caressed her skin like a whisper-soft feather. "Have more faith in me."

He pressed a button and the shaft moved within her. She sucked in a breath. It rotated around and around, stroking her vaginal walls, sending thrilling sensations through her.

Jake nuzzled her temple. "You like?"

"Oh, definitely." Her words came out hoarse, then she squeaked as a mild vibration quivered against her clitoris. Her eyes rolled back and her lids closed. "Oh, baby."

A storm of energy built within her, drawing her senses to peak awareness. Jake drew the toy away, sliding it out of her until the cock head swirled around the mouth of her vagina. His fingertip pulsed on her clit; then he sank the cock into her again. Riotous sensations flickered through her as the pleasure rose higher and higher.

"Oh, God, yes," she cried.

She wrapped her arms around him and slammed her lips against his, jabbing her tongue into his mouth in wild thrusts. He stroked his tongue against hers, then leaned down to lick her nipple, then the other, as he pressed the vibration to her clit again. His mouth closed over her nipple and he sucked hard. Joy pounded through her as she catapulted into a mind-blowing orgasm, blissful pleasure ricocheting through every part of her.

Finally, gasping for breath, she slumped against the cupboards behind her. Her eyelids flickered open to see Jake grinning at her.

"And you thought it didn't work."

He drew the purple penis from her depths. The whirring mechanism seemed incredibly loud now. He silenced it with the press of a button, then tossed the device into the empty sink.

"Silly me." She smiled.

He captured her mouth, his tongue dipping in to stroke the inside of her lips. She curled her arms around his neck and drew him close, pressing her naked breasts to his fully clothed chest.

He cupped her breast and gave a light squeeze.

"Now, my dirty girl, this powerful businessman wants to have his way with you."

She pressed her arm against her head in the classic damsel-in-distress gesture. "I'm helpless against you. What are you going to do to me?"

He dabbed lightly at her clitoris and murmured in her ear, "I'm going to drive my *enormous* cock into your dripping wet pussy."

Shivers pulsed through her.

"No, you mustn't," she cried in mock concern.

His cock head rubbed against her intimate flesh and she moaned. He thrust forward, and she cried out at the exquisite feel of his cock propelling into her. She wrapped her legs around his waist as he pushed deep inside. She ran her hands across his incredibly tight butt muscles.

As soon as he started moving within her, she felt an orgasm blossoming again.

"Oh, God, Jenna . . ." He gasped. "I hope . . . you're close . . . because I won't . . . last . . . long." The cadence of his speech was broken by his steady thrusts.

The heat in her core expanded, quivering through every part of her.

"Jake . . ." His name came out as tight as her fists, which clenched the fabric of his shirt. "I'm going to . . ." She gasped as he spiraled inside her. "Oh, yes." The waves of pleasure rippled over her. "I'm coming."

He grunted, pausing deep inside her for a second as she clung to him. He began to move again, thrusting faster, kissing the side of her neck. He accelerated her pleasure to new heights.

"Yes," she wailed, her voice trembling, as she fell into total bliss.

Slowly, she floated back to the real world, as he held her close, her head against his chest, and tenderly stroked her hair.

"Wow." It didn't seem sufficient but it was all she could think to say.

He kissed the top of her head.

"Absolutely, wow," he agreed.

She smiled and tipped her head up for a kiss. He met her lips hungrily, his arms tightening around her.

"My, God, Jenna. I love you so much."

Her insides quivered as she realized she was in love with Jake, too. Despite the deep sense of security and love she felt with Ryan, she knew that she felt something just as deep with Jake. It was too powerful to be just an echo of her feeling for Ryan.

My God, am I really in love with both men?

CHAPTER 14

JAKE'S STRONG, WARM hands encircled Jenna's waist and he lifted her from the counter. She held his hand as he led her through the bedroom toward the ensuite bathroom. Her gaze followed the curve of his sexy, hard butt as he walked ahead of her.

She still basked in the glow of love, but a nagging voice reminded her that Ryan still loved her and waited patiently for her answer—an answer she was farther from than before.

Jake stopped in front of the shower and she smiled up at him. He smiled and kissed her tenderly.

She stroked her hands across his shoulders, then under the collar of his shirt, stroking across his upper chest, loving the feel of taut, well-formed muscles under her fingertips. She unfastened his buttons and pushed his shirt off his shoulders and let it drop to the floor. He tugged off his briefs and socks, then led her into the large glass shower stall.

The warm water beat down on them as he soaped her body from top to bottom. He paid particular attention to her behind, stroking around and around the curve of each cheek with slick, soap-covered hands.

"My turn," she insisted. She grabbed the translucent amber bar of soap and rubbed it until her hands were covered with suds. She wrapped her hands around his penis and slid them up and down. His skin felt slick and satin-smooth. He hardened within her grasp. His slick hands swirled over her breasts. Once he'd soaped them thoroughly, she leaned forward and rubbed against him, her breasts sliding up and down his chest, leaving a path of suds.

His hand slipped between her legs, lathering her up. The erotic feel of his hands gliding over her made her vagina ache with longing. She became impossibly slick, a combination of soap and her natural, intimate lubricant. As he stroked her pussy with one hand, slipping one finger inside her, his other hand caressed her butt. She tossed her head back, the water streaming through her long hair, plastering it to her back. He pulled her pelvis tight against his and leaned down to plant his mouth on her nipple.

"Oh, Jake, yes."

He slid another finger inside her and stroked in circles, stimulating all kinds of interesting sensations. She grasped his cock again, pumping him in time with the circles of pleasure he stirred within her. He curled his fingers and stroked her vagina, finding her G-spot. He eased her back against the tile wall.

Her breathing accelerated as the pleasure increased. With infinite patience he stroked her, up and down.

"Oh, that's so good."

She gasped for breath. Warm water rushed over her left shoulder and streamed down her body.

"Yes. Oh, yes." Flashes of intense joy followed by spikes of bliss shot through her; then they coalesced into one brilliant sweep of overwhelming pleasure in a powerful, mind-numbing orgasm.

Before it waned, he slid his hands around her thighs and lifted her. She wrapped her legs around him as he drove into her in one deep, hard thrust, propeling her toward heaven. She clung to his wet shoulders as he pounded into her, her wail of pleasure echoing around them in the tiled shower stall. He grunted and held her fast against the wall. She felt his hot semen filling her womb and she wrapped her legs tighter around his waist, welcoming every drop.

She nuzzled his neck, then across his shoulder, and reveled in the heat of his body and the warmth of the water still streaming over them.

After they rinsed off, he patted her dry with a big blue fluffy towel, then helped her on with his robe. The phone warbled in the next room.

"I'll get it." Jake planted a kiss in the crook of her neck.

She watched his fabulous retreating butt as he walked into the bedroom totally naked. She wrapped a towel around her hair and twisted it on top, then followed him into the other room.

Jake held the receiver out to her, his expression sour.

"Who is it?" she asked.

"Ryan."

Ryan. Oh, God, she'd forgotten he was going to call. He'd said he wanted to see her tonight.

She shuffled toward Jake, then sighed and tucked the robe tighter around herself as she took the receiver from Jake's outstretched hand.

"Hello, Ryan." She shoved one hand in her pocket and gazed down at the spiral telephone cord.

"Hi. How are you doing?" he asked.

"Fine." Her gaze flicked up to Jake, scowling on the other side of the room as he pulled on a pair of pants. She sat down on the edge of the bed.

"Is everything alright?"

"Uh-huh." She understood that her tight words didn't make it sound like everything was alright, but she was self-conscious with Jake staring at her. Her free hand stroked back and forth over the smooth burgundy-and-navy patterned duvet.

"Jake's right there, isn't he?" Ryan asked.

"Yes."

"Listen, Jenna. I really need to talk to you about something. I've checked into the Marriott downtown. Would you join me for dinner?"

She lowered her voice. "Ryan, you promised Jake you'd leave us alone for a month."

"That's right," Jake grumbled in the background.

"I know. I wouldn't have broken that promise if it wasn't important. Please, Jenna, I drove all the way here."

She ran her hand over her face and glanced up at Jake. Noting the tight line of his mouth, she stood up and paced a little, then turned toward the window.

"Yeah, okay. What time?"

"I'm leaving right now to pick you up."

"What's going on, Jenna?" Jake demanded.

She covered the mouthpiece.

"Ryan needs to talk. He's coming over to pick me up for dinner."

Jake reached for the receiver. "What the hell are you doing?" he demanded into the phone. "Yeah?" He stood in silence for a moment, scowling. "Yeah." A few more seconds passed and Jake's scowl deepened. "Okay, fine, but I'm driving her over."

He grabbed a pen and paper from the bedside table.

"What's the name of the restaurant?" His fingers clenched around the pen so tightly Jenna was sure it was going to snap. "I don't think so." He tapped the pen on the paper. "Yeah, I'll say it's private."

He glanced at Jenna, then he turned away.

"Damn it, Ryan. Don't put me in this position." He listened for a moment longer, then slammed down the phone.

He glanced at her, his lips a tight line.

"Is there a problem?" she asked. From what she'd heard on this side of the conversation and Jake's reaction, she had a pretty good guess what Ryan had suggested.

"He wants you to eat in his room."

Bingo.

"Says he needs to talk to you *privately.*" He took her hand and locked gazes with her. "You don't have to go, Jenna."

She squeezed his fingers. "Yes, I do. He and I dated for over a year. He asked me to marry him and at one point I said yes. I won't deny him dinner and a conversation."

His expression went grim. "Will you deny him sex?"

"Jake!"

He tugged her into his arms and held her tightly against his body, his hands firm against her back.

"I'm sorry, baby," he said as he stroked her hair. "I just can't stand the thought of you making love with him." He tipped her chin up. "I love you too much."

Tears welled in her eyes.

"And I love you."

His eyes softened and a smile spread across his face. He

drew her close for a sweet, tender kiss. Ardently, his lips moved over hers in silent persuasion.

"Does that mean you've decided between us?" His dark eyes, so filled with hope, stared deep into hers.

"I . . . uh . . ." Queasiness undulated through her.

She sank onto the bed. He sat down beside her and took her hand.

"Jake, I do love you, but—"

"But?" Alarm skittered through his eyes.

She squeezed his hand. "I'm worried that you'll grow bored of me."

Puzzlement crinkled his features. "Why the hell would you think that?"

"Because yesterday morning you were so wrapped up in your papers you hardly noticed me. I mean, I understand that everyone needs time to themselves, but it *was* the morning after the first time we'd ever made love. It just set off warning bells, that's all."

"Jenna, I wasn't ignoring you."

She stared down at their joined hands. "It certainly felt like it."

He shook his head. "I didn't want to tell you this. I didn't want to make you feel bad."

Her eyes widened and her stomach tightened. He took her hand between his. "I wasn't ignoring you, I was trying to deal with my own feelings. I was hurt."

"Hurt? I . . . I don't understand."

"The night before, just before you fell asleep . . ."

"Yes?"

He sighed.

Her thoughts were going a mile a minute. What had she done? Suddenly, a dim memory wobbled through her brain. Her jaw dropped open and she covered her mouth with her hands.

"No, I didn't . . ."

"You called me Ryan."

"Oh, God. Oh, Jake." She stroked his cheek, her eyes pleading with him to forgive her. "I'm so sorry."

He hugged her to him.

"I didn't want to tell you because I didn't want to make you feel bad."

"But I *hurt* you."

He raised her hand to his mouth and kissed it.

"You didn't mean to. Look, Jenna, you've been through a lot, I know that. I'm only mentioning it now because . . ."

He slid his hands to her shoulders and drew her around to face him.

"Because I'll be damned if I'll let you believe I'd ever be bored with you. Or neglect you. I love you too much."

He brought his lips to hers, and in that loving, tender kiss, she knew she'd found the man she would spend the rest of her life with.

AS JAKE NEGOTIATED the car through the highway traffic into the city, Jenna's thoughts turned to Ryan.

How could she face him now that she knew she was in love with Jake?

She ran her finger along the dash then fiddled with the button on the glove compartment door.

She glanced over at Jake and watched his profile flickering

in and out of light as cars passed in the opposite lane. Jake definitely loved her and he would make time for her, and she knew he would make a fabulous father when the baby came.

With Jake being the baby's true father, things really had worked out for the best.

Except for Ryan.

Her heart sank a little as she realized it wasn't fair to keep Ryan's hopes up. Somehow, tonight, she had to find a way to tell Ryan that it was over between them.

If only she didn't have to choose.

JAKE PULLED UP in front of the hotel. A doorman in an elaborate burgundy and gold uniform opened the car door for Jenna. Jake walked her into the lobby, his arm around her waist. Jenna spotted Ryan immediately, walking toward them.

"Jenna." Ryan leaned forward and kissed her on the cheek.

He rested his hand on her lower back and drew her away from Jake.

"I'll come back to pick you up in two hours, Jenna," Jake said firmly.

"I'll drive her back," Ryan responded.

"I don't think so." Jake glared at his brother.

Jenna put her hand on Jake's chest. "It's okay, Jake. Ryan can drive me."

Jake scowled but didn't argue with her. He did pull her into his arms and kiss her, hard and passionately, leaving her breathless. Before he let her go, he murmured against her ear, "Remember that while you're up there."

Ryan narrowed his eyes, but said nothing. He took Jenna's

arm and led her to the elevator. A few minutes later, he opened the door to his room on the eighteenth floor.

A suite, actually, she saw as she entered. Decorated in soft shades of brown, punctuated with the odd splash of tomato red in the artwork and silk flower arrangements, it looked quite elegant. She sat down on the light beige leather sofa.

Ryan pulled a wine bottle from a silver ice bucket on a stand and poured two glasses.

"It's nonalcoholic wine," he explained as he handed her one. "I went ahead and ordered dinner. It's getting late and I didn't want you to have to wait for food, with the baby and all. Shall we?"

He gestured toward the window. Plates covered with silver domes, tall tapered candles, and stemmed glasses filled with ice water sat on a round table overlooking a spectacular view of the city skyline.

He pulled out her chair and once she was seated he removed the coverings from the plates. Wonderful aromas had her mouth watering. He had a large T-bone steak with broccoli and baked potato. He had ordered her chicken Marsala, small pieces of chicken in a sauce with the distinct flavor only Marsala wine could provide. It was one of her favorite meals, reserved for special occasions.

She smoothed the green linen napkin over her lap.

"So what did you want to talk to me about?" she asked.

He lit the tall, tapered candles standing in silver holders on the table.

"Let's enjoy our meal first, then we'll talk."

She nodded, rather glad because she was very hungry.

"I phoned you a couple of times after I checked in but no

one answered," he said as he picked up his knife and fork. "Did you and Jake go out?"

She hesitated and her cheeks flushed. "No, I . . . uh . . . was in the shower."

His smile faded as the implication hit him. After all, Ryan hadn't answered the phone either. She concentrated hard on her plate. Well, what did he expect, given the situation when he'd left the house?

They ate the rest of the meal in silence.

After dinner she settled in one of the armchairs, not wanting Ryan to cozy up beside her on the couch.

He poured steaming tea from the silver thermal pot into a cup and added milk and sugar. He handed her the cup and saucer. The aroma of Earl Grey wafted to her. Another favorite.

He sat on the couch across from her.

"How are things going with you and Jake?" he asked.

She stirred the tea with the teaspoon he'd left on the saucer, even though he'd already stirred it for her.

"Good. Really good."

"Not too good, I hope."

She laid the cup down on the coffee table.

"Ryan . . ."

"No, I just want to know, are you actually starting to consider Jake over me?"

Guilt shuddered through her. She sucked in a deep breath and released it with a sigh. She knew she had to tell him tonight, and now he'd given her the opening.

"I—"

He slammed his fist on the table.

"Damn it, you are."

Her fingers twined around each other. "He loves me."

"Do you love him?" He held up his hand in a halting gesture. "Never mind. Don't answer."

He pushed himself to his feet. "All my life Ryan has always won the girl." His fists clenched as he paced back and forth across the room. "Well, not this time. There's no way in hell I'm leaving you and him alone out there again."

"I promised Jake a month," she said weakly. Tears prickled at her eyes.

"He'll have his month, but I'm going to be there, too. I'm going to fight for you."

He looked so fierce, and all for her. She'd never seen him so adamant. Not even about the business. But she didn't want to be a prize to be won for the sake of settling old scores.

"Ryan, this isn't about winning against your brother. This is about love . . . and life."

His gaze locked on hers, hard and intense.

"Don't you think I know that?"

CHAPTER 15

JENNA DREW IN a deep breath.

"Ryan, deep down you must know it isn't really going to work out between us."

"The hell I do."

"Your first love is your career. There's no room in your life for a serious relationship right now."

"I told you I was changing that."

"I know you're trying, Ryan, I really do. But it doesn't happen. And I understand. Your business is important to you."

"Not more important than you are."

She tucked her hair behind one ear. "I'm not sure that's true."

He knelt in front of her and took her hand.

"Jenna, nothing is more important than you."

He stroked her fingers with a sweet tenderness that reached into her soul. At the sensual feel of his lips brushing the back of her hand, like the brush of butterfly wings, she thought she would melt. His midnight eyes had gone from brittle ice to warm pools of longing.

"Remember the good times, Jenna? When we were first dating? Remember when we went to the ski resort that first December? The evening we went to the hot tub?"

She remembered. It had been a beautiful, crisp, clear night. The lights on the neighboring mountain had glittered and the full moon reflected off the snow. Then big, fluffy snowflakes had fallen from the sky, landing on their hair and faces.

"When we returned to the cabin," he continued, "our key card didn't work."

She smiled. "And you had to traipse across to reception with only a towel around your waist to get another one."

He'd actually had a bathing suit under the towel, but when she conjured the image in her head, only the towel remained, and the sweet possibility of it slipping free.

"And, as I recall, you met my return with a snowball to the chest," he said.

She laughed. "Which you returned with a handful of snow down my top."

He'd chased her, then grabbed her from behind and wrapped his arms around her, to her giggling protests, then scooped up plenty of white, powdery snow. Now, as she remembered the cold, wet snow spilling between her breasts, her nipples leaped to attention.

That trip had been the first time they'd gone away together—and the first time they'd made love. Ryan had wanted it to be special. That's why he'd suggested the trip. After the snow incident, he'd carried her into the cabin and they'd made wild, passionate love in front of a roaring fire. She remembered waking up in the morning, in the warmth of his arms, thinking that this was the man she wanted to spend the rest of her life with.

"Don't you see, Jenna? It's not hard for me to spend time *with* you, it's hard for me to spend time *away* from you."

"I don't understand."

"When I'm with you nothing else is important. *Nothing.* Not my business, not my family, not myself. That used to scare me. That's what I was running away from, but I'm not afraid anymore. I realize now that with you I'm more than I could ever be alone. With you I see past my business and the traditional forms of success I used to strive for. I see a life filled with love and happiness. Through your eyes I see a better world and a better me."

He drew her hand to his mouth. The tender touch of his lips upended her composure.

"I love you. I can't imagine my future without you."

His words spiraled through her, touching her deeply, confusing her whole sense of order. She'd come to a decision, one that would keep the baby with his father, and now Ryan had to ruin it all by being so . . . so wonderfully in love with her.

But she loved Jake.

And she loved Ryan. Gazing into his loving eyes, she couldn't believe how much she loved him.

But it was Jake's baby and that fact tipped the scales in his favor.

Didn't it?

"Jenna, I'm ready to move forward and build a life with you"—he placed his hand on her stomach—"and our baby."

She rested her hand on top of his. "But, Ryan, it's Jake's baby."

"If you and I are married, any baby you have is mine, too. I will raise Jake's son as my own."

Son?

"Ryan, you heard from the doctor? He knows it's a boy?"

"Yes. In fact, both babies are boys."

She tried to speak but her throat closed up. She coughed, then tried again.

"Twins?"

"That's right."

She shook her head, feeling numb all over.

"They're fraternal twins."

Jenna trembled uncontrollably. She was going to have twins. Elation surged through her.

"Jenna." Ryan took her hand and his lips brushed her knuckles, then he pressed her palm to his cheek, holding it against his clean-shaven skin. "I love you more than life itself. And no matter how many babies of Jake's you're carrying, I will raise them all as my own. I will *love* them as my own."

He kissed her hand and cradled it between his palms. His warm gaze settled on her, full of love and tenderness, and she felt an answering love swell inside her.

"And there's something else I have to tell you."

"What is it?"

"I know you're concerned about how much time I spend at work, but that won't be a problem. I no longer have a business to run."

Her heart did a little flip-flop.

"You sold your company?"

"No, I'm still the majority stockholder, but I'm stepping down as president. I've promoted Ken Harvey. He'll run the company from now on. I'm going to spend all my time with you and the babies."

She withdrew her hand from his and stood up, then walked to the window and stared out. Confusion swirled through her. And fear.

She could see his reflection in the glass approaching her. His hands settled on her shoulders.

"What's wrong, sweetheart? I thought you'd be happy."

"You can't give up your business for me. What if you start resenting me for it? Resenting the babies?"

"Never." He turned her around to face him and captured her mouth with his, his lips working a potent magic on her. She melted against him as his tongue parted her lips and curled inside.

He released her mouth but kept her in the solid embrace of his arms.

"I could never resent you. I love you too much. That goes for our babies, too."

"Oh, Ryan . . ." But what could she say?

"Jenna, you fell in love with me long before you met Jake. You agreed to marry me. Don't let a case of mistaken identity destroy what we have."

Mere hours ago she'd had everything sorted out. Jake loved her and she loved Jake. She was having his baby. Marrying him made sense.

She loved Ryan, too, but she'd convinced herself he didn't really love her. Now he'd totally thrown that idea by the wayside and, in fact, had proven he loved her more deeply than she could imagine anyone loving her.

Ryan slid his hands around her waist.

"Poor Jenna. I know this is hard on you, but please tell me you'll marry me."

"I . . . I don't know what to do."

"Do you love me?"

She gazed into his eyes and knew she did. A tear swelled from her eye.

"Yes," she whispered. Her heart started thumping erratically. "But I need time." Words rushed from her mouth. "So many things are happening and I'm so confused and—"

He rested his fingers over her lips, stopping the flow of words.

"I know, love. It's okay. Let's take it one step at a time. Right now I'll settle for knowing you love me."

As he smiled at her, he looked so boyishly handsome, her heart melted. At the soft adoration in his eyes, love welled up inside her, overpowering her senses. He leaned toward her. The tender brush of his lips on hers touched something deep inside her. She slid her arms around his neck and deepened the kiss. The tip of his tongue gently probed her lips and she opened for him, inviting him in with a sweep of her own tongue around the inside of his lips.

He groaned and clutched her to him. Her breasts crushed against his solid chest, the nipples puckering with arousal. He swept her hair behind her shoulder, and his fingers curled around her neck to cup the back of her head.

"I love you. You are my whole world," he murmured into her ear. The wispy words sent quivers through her.

Her breasts ached and a throbbing started between her legs.

"Jenna, I want to make love to you."

Need shuddered through her.

"Yes." She breathed the word. "Make love to me, Ryan."

He slid his arms under her legs and lifted her. She clung to him as he carried her to the bedroom. He laid her on the bed and sat down beside her. He undid the tie on her wraparound dress and peeled away the fabric.

His gaze, warm and loving, traveled the length of her reverently.

"You are so beautiful, my love."

Ryan couldn't believe Jenna was letting him make love to her. He'd been afraid she would turn him down. Her decision encouraged him. He ached with love for her.

She sat up, dropped the dress from her shoulders, and tossed it aside, then unfastened her bra and peeled it away. Her breasts, round and creamy, spilled out.

He sucked in a breath as he reached out and ran his finger along the swell of one breast. Incredibly soft. She took his hand and cupped it over her. The nipple pressed into his palm.

He nibbled at the crook of her neck. Her breathing accelerated, as it always did when he touched her there. He nuzzled around her throat, then kissed along her collarbone, the whole time stroking her breast. Blood sped to his groin as she arched against his hand. Her fingers worked at his shirt buttons and she pushed his shirt off his shoulders. He shrugged it away as she unzipped his pants. As her fingers slipped inside his boxers and grasped his growing erection he held his breath, then exhaled as she wrapped her fingers around him and stroked up and down.

Her touch felt so good he thought he'd die from the pleasure. He stroked her other breast, loving the little murmuring sounds she made; and then he licked the tip of her nipple and drew only the nub into his mouth and teased it with the tip of his tongue. She loved it when he did that.

She squeezed harder on his cock and sped up her movements. He drew the pebbled areola into his mouth and sucked gently.

"Yes," she moaned softly.

Her hot hand pumping up and down on his cock was getting him too hot too fast. He eased away from her.

"I'll be right back, honey." He discarded his pants and boxers and strode into the other room, grabbing the iced bottle of wine and one of the stemmed glasses.

He set them down on the bedside table and filled the glass.

"Thirsty?" she asked.

"Not exactly." He dipped his finger into the translucent liquid and brought it to her breast, then allowed a drop to fall onto her nipple.

"Oh!" Jenna's eyes widened.

He dabbed his cold, wet finger on her nipple, then drew it into his mouth, warming it with quick swishes of his tongue. At the same time, he dripped and dabbed the other nipple, then switched his mouth to that one. Jenna arched her pelvis upward, signaling him she wanted attention lower down. He stroked his hand downward, over her still flat stomach, over her navel, and slid under her panties. He continued past her silky, dark curls and slipped over the clitoral hood and dipped into her. Dripping wet. His cock twitched. He slid back over the clitoral hood, lightly, and she groaned and widened her legs. He hooked his fingers under the delicate lace of her panties and drew them down her hips, savoring the view of her glorious, naked pussy. He gave it a quick kiss, then dragged the panties the rest of the way down and off. He stroked up her thigh, over her hip, then cupped her breast again. The nipple thrust into his palm.

He took a sip of the wine, keeping it in his mouth. He drew her hard nipple into his mouth with it. Her whole body tensed as the cold liquid surrounded her, the nipple hardening even more.

"Oh, Ryan, that's wicked."

He swallowed and lapped at her nipple with his tongue, warming it. She smiled and pressed him down into the bed, then climbed over him.

"My turn." She encircled his cock with her hands and lowered her mouth onto it.

The feel of her hot mouth surrounding his cock head sent sparks shooting through his bloodstream. She slid down over the shaft, taking it deep into her throat, then slid up again and circled his ridge with her tongue. Her other hand slid between his legs and fondled his balls.

"Is it nice and hot?"

He nodded. "Oh, yeah, baby. Really hot."

"Good." She took a sip of the nonalcoholic wine and approached him with a grin.

Knowing what was going to happen didn't prepare him for the incredible sensation. Cold liquid surrounded him as she slid her lips around him, flooding him with the cold wine trapped within her mouth. She swished it around him, then ran her hot tongue around his ridge. Hot and cold. Swishing and swirling.

Then the cold liquid disappeared but her mouth warmed slowly. She released him, then licked his shaft. Up and down. Up and down. He felt like a lollipop, and he loved it.

He stroked his hand up her neck and cupped her jaw, gazing at her lovingly.

"Come here, honey."

She leaned toward him and he kissed her, drawing her

across his body. Their lips moved together, then their tongues danced. He rolled her over and prowled over her.

He kissed her breasts, nuzzling gently, then slipped down to her pussy. He slid his tongue into the labia, then nudged through the folds until he found the little button buried inside. She shuddered. He flicked and dabbed. She arched up against him. He stroked her wetness with his finger, occasionally dipping inside her velvet opening, knowing that's what she liked.

She sucked in a deep breath and started a low moan. He sped up his movements and her moan grew louder. It curled through him, setting his excitement on a tight edge. His finger slipped deep inside her and she clamped around it, grasping him in her silky wet softness.

Her orgasm shuddered through her until finally she collapsed back on the bed. He smiled as he stroked up her body and stared down at her. She smiled back as she grasped his penis in her hand and drew him forward, letting him know it was time. She spread her legs and he positioned his erection against her slick opening.

He pushed into her, slowly, his cock head opening her to him. Once his cock was fully sheathed inside her, it twitched, nearly ready to burst. He pulled out, feeling her slickness slide over him, then he pushed back in.

"Faster," she murmured as she wrapped her legs around him.

He thrust again, deeper, then again.

"Make me come, Ryan." Her voice had that edge that told him she was nearing climax again.

He thrust again and again, feeling his own climax nearing rapidly.

"Baby, you are so hot," he exclaimed.

"Oh, God. Oh, yes." The words were short little pants, then she moaned, long and hard.

He stiffened and spurted into her soft, womanly heat. A moment later, they both collapsed. He rolled them to their sides, not wanting to crush her with his weight.

He held her close, stroking her hair, never wanting to let her go.

CHAPTER 16

JAKE WATCHED STONE-FACED as Ryan's car pulled up in front of the house. Jake had called the hotel, but the hotel operator had refused to put the call through, saying that room eighteen fifty-two had requested a do-not-disturb flag. As Jake had seethed over that, he had considered driving to the hotel and hammering on the door until they answered, but he realized that Jenna would not appreciate that.

Ryan opened Jenna's door and put his hand on the small of her back as they walked toward the house.

Damn it, she had told Jake she loved him, yet she had spent the night with Ryan.

He heard a key in the lock and Jenna pushed open the door.

"Oh, Jake, you're here." She stepped inside, Ryan right behind her.

"Yes, I was here all night. Why weren't you?"

Immediately, he wished he hadn't said it. It sounded petty and, from the stiffening of her shoulders, had put her on the defensive.

"Jake, I have something to tell you."

He felt the blood drain from his face and his gut clenched. He was going to lose her.

"Why don't you sit down?" Jenna suggested.

Jake sat down on the couch, sending a harsh glare toward Ryan, who sat on the easy chair as if he owned the place. Jenna sat down on the couch beside Jake.

"First," Jenna began, "I want to tell you that..." She gazed at him, a trembling smile on her lips, her face alight with a soft glow.

Like a woman in love. His heart sank. Somehow Ryan had won. Jake just knew it.

"I'm going to have twins."

Her words sank in slowly. They were going to have twins? Elation pumped through him and a smile overtook his face. He grasped her hands.

"My God, Jenna. That's wonderful."

She squeezed his hands and, for a moment, he felt everything would be alright. Until she let go, folded her hands in her lap, and stared down at them.

"That's the good news."

Which meant there was bad news. With teeth clamped together, Jake waited for her to tell him she was returning to Ottawa, and Ryan.

"Ryan has convinced me that..."

Here it comes.

"... he should move in here for the next few weeks. I still need time to make my decision and he doesn't think it's fair that you have the edge by having me all to yourself."

Jake glared at Ryan. "What about the business?" he demanded.

"Don't worry about that, bro." Settled back on the chair,

one leg carelessly crossed over the other, Ryan looked more re-laxed than Jake had seen him in years. "I passed control to Ken Harvey. Now I have all the time in the world for family visits."

Pain corkscrewed through Jake's gut.

Ryan had made the grand gesture of walking away from his business to spend all his time with Jenna and the babies. How could Jake compete with that?

Not that Jake wouldn't sell his business in a second if he thought it would win Jenna's heart, but it would seem like a cheap ploy now.

"So what do you think?" She gazed at him, her hands clasped in her lap.

"About Ryan moving in here?" He hated the idea. "Is that what you want, Jenna?"

"Well, I think it's only fair to Ryan."

He had very little choice. If he said no, Jenna was likely to pick up and leave. He had no leverage whatsoever.

"Fine, then that's what we'll do," he answered.

JENNA'S HORMONES WERE in an uproar. She sat on the couch, Jake to the left of her, Ryan to the right, watching a movie—some sci-fi thriller that she'd lost interest in an hour ago. Ordinarily, she would have been totally engrossed, but with her pregnant body playing havoc with her libido, she had a hard time sitting between these two sexy hunks, both of whom she'd been intimate with, both of whom she was in love with, and not grabbing one of them and dragging him off to bed with her. Hell, why not both of them? The thought of both gorgeous men touching her, kissing her, stripping the clothes from her body, sent her pulse dancing wildly.

She shifted uncomfortably, trying not to brush against either of them. Unsuccessfully. She came into contact with Jake's thigh and a tremor catapulted through her. While shifting away from him slightly, her elbow brushed Ryan's arm, sending goose bumps along her flesh.

She dragged her hand across her forehead, feeling dampness on her palm.

"Jenna, honey, are you alright?" Ryan asked.

Jake turned to her. "You're flushed." He placed his hand on her forehead. "You feel a little warm."

"I'm fine. A little hot, that's all."

Hot. She was steaming.

"I'll get you some water." Ryan stood up and walked toward the kitchen.

"Are you sure you're alright?" Jake asked, concern in his navy eyes.

She nodded. Ryan returned with the glass and she gulped the water down.

"Do you need anything else, Jenna?" Jake asked. "Something to eat?"

She shook her head. "Let's just finish watching the movie."

When the movie ended, Jake turned off the DVD player, but switched to the TV. Some late-night talk show was on and they all stared at the large screen. Man, she wished one of them would go to bed. Then she could drag the other off to her room.

When the show ended and another started, no one made a move. She glanced toward Ryan. He rarely stayed up past midnight, yet here it was two A.M. and he still sat here. Suddenly, it dawned on her that maybe each of them was waiting for the other to go to bed so he would be left alone with her.

After they had discussed Ryan staying here that morning, Jake had assigned Ryan to the couch in the basement—a very comfortable and luxurious rec room. The third bedroom upstairs was set up as a den and the only other sleeping option was the fold-out couch in the living room, which afforded no privacy.

They had discussed sleeping arrangements. What they had not discussed was sleeping-with-Jenna arrangements—as in climbing into Jenna's bed and making wild, passionate love to her. Right now she wanted wild, passionate love made to her.

She glanced at Ryan out of the corner of her eye, then at Jake.

Damn it. One of you go to bed. I don't care which!

Another twenty minutes dragged on.

She pushed herself to her feet.

"Good night," she said through clenched teeth and marched down the hall to her bedroom.

"What's with her?" she heard Jake murmur quietly.

"I don't know. Mood swings, maybe?" Ryan answered.

She shoved the door closed behind her.

JENNA STARED AT the moonlight reflected on the wall and the shadows of tree branches swaying up and down in the breeze.

Her body ached for a man's touch. She longed for Ryan or Jake to join her, to stroke her and kiss her and take her to heaven.

She heard footsteps in the hall, coming from the living room, getting louder, then stopping outside her door. She held her breath.

"What are you doing, Jake?"

She had to strain to hear Ryan's hushed voice.

"I want to check on her, make sure she's okay," Jake answered.

"No, she's my fiancée. I'll make sure she's okay."

Jenna's fingers clenched around the bedclothes.

"She stopped being your fiancée the minute she found out whose baby she was carrying."

The voices stopped and a tap sounded at the door.

"I'm fine. I don't need anything," she lied.

She did not want the two of them sticking their heads in here. She might just forget herself and seduce the heck out of both of them.

She heard their retreating footsteps, going in different directions, and her clamped fingers relaxed.

Damn. Here she was within calling distance of two incredibly hot lovers, yet here she lay, totally frustrated, staring at the ceiling.

It was going to be a very long night.

THE NEXT MORNING, she took a long, warm shower, covering her body with suds and soaping every part of herself with long, slow strokes. She thought about Jake caressing her breasts. She ran the massaging showerhead all over her body. She thought about Ryan kissing down her stomach, then his tongue pushing between her folds. She parted her legs and swirled the showerhead over her clitoris, flattening her back against the wall and glorying in the intense stimulation. Within moments an orgasm flooded over her. An empty, frustrating orgasm. God, she wanted one of her men inside her.

She dried herself off and pulled on Jake's soft, fleecy robe, tying it securely at the waist. As she opened the bathroom door, Jake's bedroom door opened.

"Good morning, sweetheart."

His arm curled around her waist and he pulled her back against his strong, hard chest. His fingers played along her stomach and she could feel his cock harden against her buttocks. Her insides ached, her vagina clenching tightly around nothing, wanting his hard cock. She leaned back against him, her eyes drifting closed.

She rested her hand over his, then curled her fingers around it, ready to drag him into his bedroom.

"Good morning."

Her eyelids flipped open and she faced Ryan's disapproving glare. *Oh, damn.* She pushed herself upright and eased away from Jake.

She cleared her throat.

"Good morning, Ryan." She slipped past him into her bedroom, closing the door behind her.

Damn it, the man could plan his timing better. Of course, she realized, from his point of view, his timing had been perfect.

This was crazy. Both men wanted sex with her. She wanted sex with both men. The situation seemed perfect, yet she found herself constantly hot and horny with no man to satisfy her, all because they were dancing around each other. There had to be a solution without anyone being hurt.

Over the next few days, neither man left her alone with the other. Jake had made a phone call to arrange things so he didn't need to go in to the office at all.

As her frustration grew, she wondered why she didn't just get up in the middle of the night and slip into Jake's room—she wouldn't consider visiting Ryan in the basement room because it felt too open and was totally visible from the stairway door—but a part of her was uncomfortable with the idea of making love with one man while the other was only a few yards away.

Damn her stupid inhibitions.

ON THE FIFTH night, Jenna couldn't stand lying in her room any longer. Her swollen breasts ached and her body yearned for the touch of one of her men. Damn it, one of them slept one door down. She wasn't going to do this to herself any longer. She threw back the covers and marched to the door. She cracked it open, then peered out. Everything was quiet. No sign of Ryan or Jake.

She slipped into the hall and quietly pulled the door closed behind her, then tiptoed down the hall to Jake's door. She felt like a teenaged girl sneaking out on an illicit date, trying not to get caught by her parents.

She stood outside his door for a moment, trying to decide if she should knock or just go inside. If Ryan was still awake—not too likely at two A.M., but still, if he was—he might hear. She didn't like just walking into Jake's room, but would he really mind?

She shrugged. Might as well find out.

She turned the knob and opened the door, then quickly slipped inside, closing it behind her. She could hear the staccato beat of her heart. Oh, yeah, she'd make a great thief. She couldn't even sneak into her boyfriend's room without practically having a heart attack.

She leaned back against the door.

"Jake?" she whispered.

Moonlight streamed across the bed and she could see the shadowed valleys of his sheets as they rose over the planes of his body. Jake pushed himself up on his elbows.

"Jenna?" His voice, coarse from sleep, vibrated through her. His rumpled hair and whisker-shadowed face, illuminated in the moonlight, looked oh so sexy. "Is something wrong?"

She drew in a deep breath as she stared at him. Her insides quivered in anticipation.

"I . . . I just wanted to be with you." Her voice came out low and sultry.

He flung back the covers and prowled across the room in a split second, his dark, simmering gaze locked on hers. His arms slid around her and he pulled her against his body. Her nipples ignited in a flash of hot need as they crushed against his chest. Their lips met in a blaze of passion, and she threw her arms around his neck, savoring the feel of his strong body against hers, loving the touch of his fingertips along her cheek.

"Oh, God, Jake, I need you."

Her hands stroked down his broad shoulders then over his muscular chest. His tongue swirled inside her mouth, then plunged deep. She fumbled with the hem of his boxers, then slid inside to touch his long, solid erection.

The clear evidence that he wanted her, too, thrilled her.

He released her lips and eased her back until she rested against the door. His hands slid up under her nightshirt and he stroked her breasts, her nipples already blossoming into solid, needy nubs.

Oh, God, she couldn't wait.

"I'm so wet, Jake." She kissed him and drew one of his hands downward so he could feel proof of her words. His fingers slipped under her white lace panties and he stroked her curls, then slid his finger inside.

"Yes, you are." His gaze never left her face. The intensity of it seared through her.

She nibbled his earlobe, then blew lightly into his ear. He sucked in a shaky breath.

"Jake, make love to me. Now. Here."

He shifted and she felt the head of his penis nudge her moist flesh. She pushed herself onto her tiptoes and opened her legs, while tilting her pelvis forward to give him easier access. He slid the crotch of her panties to the side, then pushed forward, his cock like an arrow gliding through her. She groaned at the delicious sensation of her hot, slick vagina opening around him. She squeezed his long, hard cock inside her.

"Oh, God, Jenna, that feels so good." He kissed her as he drew out, then plunged forward, burying deep into her again.

She tightened intimate muscles around him, trying to draw him in even deeper, reveling in the feel of his hard shaft inside her. Solid. Unyielding.

He grasped her thighs and lifted her. She wrapped her legs around him. He drew back and pushed forward, slowly, again and again. She clung to his shoulders, her breathing quickening, her pulse thrumming through her body.

"Yes, Jake. Oh, God, I want you."

He thrust harder, faster. She moaned at the sweet feel of his cock sliding into her, sending pleasure ricocheting through every part of her.

"Yes. Oh, God, yes," she cried as she felt the first tendrils of the exquisite, intense pleasure of orgasm coiling through her.

"I'm going to come," she cried joyously.

He accelerated to quick, hard thrusts, knowing her so well. She gripped him tighter in her velvet vise, intensifying the friction, and the pleasure.

He pounded her against the door as she wailed in release.

"Oh, Jake . . . Oh, God, yes!"

"Oh, Jenna . . . Oh, Jenna . . . Oh—"

She felt the flood of hot liquid inside her. They both stood frozen, him spurting into her, her intimate muscles repeatedly clenching around him, while they held each other tightly and rode the wave of their orgasm together.

As she slumped against the door, she realized that she had not been quiet while they'd made love.

"Do you think Ryan heard us?" she murmured against his ear.

Jake nuzzled her neck.

"What if he did?"

"I don't know, I . . ." She shrugged.

He kissed her. "Is that why you waited so long to come to me? You were worried about him hearing us?"

"Well, I . . . didn't feel comfortable . . ." She shrugged. "You know, with him so close."

"And me so close. You haven't gone to him, have you?"

She shook her head.

"So you've been hiding out in your room, frustrated." He stroked her hair back from her eyes. "Look, Jenna, we're both big boys. You have to think about what you need and let us worry about ourselves."

She arched her eyebrows upward. "So you don't mind if I bring Ryan into my room, or go downstairs and spend the night with him?"

"I didn't say I didn't mind, but I'll get over it. If you're looking for permission, don't. You don't need it. Do what you need to do."

Her heart warmed at his words, so full of concern for her needs.

She kissed him. "Thank you."

A knock sounded on the door behind her and she practically jumped through her skin.

CHAPTER 17

"JAKE, IS JENNA in there?"

Her chest constricted, knowing Ryan stood inches behind her, only a thin wooden door between them, while she stood here with Jake's cock still buried inside her.

"That's none of your business, Ryan."

He knocked louder. "Jenna, are you in there?"

She locked gazes with Jake and chewed her lower lip, then sighed.

"Yes, I am, Ryan."

Jake eased away from her. She felt cold as he slipped from inside her. She straightened out her nightshirt then pulled open the door.

She smiled sweetly. "Yes?"

"Oh, uh. I heard noises. I just wanted to make sure you're okay."

"Yeah, I'm okay. Jake and I were just . . ." She hesitated, watching Ryan's face tighten. She sighed. "We were just making love."

His jaw dropped. Clearly, he'd been expecting her to lie.

"Look, Ryan. I've been lying in my room every night, wanting you."

"Wanting me?"

"You." She waved at both of them. "But I haven't acted on it because . . . well, if I go to bed with one of you, I'm afraid I'll hurt the other."

"So you decided to go to bed with Jake?"

"He was closer."

"Thanks," Jake muttered.

She turned back to Jake and stroked his arm gently.

"Please, don't be offended. I want both of you."

She turned back to Ryan.

"I don't want to decide between you." She felt tears pushing at her eyes. "I never asked to be put in this position. I never wanted to hurt either one of you. There is no good way to choose between you." Tears streamed freely down her cheeks now. "I love you both."

"Oh, Jenna." Ryan drew her into his arms.

She snuggled her face into his neck. Jake stroked her back.

"This has got to be hard on you, Jenna," Jake said. "What can we do to make it easier?"

She snuffled, then wiped her eyes. The heat of their touches sent streamers of arousal through her.

"I don't know, but . . ." Without conscious thought, she arched her body against Ryan, her breasts pressing into him. She felt dizzy with need. "Damn it, my crazy hormones . . . I'm getting turned on again."

Her fingers tangled in Ryan's robe, as she glanced up at him.

"I want you."

She shifted her gaze to Jake.

"Both of you!" she wailed, then her snuffling overwhelmed her. She tucked her face against Ryan's chest again.

Ryan handed her a tissue and she wiped her eyes, then blew her nose.

"Do you mean both of us? At the same time?" Ryan asked.

Both of them? At the same time? Her hormones shifted into high gear. Her heartbeat accelerated.

"Yes. No . . . I mean . . ." She blew her nose again and sucked in a deep breath. "I . . . uh . . . have thought about it."

It had been one of her most exciting fantasies.

Now that they'd brought it up, the idea was burrowing into her, becoming an itch that defied scratching. She knew this yearning would not go away, but the looks on their faces told her they'd never go for it. Not that she'd ever thought they would.

Still, Jake had told her to attend to her own needs and let them deal with theirs. She stroked her hands across her breasts, deciding a little coaxing was in order.

"I've had fantasies. I've thought about what it would be like to feel the two of you stroking my breasts, one on each." She stroked the tips of her breasts. The nipples poked up clearly through the thin cotton of her nightshirt. "To feel your mouths on me at the same time."

She stroked one hand downward, past her belly. Both pairs of eyes watched her movement as she stroked over the mound and between her legs.

Oh, God, she felt so wicked. And so sexy.

"I've fantasized about one of your long, hard cocks thrusting into me here while I sucked the other cock into my mouth, swirling my tongue around the head."

She saw both cocks swell at her words.

"Jenna, you and your fantasies." Jake's voice sounded hoarse.

She stroked over her breasts again, then reached for Ryan's hand and planted it over her right breast. She felt his hand tighten on her as he watched her grasp Jake's hand and place it over her left breast.

"Jenna. My God . . ." Ryan's gaze locked on Jake's hand.

Jake stroked in a circular caress. Ryan squeezed her gently, then twirled his finger over her nipple.

She drew her nightshirt up, revealing the lower swell of her breasts, then led Ryan's hand under the fabric to one naked breast. He sucked in a breath as her flesh conformed to his gently squeezing hand. Jake slid his hand down over her bare stomach, then slid his finger inside her panties, brushing lightly over her slick pussy.

His delightfully arousing touch fogged her brain. She wanted to sink down onto the floor right here, open her legs, and invite them both in. Beg them to plunge their cocks inside her, one after the other.

Ryan's gaze remained fixed on Jake's hand and his breathing became labored.

Was it possible she could convince them? Excitement spiked through her at the thought.

Jake's finger brushed against her clitoris. Mmm. He definitely seemed close to a yes.

As she glanced at Ryan's face drawn into rigid lines, however, even through the haze of pleasure she realized she was asking too much. She didn't want to push either of them into something they'd regret. In the light of day, she'd probably regret having said any of this.

Jake's finger slipped into her slick passage and her insides fluttered. Her nipple ached as it thrust into Ryan's palm. Oh, heavens, she wanted sex. Again. She'd just been with Jake, so she slid her hands around Ryan's forearm and leaned close to him.

Nuzzling his ear, she murmured, "What about a pirate fantasy?" Her teeth grazed his earlobe. "Just you and me."

"Hmm?" His eyes lit up.

"Well, Jake and I just had some *quality* time together. I'm sure he won't mind if you and I share an adventure now."

Jake reluctantly removed his hand from her panties.

"If that's what you want, Jenna," Jake said.

"You know what I want, Jake." Her voice sounded low, husky. "But this will be good, too."

Ryan untied his robe, letting it fall open, revealing a raging hard-on beneath navy blue pinstripe boxers. He took Jenna's hands and coiled the satiny belt around her wrists, then tied them together. He tugged her toward him, then slid his arms around her and murmured in her ear, "Maybe we'll let Jake watch."

Her eyes widened. Jake's face broke out in a broad, unbelieving smile.

Ryan bent down and nudged his shoulder against her pelvis, curled his arm around her thighs, then stood up. She folded over his shoulder and he carried her into the living room toward the patio doors.

His free hand stroked up her thigh, then cupped her buttocks.

" 'Ere, me pretty. I've got plans for ye," he said. He slid open the door and carried her into the warm night air.

The lights in and around the pool turned on and she realized Jake must have flicked the switch inside. The kidney-shaped pool looked like a blue jewel in the darkness.

Ryan's hand slid down her butt and between her thighs, stroking lightly over her heated pussy. She almost cried out at the intensely erotic sensation. He carried her to the diving board, then set her down on it.

"I think maybe I'll have ye walk the plank."

"Oh, no, not the plank," she pleaded, loving how he'd fallen right into the role.

He tugged the belt from around her wrists and tossed it aside, then stepped forward. She stepped back, toward the diving end of the board.

"Aye, the plank." He looked mock ferocious, with a gleam in his eye and a savage grin.

Her heart went pitter-pat. My God, Ryan made a sexy pirate.

He took another step and so did she. She glanced behind her.

She fell to her knees and grabbed handfuls of his robe.

"What can I do to convince you to free me?"

"Well, I won't free ye, lass, but I might keep ye around, if . . ."

"If?"

"Well, I'll just be leavin' that to yer imagination. Let's just say, yer in a good position."

His erection pushed at the thin cotton of his boxers right in front of her face. She knew exactly what he wanted.

She glanced toward the house and noticed Jake's silhouette framed in the patio doors. Adrenaline rushed through her. He was watching them.

She stroked her hands under Ryan's robe, climbing up his chest to slide over his tight nipples, then traveled back down to his boxers. She hooked her fingers under the waistband and slid around his waist to his back, then caressed over his muscled buttocks as she drew the boxers down slowly, licking her lips. She slid her hands to the front and drew the elastic forward. His erection popped out; then she tugged the garment down to his knees.

Her fingers encircled his cock and she stroked gently.

"You want me to touch you here?"

"Aye, but ye'll be doin' more than touchin', missy."

She lapped her tongue around her lips, then opened her mouth and curled her tongue out and up.

"Like what?" she asked in exaggerated innocence.

"Like lickin' it."

Seeing Ryan like this, opening up, acting outrageous, warmed her heart. He needed to set himself free more often.

She curled her tongue out and dabbed at the base of his penis, then stroked up to the tip.

"Like that?"

"Aye. Now suck it into yer mouth."

She glanced toward Jake as she covered the tip, flicking the tiny hole with the tip of her tongue, then swirled her tongue around the ridge below the head. She sucked. Ryan groaned, then she slid her mouth over him, swallowing him deep into her throat. She squeezed and sucked hard.

"Ohhhh." His hands stroked her hair.

She tucked her hands under his balls and fondled them gently. He tried to widen his legs to give her better access, so she dragged his boxers down to his ankles. She was afraid he was going to topple over.

She removed her mouth and coaxed, "Mr. Pirate, shouldn't you be comfortable while I pleasure you?" She tugged lightly downward on his cock, then swirled her tongue out and around the tip.

He smiled, taking her hint, and lowered himself onto the diving board, lying back. She glanced toward the house as she tugged the boxers off and tossed them onto the grass. Jake still stood watching. It was hard to tell, but she thought she could see his hand moving at his groin. As she licked over Ryan's rock-hard cock, she could imagine Jake had taken out his equally hard cock and was stroking it now. The thought that she was turning on two incredibly handsome studs at the same time turned her on immensely. She could feel slickness between her legs, dripping down her thighs.

She sucked Ryan into her mouth, drawing hard and strong. She slid her mouth up and down on him, swirling her tongue along the shaft. His balls tightened in her hands. She slid off the end of his penis and licked downward, then over his tight testicles. She drew one ball into her mouth, then the other, sucking them in her warmth, dabbing them with her tongue. She released them, then swallowed his cock again.

"Oh, sweetheart, I'm so close," Ryan murmured.

She tucked her finger under his balls, then stroked his perineum while she sucked and stroked his cock in her mouth. She felt him tense. She glanced toward Jake as she slowly slid her mouth up Ryan's penis, following her progress with her hands. She held his cock in the warm cradle of her hands and drew her mouth off the tip of him just as he started to ejaculate. Long, white streams of liquid pulsed over her shoulder. She licked his balls as the semen fountain continued.

She prowled over him, then kissed his mouth.

"You've got quite some distance there." She winked at him. "I bet your brother was impressed."

JAKE WATCHED JENNA sucking his brother's cock down her throat and his own cock throbbed painfully. He stroked it in his hand. Ryan lay down on the diving board, his erection sticking straight up like the mast of a ship. Jake pumped himself harder as Jenna moved her mouth up and down his brother's pole.

Oh, God, he longed to feel her lips on his cock. Damn, why hadn't he and Ryan jumped at Jenna's suggestion? Two of them making love to her.

A threesome. She had offered a dream scenario and they had turned it down. Idiots.

He continued to pump his cock as he watched Jenna going down on his brother. Finally, she drew her mouth away from Ryan and a fountain of semen spewed from his cock. Jake's balls tightened and he released his own fountain, wishing it was in Jenna's hot, sexy mouth.

RYAN DRAGGED JENNA on top of his body and kissed her, then sat up.

This woman was incredible, and her fantasies had brought an exciting element to his life.

"Well, missy . . ." He winked at her. "Ye've bought yerself some time."

He stood up and grabbed her hands, then pulled her to her feet. He hung on to her arm as he retrieved his belt from the grass, then coiled it around her wrists again. He held the middle of the belt and used it like a leash to lead her to the patio doors.

Jake no longer stood at the door. Ryan had been well aware of Jake watching them the whole time and it had been a real turn-on. Maybe it was knowing Jake saw how excited Ryan made Jenna. He wasn't sure. He just knew it had added spice to the whole thing.

Ryan slid the door open and drew Jenna inside. Jake caught his attention from the kitchen and pointed toward his bedroom. Ryan led Jenna down the hall. Inside his brother's room, he saw four Velcro cuffs attached to the headboard and footboard, aligned so that Jenna would be spread-eagled on the bed. He smiled and his cock twitched.

"Lie down, wench," he instructed Jenna.

She glanced at the cuffs, then turned back to him, wide-eyed.

In mock horror, she cried, "No, please, don't tie me up."

"I said lie down, wench." He glared at her, a half-smile crossing his lips as he slapped the end of the cloth belt against his hand. "Don't be makin' me say it again."

The thought of slapping the fabric across her backside, watching the round, white flesh of her buttock flush under the strokes, sent his cock twitching again. Would she defy him? Maybe being spanked was part of Jenna's fantasy.

As she lay down on the bed, he realized it wasn't. At least, not this time.

He took one of her wrists and fastened a cuff around it, then the other. He took her ankle and pulled it sideways, until it reached the footboard and the cuff there. He bound it, then took her other ankle and slid the final cuff around it.

He sat back and stared at her, lying with her arms and legs

wide open, ready for him. She stared back, wide-eyed and breathing heavily. The only problem was, she still had her big T-shirt thing on. He could take off the wristbands and tell her to take off the shirt, but that's not what a pirate would do. He sent her a devilish smile, then grabbed the hem of her shirt and ripped it open, from hem to neckband.

She gasped.

He pulled the fabric back, revealing her round, white breasts. The nipples peaked, beckoning him to swallow them into his mouth. Her panties, so dainty and white, were the next to go. The delicate lace shredded as he tore them free. He tossed them onto the floor.

The short sleeves of the T-shirt still hugged her shoulders, so he tore each of them free and left the tattered garment lying beneath her.

"What's going on in here?"

Ryan turned to see Jake standing in the open doorway.

"Are you here to rescue me?" Jenna asked.

Jake smiled. "If I rescued you, I'd have to untie you."

Ryan saw the excitement in Jenna's eyes and he remembered what a turn-on it was to know Jake was watching them on the diving board. In fact, earlier it had been extremely exciting hearing Jenna while Jake made love to her against the door. Ryan still remembered the banging sound as Jake had repeatedly thrust her against the door, and her sweet whimpers of delight as his brother had pounded into her. Her moan as she'd reached orgasm still shuddered through him.

If they both made love to her, he was sure she would be more excited than she'd ever been. How could he deny her such pleasure?

How could he deny himself such excitement?

"Untying her would be a shame," Ryan said. "Come, brother, share the wealth."

Jenna's eyes widened and Jake's face broke into a broad smile.

"As you can see, wench, the brother of a pirate is a pirate. I think we'll both be having our way with you."

CHAPTER 18

JENNA FELT FAINT as she realized her most sublime fantasy, being with two men—these two men—was about to come true. She could hardly believe it. Excitement spiked through her and she could barely catch her breath.

Jake knelt down beside the bed and stroked her right breast. The nipple thrust upward. Ryan sat on the other side and stroked the left breast, then leaned forward and drew her pebble-hard nipple into his mouth.

"Ohhhh, yes," she moaned.

When Jake also took her nipple in his mouth, she almost fainted at the exquisite pleasure. Soon they were both sucking and licking, cajoling and dabbing.

"Our captive is surprisingly cooperative," Ryan said.

Oops. She was the one who'd suggested the fantasy and she wasn't keeping up the act. She widened her eyes and struggled.

"No. Let me go."

"I don't think so, me pretty," Ryan said.

He stroked down her belly, then slid between her legs. Jake leaned in close and licked her slit. Ryan's fingers separated her folds and Jake's tongue lapped across her exposed clit.

"Ohhhh."

Jake settled between her legs and lapped at her clitoris in earnest, then sucked it into his mouth. Ryan shifted upward, capturing her nipple in his mouth again. His hand drifted to her other breast and he stroked it gently.

It was so incredible, feeling both their hands and mouths on her.

She arched upward against Jake's mouth. Ryan covered each breast with a hand, then licked up her chest and nuzzled the base of her neck. Jake's tongue rippled against her.

Pleasure quivered through her as Jake swirled his tongue inside her, round and round, then fluttered on her clit. His hands stroked along her inner thighs. Ryan sucked her nipple hard and deep, then slid under her back and cupped her butt. As Ryan stroked and squeezed, her muscles clenched and she arched forward, pressing herself harder against Jake's tongue. Ryan nibbled her other nipple between his lips and Jake dabbed while sliding his fingers inside her.

"Oh, yes. Oh . . . yes . . . ," she moaned.

"Jake, I think you're making her come," Ryan crooned.

Jake's tongue spiraled on her clit and she exploded in orgasm. Ryan stroked her breasts as she arched in blissful contortions.

"Yes, you're definitely making her come."

The pleasure pulsed through her in waves. As her body relaxed, Jake's tongue slowed and she slumped back on the bed. Ryan's large, solid cock bobbed in her view as he stroked it with his hand, obviously extremely turned on. She glanced down at Jake and saw his huge cock standing proud.

She needed one of those inside her—Ryan's, to be fair, since she had last made love with Jake. She'd keep Jake otherwise occupied.

"Oh, Mr. Pirate's brother?" She fixed her gaze on Jake. "Whatever will you do to me now?"

She opened her mouth, then slid her tongue around her lips suggestively. Jake smiled then shifted to her side and leaned his cock head close to her mouth. She licked the top, then swirled the tip of her tongue around his ridge.

"More," she murmured and he leaned closer, allowing her to swallow him inside.

"Our captive is becoming very cooperative again," Ryan observed, his hand gliding up and down his bulging erection. Oh, God, she wanted that inside her.

She let Jake slip from her mouth.

"No, you beasts. Leave me alone. Don't thrust your *enormous* cocks into me. Don't drive them into me hard and fast. Don't make me scream in ecstasy."

They watched her, broad smiles on their faces, but neither made a move. She squirmed beneath their gazes.

"I said don't do it . . . and don't do it right now," she insisted.

Jake slid his rod into her mouth again and Ryan shifted lower on the bed. He kneeled between her wide open legs and skimmed his hands down her body, from bound wrists to waist. His touch felt like electricity shimmering over her body. He leaned forward and sucked her nipple into his hot mouth. She almost cried out around the huge pole of flesh inside her mouth.

She stretched her thighs wider apart, arching her pelvis upward as she sucked and stroked Jake with her tongue. Ryan placed the tip of his cock at her damp opening. She pushed forward, trying to draw him inside, but he held back.

"Easy, love." He dabbed at her clitoris with his thumb, then stroked gently. She moaned out loud, then sucked Jake deep into her throat.

Ryan drove into her, hard and fast, and she gasped. Oh, sweet heaven, it felt incredible, his hot, rigid flesh inside her. She squeezed Jake tight in her mouth as Ryan slid forward and back, building up to deeper and deeper thrusts. She sucked hard on Jake as she rode the wave of passion. She knew Jake was close but he pulled out of her mouth just as she felt the pleasure mount. She started to moan and Ryan jerked forward and grunted, spewing hot semen inside her. She wailed in release as they climaxed together. She fell back, panting as Ryan pulled out of her.

Her gaze met Jake's, the echoes of her orgasm still shuddering through her, and anticipation flared.

"Now, Jake. Let me feel you inside me," she said, her voice throaty and full of need.

He smiled broadly. "My idea, exactly."

Jake positioned his steel rod against her, then thrust inside, and kept on thrusting while she plummeted into an immediate orgasm. She screamed in ecstasy and he erupted inside her, his semen mingling with his brother's.

Jake collapsed on top of her, then rolled sideways. She lay panting, gazing at her two incredible lovers.

"What else should we do to our lovely captive, brother?" Jake asked Ryan.

"Well, we probably don't need these anymore." Ryan removed the bindings on her ankles and Jake removed the cuffs on her wrists.

Ryan leaned against the headboard and drew her onto his lap.

"I think you should have first try this time." Ryan drew her legs apart, presenting her to Jake.

Jake kneeled in front of her and licked her dripping pussy, then drove his tongue into her clit.

"Oh, God." She was still so sensitive, still so turned on, she moaned as another orgasm swept over her.

"I want both your mouths on me again." She sucked in a breath. "One on each breast."

Ryan laid her on the bed and each man sucked her into his mouth. Her hard nipples elongated even more.

"Oh, God, yes. Suck them hard."

Ryan sucked her deep and squeezed her between the roof of his mouth and his tongue. Jake nipped lightly, making her gasp, then gently licked.

The different rhythms and sensations were incredible. She pushed herself to her knees, then kissed Ryan. As his arms came around her, she pushed him down onto the mattress, his head near the foot of the bed. She lifted her derriere and waved it toward Jake's face. She felt his hands stroke along her hip and over her buns. A second later, his hot tongue licked her wet opening.

She glanced over her shoulder, sending him a sultry stare.

"I want you inside. Right now." She crawled down Ryan's chest and sucked his big, hard cock into her mouth.

Jake slid his member into her and she groaned, then started to suck cock like there was no tomorrow.

Jake slid in and out, stroking her intimate flesh with the ridge of his cock.

"Oh, yeah. Oh, yeah. Faster. Mmm."

"Oh, baby, you are so hot," Jake moaned.

She ran her fingers under Ryan's balls, feeling them

tighten, feeling his cock swell and his body stiffen. He was going to come soon. She slowed her movements a little on his gorgeous erection and thrust back against Jake's pounding body, urging him to go faster. She could tell Jake was close, too. She sucked harder and faster on Ryan while pounding back against Jake.

Adrenaline rushed through her and a wave of bliss began. She moaned around the rigid flesh in her mouth, then swirled her tongue around the ridge of his cock while stroking behind his balls. Ryan erupted inside her, his hot semen flooding down her throat. At Ryan's groan, Jake stiffened behind her, then moved in short, hard thrusts. Hot liquid filled her womb as ecstasy washed over her.

She slumped down on Ryan's chest and Jake's cock slipped from inside her. She felt his head rest on her lower back, his hand stroking her thighs. They fell asleep in a tangle of limbs.

JENNA WOKE UP on her back between two hard, warm bodies, Jake's arm curled around her, his hand cupping her breast, and Ryan's arm across her hip, his fingertips resting on her pubic curls. Each of her arms was wrapped around a man.

She glanced from one handsome face to the other. Her nipple swelled under Jake's hand, pushing into his palm. An ache started in her groin and she shifted a little. Ryan's fingers slipped a little lower.

Oh, man, she wanted them to wake up and ravish her again. Last night had been the most incredible experience of her life—and given the sexual adventures she'd had ever since Jake had fulfilled her first sexual fantasy, that was saying something.

Each of her hands stroked lightly up and down a strong back. Jake's eyes opened first and he gazed at her.

He leaned in and kissed her cheek. "Morning, sweetheart."

Ryan woke up next, his gaze locking on Jake. Jake seemed to notice Ryan for the first time. Shock ripped across both their faces, then they both jerked back. Jake pushed himself to a sitting position.

"What the heck . . . ?" He rubbed his hands over his face, then memory seemed to dawn.

"Hell." Ryan sat up and dropped his legs over the edge of the bed. He pushed himself to his feet and strode out of the room, slamming the door behind him.

Jake stared after his brother, then shook his head and strode away, exiting into the bathroom.

"I take it the party's over," Jenna grumbled.

AFTER SHE'D SHOWERED and dressed, Jenna strolled into the kitchen. Sam stopped eating from her bowl to glance at Jenna. Jake sat at the counter sipping a cup of coffee.

"Where's Ryan?" she asked.

He nodded toward the door. "He went out."

"Out?" she asked in disbelief. The whole time he'd been here, he'd never left her alone with Jake, and vice versa. "I guess he's pretty upset."

Jake said nothing. She poured herself a glass of orange juice and sat on the stool beside him.

"Are you . . . um . . . okay with what happened last night?"

He dragged his hand through his hair, his face drawn into tight lines.

"I don't know, Jenna." He gazed at her. "I mean, don't get

me wrong. You were sexy as hell. The whole thing was sexy as hell." He rubbed the back of his neck. "It's just that . . ."

She waited, embarrassed at the thought of what they'd done last night, yet excited when she thought about how they'd both touched her at the same time, about how she had touched both of them at the same time.

Jake's fingers clenched his coffee mug.

"Damn it, I never thought I'd wake up next to another guy, let alone my own brother."

"I don't understand. It's not like you were making love to each other. You were making love to *me*."

He shook his head. "It's hard to explain." He pushed himself to his feet and strolled to the sink, then set his cup on the counter. "I've got some stuff to do."

With that, he left.

She propped her elbow on the counter and rested her chin in her hand, staring out the back window at the pool sparkling in the morning sunlight. Sam jumped up on the stool beside her and meowed. Jenna petted her distractedly.

Well, clearly the guys could not cope with the idea of the three of them together. That put an end to one wonderfully exciting possibility for a solution to her dilemma. Not that she'd ever seriously entertained the idea that the three of them could form a long-term relationship together. Still, it was too bad.

OVER THE NEXT few days, things simply got worse. The two men avoided each other. If one walked into a room, the other left. Jenna insisted they all eat dinner together, but the meals were quiet and didn't last very long.

Her heart ached watching what was happening. She'd

thought they just needed a few days to get over it, but they seemed to be drawing further apart. Despite her continued state of arousal, she hadn't gone to either of them during the night for fear of alienating one or the other even more.

After a week, Jenna filled with guilt as she realized she might have done irreparable damage to Ryan and Jake's relationship.

They were brothers. They were supposed to love each other. Now, because of her, the close bond that should exist between them had been strained to the breaking point. On top of that, she realized that once she made the decision they were both waiting for—which brother she would marry—the other brother would grow to hate the one she chose.

Not only that, no matter which one she chose, she would still ache for the other.

Depression claimed her as she realized there was no solution to her dilemma. She loved both of them. Deeply.

There was no way she could choose one over the other.

CHAPTER 19

JENNA OPENED THE kitchen door to see Jake washing up some dishes. She hadn't seen Ryan on her way from her bedroom to the kitchen.

"Good morning." Jake dried his hands, abandoning the dishes to give her a kiss. She allowed a light brush of lips but when he tried to deepen it, she stepped back.

"Where's Ryan?"

"I don't know. I think he's outside."

Jenna pulled back the drapes on the small side window in the kitchen and saw Ryan, wearing a short-sleeved shirt and shorts, sitting on a lounge chair by the pool, reading a book in the sunshine. She stepped into her slip-on sandals sitting at the patio door, and went outside. Jake watched her from the door. She walked across the soft grass until she reached the stone pool deck.

"Ryan, would you come in for a minute, please? I need to talk to you."

He glanced up and smiled, but when he saw her serious expression, the smile faded.

"We could talk out here."

She shook her head. "Please."

He stood up and followed her back into the house. The two men avoided each other's gaze.

"Jenna, can I get you some breakfast?" Jake asked.

"No, I'm not hungry." In fact, she couldn't stand the thought of putting anything into her churning stomach.

"But the babies need—" Jake said.

"The babies need a lot of things." She clasped her hands together and stared down at them. Even she noticed the profound sadness in her voice. "Unfortunately, they can't have everything they need."

Ryan stepped behind her and stroked her shoulder.

"Jenna, are you alright?" he asked.

She shrugged him away, then hugged herself.

"Yes, I'm fine," she said tightly, then took a step away. "Actually, no, I'm not."

"What is it, sweetheart?" Jake asked, approaching but not getting too close, clearly sensing she needed space.

Tears welled in her eyes but she blinked them back. She had to keep a clear head to explain to them.

"I need to talk to you both. I've made a decision."

The two men exchanged glances for the first time in more than a week.

Ryan pulled out a kitchen chair for her and she nodded in thanks and sank into it. Jake pushed himself onto the counter, his legs dangling over the edge. Ryan leaned against the refrigerator.

"Ryan, I love you."

Ryan's lips turned up in a wide smile, clearly believing he

had won. When she turned to Jake and saw the pain in his eyes, her heart broke.

"Jake, I love you, too."

Confusion crossed both their expressions.

"That's the problem. I love you both. Deeply." She clasped her hands on the table and stared at them. "If I choose one of you, I will still ache for the other. And whichever one of you I don't choose will hate the one I do." One tear escaped her eye and she dashed it away, hoping they hadn't seen. "That means by picking either one of you, I'm breaking up a family, and I just can't do that." Her voice ended in a choked sob.

"You really shouldn't worry about that," Jake said. "We can handle whatever decision you make."

Her gaze locked on his.

"Fine, Jake, so if I tell you I'll choose Ryan over you, you'll be fine with it?"

She watched his lips tighten into a straight line and his eyes darken in pain.

"Even if you could handle it, I couldn't. When I make love with my husband, I'll think of the brother I couldn't have. That wouldn't be fair to either of you."

Ryan shoved his hands in his pockets. "But, Jenna, you said you'd made a decision."

She nodded, flicking a tear from her eye. "I have." She sucked in a deep breath. "I really think it's best if I don't marry either of you."

The two of them stared at her in astonishment.

Tears streamed steadily from her eyes and she shook her head helplessly. "I just can't choose between you."

She stood up and hurried from the room.

. . .

JAKE STARED AT Ryan and Ryan stared back.

"We can't let her do this," Jake said.

"Are you willing to step aside so she doesn't have to?" Ryan asked.

When Jenna had asked Jake how he'd feel if she chose Ryan over him, his heart had turned to stone and he'd gone numb inside. He could never willingly step aside.

"Are you?"

Ryan's face hardened. Of course he wouldn't, either. They both loved her.

"Maybe she doesn't really mean it. In a few days, when she's thought a little more about it—"

The door opened and Jenna entered with her suitcase in her hand. "Jake, would you call me a cab, please."

The sight of her with her bag in hand, ready to leave his house forever, sent Jake's thoughts spinning. He had to find a way to make this work.

"Jenna, when this all started, you asked for time to decide. You granted me time to spend with you and get to know you. You've been extremely patient. Would you be patient a little while longer and allow Ryan and me time to work something out?"

"Jake, there's nothing to work out. I just can't . . ."

Her tears started again. He stroked her back.

"I know, honey. I know. Just trust me, okay?"

"Please give us a little more time?" Ryan implored.

Jenna stared at him with big, dewy eyes, her lids a little puffy. She hesitated.

"If you're hoping the two of you can agree on which one I should marry, that won't help."

Jake took her hand. "Jenna, please."

Finally, she nodded.

"Alright."

He picked up her suitcase, then placed his hand on her elbow and led her back to her bedroom.

"Why don't you just sit and read a good book? I'll bring you some breakfast. That'll give me a chance to talk to Ryan."

JENNA SAT PETTING Sam, who was happily curled up on her lap. She glanced at the clock. The men had been talking for two hours now. She sighed and continued reading.

About twenty minutes later, someone knocked on her bedroom door.

"Come in," she called.

Ryan pushed open the door. Sam leaped onto the floor and scampered out of the room.

"Jenna, I have an idea I'd like to discuss with you. Would you follow me?"

He held out his hand. She stood up and folded her hand in his. He led her out into the hall, but instead of turning left toward the main part of the house, he turned right. Toward Jake's bedroom.

She slowed down, tugging back on their joined hands.

"What are you doing, Ryan?"

He turned to her and smiled warmly. "Come on, Jenna. Just trust me."

What was she worried about? He wasn't going to take her

into his brother's room and ravish her—especially with his brother still in the house. She nodded and followed him into the room. At least, she assumed Jake was still in the house. He wouldn't leave when they still had so much to sort out.

Unless their answer was to share her, one at a time, sort of like joint custody—and Ryan got her first.

As she passed through the doorway, she remembered how Jake had made love to her right there, how he'd banged her against the door with his strong, steady thrusts.

Ryan led her toward the bed, then stopped in the middle of the room.

"Now what?"

He turned to face her.

"Jenna, we can make this work."

"You and me, Ryan? But what about Jake?"

"When he said 'we can make this work,' he meant all three of us, Jenna."

She turned to see Jake standing in the doorway. Her heart rate leaped.

"Make what work, exactly?"

"Well, this for one." Ryan stepped close behind her and slid his hands around her waist, then drew her back against his body. His lips pressed lightly against the back of her neck.

She stiffened.

"But, Ryan . . ."

"And this," Jake said, stepping toward her.

He moved close, sandwiching her body between his and Ryan's. Jake cupped her face and brought his lips to hers. His tongue spiraled inside her mouth, sending her senses into a frenzy. All she could feel was hard male muscle all around her, and soft, masculine lips teasing her mouth and neck.

"But when we did this before, the two of you freaked out. I don't want you to do something you're uncomfortable with."

"Jenna, we discussed it," Ryan responded. "For the first time, we sat down and really went over it. We realize that it was just stupid male conditioning."

"As you said that morning," Jake continued, "we'll be making love to you, not each other. We both love you and you love both of us. It's sex between loving partners. A man and a woman and a man."

Ryan stroked along her shoulders, sending tingles through her.

"Sure, it might be a little unconventional, but if it works for us . . ."

Her body ached for their touch. She gazed into Jake's eyes, dark and serious. She glanced over her shoulder at Ryan, and saw the same intent gaze.

"Will it work for us?" she asked.

"I'll do everything in my power to make it work," Ryan stated. "Because I don't want to lose you."

"Me, too," Jake agreed.

Could she really do this?

"What do you think, Jenna?" Ryan murmured against her right ear.

"Can we give it a try?" Jake nestled his lips against her left temple.

At her hesitation, Jake nuzzled her neck. "We're talking both of us at the same time. Anytime you want."

Ryan blew in her ear. "You'd like that, wouldn't you, sweetheart?" His hands glided under her T-shirt, then stroked over her ribs and covered her breasts.

"After all—" Jake smiled down at her, "—you are our wanton little sex kitten."

He cupped her bottom and pulled her pelvis against him, pressing the bulge of his fabric-encased cock against her. Ryan's erection pressed into her bottom.

Oh, God, if she agreed, in a few moments she'd feel both those cocks bringing her pleasure. Right now she wanted both of them in her hands.

"I don't know," she teased. "How do I know you both want me?"

Jake chuckled as Ryan protested, "But, Jenna . . ."

"No, bro, this is what she wants."

He stepped back and peeled off his pants, then slipped the waistband of his black briefs down, tucked under his balls so she could see his fully erect cock.

"Ohhh." Ryan released her breasts, leaving them cold and needy, but the sight in front of her kept her brain in forward gear.

Ryan kicked off his pants and matched his brother's pose, tucking away the top edge of his charcoal gray boxers.

At the sight of two, huge, red-faced cocks standing at full attention in front of her, the pace of her breathing increased.

"Oh, my. You both sure are happy to see me."

She smiled as she tugged her T-shirt over her head and tossed it aside. Both men watched intently as she unfastened the button on her jeans, then eased down the zipper and dropped them to the floor, kicking them aside.

She stepped forward and touched the tip of each lovely cock with an extended finger. At the pained expressions on their faces, she closed a hand around each one and pumped a couple of times.

"However will I find a way to satisfy two such lovely examples of excited manhood?"

"Why don't you leave that to us?"

Jake nodded to Ryan and they each grabbed one of her arms and rushed her backward toward the bed. A second later, she found herself flat on her back, her front-opening bra unsnapped and peeled open, a male mouth firmly planted on each breast. Her nipples rose instantly, the exquisitely erotic feel of hot man-mouth on both at the same time driving her insane with need.

Their cocks were still in her hands, so she started stroking them, toying with the head of one, sliding under the testicles of the other. Jake stripped off her panties in one swift motion. She felt his tongue slide down her ribcage, over her navel, then down farther. She opened her legs and he lapped at her inner thighs. She pulled on Ryan's cock, drawing him to her mouth. He released her nipple and shifted on the bed, turning over on his side with his feet resting on the pillows at the top of the bed, aligning his beautiful, erect cock with her mouth. She tugged off her bra, then turned onto her side to face him. Jake helped by lifting her leg and draping it over his shoulder. As Ryan's cock slid into her mouth, Jake slid his tongue inside Jenna.

She moaned her appreciation. Her tongue circled around and around the corona of Ryan's penis while Jake dabbed at her clitoris. Ryan toyed with her breasts, stimulating the nipple of one, cupping the other in the warmth of his hand.

As Jake lapped at her highly sensitive clit, she felt waves of pleasure waft through her. She pressed the roof of her mouth down on Ryan's rod and sucked hard and long. Her fingers curled around his testicles and she fondled them as the pleasure built within her.

"Oh, Jenna, I'm getting close."

She bobbed her head up and down, squeezing her mouth around him, giving him strong, arousing friction.

Jake sucked at her bud, then twirled his tongue against her, hard and fast. The waves came faster and harder. Her fingers spiked through Jake's hair as she sucked harder on Ryan.

"Oh, God, I'm coming, Jenna."

Ryan groaned as hot liquid spurted against the back of her throat. She continued sucking as he spewed inside her, riding her own waves of pleasure. He slipped from her mouth and immediately planted his mouth on her nipple. Intense heat shot straight from her breast to her vagina, blasting straight into the building fervor from Jake's hot tongue, which now jabbed into her depths.

She moaned. Jake's mouth slipped over her clit and he sucked hard, matching Ryan's sucking on her nipple.

The intensity skyrocketed through her and scorching pleasure erupted through her in the most potent orgasm of her life.

She flopped back on the bed and sucked in air.

"That was incredible."

"We aren't done yet."

She opened her eyes to two bright-eyed faces. The two incredible men in her life.

"Jake will be awfully frustrated if we stop now. Look how much he still wants you," Ryan said.

Jenna eyed his huge, purple-looking member.

"You're right. We can't leave it like that." She pulled herself higher on the bed, then settled back on the pillows and opened her legs. She curled her finger in a come hither gesture. "Jake, I need you."

He grinned and crawled up the bed. He positioned his knees between her legs and kissed her firmly on the lips.

"Now, Jake." She arched upward.

His long, hot cock fell against her belly.

"Mmm."

He pressed the head to her soft folds, then slid the tip inside.

She noticed Ryan on the end of the bed, his fingers curled around his fully reanimated cock as he slid his hand up and down, pumping as he watched.

"Jake, I want you fast and hard. Drive that *enormous* cock deep inside me, again and again."

Ryan chuckled. Jake complied.

She moaned as his penis thrust into the depths of her, surrounded tightly by her wet vagina. He pulled out and drove in again. She could see Ryan pumping faster on his own rod. Jake plunged in again. And again.

"Oh, God, yes. Give it to me, Jake." An orgasm rolled over her, totally catching her off guard. Intense. Frantic. Excruciating in its perfection.

Jake groaned and his seed pumped inside her.

After a few moments, Jake kissed her sweetly, then rolled to her side, his deflated member sliding out of her.

Her eyes dropped closed, then fluttered open again as lips tickled her neck. Ryan hovered above her.

"Room for one more, sweetheart?"

She smiled. "Of course."

She wrapped her arms around his neck and pulled him in for a deep, passionate kiss. She felt his knees settle between her legs and the tip of his cock press into her opening. He entered her in one strong thrust. She gasped, then wailed as another orgasm overtook her immediately. He pumped and pumped inside her, pushing the pleasure longer and longer. Time became tenuous. She heard him groan, felt his semen flood into her, but still the pleasure poured through her. It built to an intense ball of fire searing through her like a comet carrying her to the farthest reaches of the galaxy. Her wail turned to a scream, wild in its intensity. More and more and more. Her throat grew hoarse. He pumped on and on.

She reached a peak, then sailed down the other side of forever. Pure, sweet bliss all the way.

She slumped back. Slowly, she realized he was still rigid inside her. He rolled her over so she lay on top of him. Jake moved in behind her and she felt his hard cock stroke between her buttocks. She moaned and leaned forward, her buttocks parting more. His finger stroked her puckered opening, then dabbed at it. He grabbed a tube of lubricant from the bedside table—she hadn't noticed it before, but then she'd been quite distracted—and squeezed it onto his finger, then stroked her opening with his fingertip.

Oh, the slick liquid was warm. He pressed firmly and his finger slid inside. She'd never had anal sex, but the feel of his finger sliding inside her made her hunger for more. He slid another finger in and spiraled both inside her. She shifted her butt toward him and moved it in a circle, encouraging him.

"More," she coaxed.

He grabbed the tube again, but this time, slathered the clear gel over his cock. He pressed the head to her opening and pushed against her. As his cock head eased forward, she stretched around him. Once the whole head was inside, his hard flesh stretching her wide, he stopped. His arms wrapped around her and he held her close to his body. Ryan's cock twitched inside her vagina.

She felt impossibly full, but she wanted more. She wanted to feel both cocks fully inside her. Filling her, pleasing her.

She leaned forward again.

"Give me the rest of it," she told Jake.

He eased forward, feeding her his cock an inch at a time.

She thrilled at the sensation of his hard rod sliding inside her. Slowly. Purposefully.

Two cocks inside her. Two!

Once she was totally full, the two men remained perfectly still. After a heart-pounding moment, Ryan started to move. Slowly. In and out. Jake followed the rhythm his brother set. In and out.

"Oh, my God." An immediate orgasm pummeled through her. "Oh, yes. Oh, my God," she wailed.

The two cocks seemed to stroke against each other as they slid inside her. The incredible sensation threw her into an intense, prolonged orgasm. Time melted away and only the sensation of the two incredible cocks, gliding inside her, pleasuring her, seemed real.

A siren sounded in her ears. No, it was her own voice, crying out in ecstasy. The cocks seemed to swell inside her.

"Jenna, Jenna, Jenna. Oh, God!" Ryan thrust forward, holding her tight around the waist.

"Baby. Oh, God, yeah." Jake held her tight against his chest, her breasts cupped in his hands.

She squeezed their cocks inside her, drawing them in tighter, flying into forever as the sweet, hot nectar of their bodies flooded her insides.

They lay frozen for several moments, breathing as one. Finally, Ryan kissed her; then Jake peeled himself off her, tumbling to her side. She rolled onto her back and her two lovers nestled their lips against her cheeks, their arms sliding around her waist.

As she lay between her two gorgeous men, warm and cozy in the glow of their love, she realized her life was now a fantasy come true.

In fact, twin fantasies.

EPILOGUE

JENNA DROVE ALONG the narrow private road past the tall, dense trees alive with the spectacular reds, oranges, and yellows of autumn. She pulled into the clearing and parked in front of the cozy-looking cedar house, the lovely, secluded hideaway she now called home. Purple, orange, and yellow chrysanthemums added bright color to the front garden.

The other flowers were finished for the season and she could tell Jake had been busy while she'd been away, cleaning up the garden and preparing it for winter. Only a few stray orange leaves littered the lawn. Near the front steps two large orange garbage bags with jack-o'-lantern faces smiled their semi-toothless grins, stuffed with the leaves Jake must have spent a full day raking.

Two pairs of bright eyes peered out at her from the huge set of windows across the front of the house. Her heart swelled at the sight of her two little angels, three-year-old Jeremy and Robbie. Suddenly, the front door burst open and the two bundles of energy flew toward her.

"Mommy, Mommy!" they shouted in unison.

"Daddy, Mommy's home!" Jeremy shouted behind Robbie as he sprinted out the door and down the steps toward her.

She laughed as they tackled her legs, then she scooped them up and kissed them each soundly.

"I have missed you both so much." She squeezed them tightly. They smooched her face wetly, then squirmed to get down.

"Jenna, you're home."

She glanced up to see Jake striding through the front door toward her. He grabbed her and hugged her close, dipping her into a deep kiss. Love swelled through her like a wellspring of warmth from deep in her soul.

Every day she had shared with him over these past few years, she thanked God for the joy he brought her.

"And *I* have missed *you*," he murmured.

"Mmm. Me, too." She kissed him again, delighting in the pressure of his strong, masculine lips on hers, her thoughts straying to the other delights they would share after the boys went to bed tonight.

She'd only been gone three days and it felt like an eternity. Now that they'd combined their efforts to form a new company, writing fun, educational software for kids, they took turns when business trips arose.

Jake grabbed her suitcase from the trunk of the car. He slid his arm around her waist as he accompanied her into the house.

"Mommy, come play the new game Daddy got us." Jeremy ran a few steps, then looked back to ensure she followed.

"Yeah, Mommy, play it with us." Robbie smiled, his eyes twinkling, knowing exactly what worked on Mommy.

"Boys, your mom has had a long flight." Jake tousled Robbie's hair. "She might want to relax for a little while first."

"Playing the game *is* relaxing, Daddy." Jeremy pulled a box from the bookshelf at the end of the counter and plunked it on the kitchen table.

"Hey, buddy, how about we sit and watch the new movie together," Jake suggested. "That might be more Mommy's speed right now."

Robbie ran to the living room door and yelled, "Daddy R! Mommy's home and we're gonna watch a movie." He grabbed Jake's hand and dragged him toward the living room. "Come on, Daddy J, let's go."

Jeremy picked up the game and took it back to the shelf.

It always amazed Jenna how the kids fell into calling the men Daddy R or Daddy J when they were dealing with both of them, but just plain old Daddy the rest of the time. They didn't question why they had two daddies.

That would come soon enough and then they'd deal with it.

"Jenna?" Ryan peered into the room and a broad smile spread across his face. He dodged out of the way as Jeremy flew past him into the living room.

A warm smile crept across her face as she stared, mesmerized, at his handsome face. He had relaxed so much over these past few years. Fatherhood became him. Any worries she'd had about Ryan not spending time with her and the kids had evaporated as soon as the boys were born. He certainly had followed through on his promise to treat the twins just like they were his own.

His face glowed when he looked at the boys. He loved spending time with them. He no longer worked all the time.

In fact, he was the one who suggested the scheme where they alternated one of them watching the boys while the other two worked. One of the great advantages of working at home.

Ryan strode toward her, opening his arms wide. "Welcome home."

She stepped into his embrace, loving the feel of his strong arms around her. He tipped her head up and kissed her soundly. Love swelled through her again.

His hand stroked lightly over her breast and her nipple peaked and snuggled into his palm. Yes, indeed, tonight she would be well loved.

He smiled down at her. "I'm glad you're back. I've missed you."

"Me, too."

At first, she'd really wondered whether this relationship would work, the three of them together, but somehow they had made it work. Every day her love grew stronger. For Jake and for Ryan. And they both insisted they were just as much in love with her.

The three of them had formed a company together, using all of their strengths to the fullest. Ryan no longer felt a need to compete with Jake, probably because now they all worked to the same end: to create a successful company and, more so, to create a successful and happy home.

"Mommy. Daddy R. We're *waiting*." Jeremy's voice rang out loud and clear from the other room.

She laughed. Ryan took her hand and they strolled into the living room.

As she sat down on the couch, Ryan on one side of her, Jake on the other, with the two kids piling on top of them, she realized they'd been successful in all respects. Joy filled this house like the warm autumn sunshine glowing in the picture windows.

She stroked Jeremy's dark blond wavy hair as he stretched from Ryan's lap to hers. Robbie snuggled into Jake's lap and clicked the remote control to start the movie.

Yes, indeed. A fantasy come true.

Read on for a preview of Opal Carew's
upcoming erotic romance

SWING

Available from St. Martin's Griffin
in January 2008

MELISSA WOODS HAS always been the self-appointed pro-
tector of her family. When she learns that her younger sister is
planning a weekend at a swingers' resort, she's determined to
dig up dirt on the establishment. Melissa, a journalist, asks
her longtime friend Shane to pose as her husband as she goes
undercover. But she isn't prepared for the storm of desire that
awaits. . . .

She was the one. Ty was sure of it.

Melissa Woods.

He watched the woman, with her pert little nose, full sexy lips, and wavy ash-blond hair, caressing her shoulders as she listened to the host outline the etiquette at the resort. She wore an alluring black dress, cinched at the waist, that revealed an enticing glimpse of cleavage and plenty of long, shapely leg. Although she fit in completely with the other wives, something in his gut told him she wasn't here for a weekend of sex.

Which was a damned shame, because a weekend of sex

with her was a hell of an exciting prospect. His body tightened in response to the thought of dragging that voluptuous body against his, her tight nipples pressing into his chest as his tongue invaded her soft, sweet mouth.

But she was the woman he'd been hired to watch. She was the woman who could well destroy the reputation of this resort. Ty was not about to let Melissa Woods, or anyone else, for that matter, ruin his closest friend's business.

She glanced his way and their gazes caught. He found himself staring into her soft blue eyes and he smiled. She was certainly an attractive woman. Maybe in this case, business could be mixed with a little pleasure. Her face glowed red and she curled her fingers around her husband's hand as she glanced away again.

"Be sensitive to others," the host said. "Always ask, and remember, 'no' means 'no.'"

"Also remember," the hostess, a tall, blue-eyed woman with raven hair, broke in, "that it is perfectly acceptable to sit back and watch." She winked. "But believe me, participating is much more fun." A few nervous giggles twittered around the group.

Melissa glanced toward the clock, carefully avoiding the gaze of the darkly handsome man who'd been watching her. And still was. Her heartbeat accelerated as his disturbing gaze slid down her body, then rested on the swell of her breasts before continuing down to her crossed legs. She forced herself not to shift in her chair.

She tightened her grip on Shane's hand. Shane smiled at her, then turned his attention back to the auburn-haired beauty with emerald eyes a few chairs away. If Shane had been her real husband, she would have been jealous at the way he flirted with the other woman, but he wasn't her husband. In fact, she *was* a little jealous, but she and Shane were just good friends and, despite wishing their relationship could be more, she had good reasons for keeping it the way it was.

His flirting, however, made their role here appear more real. She should be doing the same thing, but there was no way she was going to have sex with a stranger.

She intended to play the "I just want to observe" card a great deal, and by "observe" she meant the rituals, not others having sex. No one should be surprised, since the host said that it was quite common for newbies to take a few days to open up. After that, she should have enough information and it wouldn't matter what people thought.

She chanced a quick glance at the stranger, who had introduced himself as Ty Adams, as he whispered something to his blond, blue-eyed, aerobic-instructor-perfect wife. The problem was, Melissa sensed this guy with the midnight eyes that could chip away at a woman's resolve would view a newbie like her as a challenge. And she had the impression that, whatever challenge this man took on, he pursued it with a vengeance.

"Now I suggest," the host said, "that you all take a look around the resort. There is a welcome dance in the ballroom. Feel free to talk to the other members and ask questions. Everyone is very friendly." He grinned. "There are various bars and"—he winked—"specialty rooms available. These are outlined in the orientation booklet. And you can always take a dip in the pool or soak in one of the four hot tubs—bathing suits optional, of course."

Melissa wrote down each of his suggestions in her notebook, ignoring her uneasiness at the thought of naked people lounging around the pool doing who-knows-what and especially trying not to imagine what went on in the *specialty rooms*.

"One more piece of advice." The hostess smiled at them. "Don't stay with your spouse this evening. Practice experiencing the club and meeting other people on your own.

"If you have any questions, we'll be circulating around the club. Now, go have fun."

Everyone took that as a cue and stood up. Couples began milling toward the door.

"Do you want me to stay with you?" Shane's eyebrows rose.

Shane was such a sweetheart, coming to the resort with her to give her moral support, willing to stay with her now when, clearly, he wanted to pursue that gorgeous redhead.

"No, they suggested we separate."

The thought of roaming around this place on her own filled her stomach with butterflies, but she was a big girl and she could handle it.

As Shane crossed the room, Auburn Hair smiled at him, her face lighting up. They chatted for a moment, she laughed, then he slid his arm around her waist and they slipped through the door.

Melissa noticed Mr. Dark Eyes standing by his wife's side as she chatted with the hostess. He smiled at Melissa. Calmly, she returned his smile, then headed for the door, relieved when he did not follow her.

She returned to the lobby, then followed the signs to the ballroom. Soft music flowed from the room. She walked straight to the bar, then sat on one of the high wooden stools and ordered an orange and cranberry juice.

"So you're a virgin," a woman's voice said.

Melissa glanced at the lady to her left. "I beg your pardon?"

The slender brunette smiled, her green-eyed gaze taking in Melissa's black wrap dress and her velvety high-heeled shoes trimmed with sequins, then returning to her face. Her red lips parted to reveal pearly white teeth. She nodded to Melissa's name badge, with the little lipstick kiss symbol on the corner.

"That's what we call new members. Virgins."

"Oh." Melissa picked up her drink and churned the straw through the crushed ice, blending the orange and red juices. "Yeah, that's me."

"It's strange being at a place like this for the first time." She smiled, resting her elbow against the bar. "I've been a member for years. If you have any questions, just ask."

This was the perfect opportunity for Melissa to find out more about what went on here, but she couldn't bring herself to ask. Not until she became more comfortable with the place. If that ever happened.

"Thanks." She took a sip of her drink.

"Sure, honey." She held out her hand. "Karen Smeed."

Melissa shook her hand. "I'm Melissa Woods."

A man stepped to the bar and Melissa cringed, fearing he was going to approach her, but he slid his arm around Karen's waist.

"Hello, sweetheart. I see you've made a new friend."

"Yes, Derrick, this is Melissa." Her voice took on a conspiratorial tone. "She's a virgin."

Melissa wished the woman would stop saying that.

"Really?" A smile spread across his rugged face and his eyes twinkled. "Isn't that delightful?"

His hand slid higher and he cupped Karen's breast. Melissa's breath caught and she kept her gaze on Karen's face, trying valiantly to ignore the way Derrick's fingers circled over her breast and how the nipple rose to a clear outline through the thin fabric. Karen arched forward, forcing her breast fully into his hand.

"This man knows how to work a pair of breasts."

Melissa gazed around and noticed a few people glancing their way. Her face heated.

"We'd love you to join us, Melissa." Karen rested her hand on Melissa's arm. Melissa stiffened at the woman's touch.

"Derrick is very good with virgins. I can just watch or—" her fingers stroked along Melissa's arm "—join in. There's nothing like a good licking from another woman, don't you think?"

"I, uh . . ." Panic overwhelmed Melissa. She wanted to pull away, but she couldn't.

"Ah, never tried it." She squeezed Melissa's arm in encouragement. "Well, that's what this place is about. Trying new things." She smiled wickedly. "And talking about new things, if you want to invite your husband along, you could try two men at the same time. You've never felt pleasure until you've had one cock in your pussy and another—"

"Melissa, there you are."

Melissa jumped at the voice and a hand clamping simultaneously on her shoulder. She glanced around and came face to face with Ty Adams, the man who'd been watching her earlier.

"I told my wife about you and she would love for you to join us." Ty held out his hand and she grabbed it like a lifeline. As he drew her to her feet, he turned to Karen. "Sorry to interrupt, but Melissa and I have a prior agreement."

Disappointment crossed the woman's face, but she smiled sweetly. "Of course. Maybe later."

Melissa just stared at her, dumbfounded, as Ty gently tugged her away from the bar. She followed him across the room, then out a door to the patio beyond. She sucked in a breath of fresh air. The rolling waves of the ocean serenaded them as they walked beneath the glittering cascade of stars in the black sky.

Finally, Melissa regained her composure and stopped in her tracks.

"Wait a minute. I'm not going to join you and your wife—"

He waved her words away. "I know that. I just thought you could use some rescuing. Not that I don't think you could have handled yourself."

"Of course I could."

But Melissa hadn't handled herself well at all. What had come over her? Shock, most likely. She had suspected people in a swingers' club were as brazen as Karen and her husband—that's one of the reasons she didn't want her sister anywhere near a place like this—but Melissa really hadn't anticipated being approached in such a bold manner.

"Apparently, Karen can be hard to escape once she's set her sights on you."

"Thank you."

For the first time, she realized how warm and comforting his hand felt wrapped around hers. Tendrils of warmth coiled up her arm into her body and spiraled downward. She remembered Karen's breast, pointed and aroused, Derrick's fingers curling over the tip of her nipple. Melissa's nipples peaked, longing for a man's touch. This man's touch. Which made no sense at all. Wanting Shane's touch—that she understood. She'd wanted to make love with Shane for a long time. But this man was a stranger. This man was a lecherous husband who frequented swingers' clubs in search of lewd sex with other men's wives.

Actually, he was a newbie, the voice of reason reminded her. Just like her. That meant he hadn't done this before, either. The difference was, Melissa wasn't really a swinger. She'd come here to find out what the club was like and prevent her sister from making a big mistake.

This guy was here for the sex.

And Melissa damned well wouldn't be the one to give it to him!

People laughed nearby, then Melissa heard a splash.

"The pool must be nearby." Melissa glanced to the right and saw a clump of bushes. Probably on the other side.

"Do you want to check it out?"

She nodded and headed toward them, then suddenly remembered the swimsuits-optional rule. She slowed, but he kept going. She peered around the bushes and saw a beautiful free-form pool with a waterfall at one end. Colored lights reflected on the falling water and people reclined around the edge of the pool, several floating in the aqua water.

To Melissa's relief, all of them wore bathing suits. Not a naked breast or any other private body part in sight.

"There's a hot tub over there." Ty pointed beyond the pool to a tub that seemed carved from stone.

"It's lovely."

As they passed another set of bushes, farther from the building, she caught sight of a second hot tub. She sat down on a wooden bench by a flowering bush, enjoying the warm night air and the smell of the ocean. Ty sat down beside her.

There were two women and a man in the hot tub, and a

man lounging on the side. As Melissa watched, one of the women stood up and Melissa realized she was topless.

The man slid his hands around her waist and drew her onto his lap, then—to Melissa's complete horror—he cupped her breasts. The woman moaned as her head lolled back, resting on his shoulder.

Melissa's gaze remained glued to the scene, despite her embarrassment, especially with Ty sitting beside her. Melissa's nipples hardened and intense need ached within her. All she could think about while watching the man's hands circle over the woman's breasts, her nipples thrusting outward in eager arousal, was that she wanted a man's hands on her breasts, too.

"Feel like a dip?" Ty asked.

His voice startled her and her gaze locked on his. Humor danced in those dark, midnight eyes.

Oh, God, he knew she was turned on. She was sure of it.